DEATH OF THE
BODY

CROSSING DEATH:
BOOK ONE

Rick Chiantaretto

ISBN-10: 940748-00-3
ISBN-13: 978-1-940748-00-9

Published by Orenda Press

Copyediting by Bev Sninchak and Kathryn Star Heart
Formatted by Willow's Formatting
Cover Design by Eden Crane Design
Production Management by Orenda Press

What if all religions were stories,
and all stories were true?

For Mike, who knows what goes on in my head
and sleeps next to me in the dark anyway.

PROLOGUE

I watched in disbelief as blood seeped through my fingers and dripped, thick as syrup, to the ground. I heard each drop thud against the ground beneath me. The echo in my ears beat louder than any drum. For the first time in my ten years of life, I cursed the connection I had with the planet. I cursed it for its betrayal. I cursed it because, with every drop of blood that spilled, the planet felt my pain and mimicked my screams with its own bleating sound that bounced around inside my already spinning head.

My legs were weak and my knees buckled but I didn't dare let my hands loosen from around the wound in my stomach. I caught the weight of my fall with my face. I rolled onto my side in order to breathe. Pain surged as the ragged edges of my wound rubbed together. I felt every last severed nerve. They were all on fire.

Blood poured quickly. Worse than seeing it, I could feel it, hot and sticky in a pool beneath me. My stomach retched but it would hurt to throw up so I tried to force down the feeling. Bile came up anyway. I turned my head and choked it out. The rusty taste left in my mouth was so sour it made my eyes water. I cried uncontrollably, feeling ashamed of myself.

I wished for the comfort of my mother and father. I longed for the company of my two best friends. It was ironic that I'd just had a conversation about death with them a day ago.

As I lay sobbing on the ground, the thought that I was going to die became more and more real. Already my blood was soaking back into the earth that I loved so much. I thought of the lessons that taught me not to fear death. I had been taught that death was a return to the larger conscious mind that is nature. This awareness made my people who they were and gave us our unique gifts.

I was afraid anyway. The thought of dying was much more terrifying now than when it was taught to me by the Elders.

The Elders. The Elders who were either dead or enslaved. The Elder who betrayed us all and who did this to me.

Rage: pure, blazing, and blinding in its fury. I was too enraged to even notice that I could feel anything besides pain. Rage boiled inside me as blood boiled from my stomach and I realized it was based in two other emotions: hate and disbelief.

Then something cold and wet hit me between the eyes. I rolled onto my back and stared into the dark and threatening clouds. Another something hit the back of my hand, and I lifted it (was my arm always this heavy?). A drop of rain mingled with my blood.

I had never experienced rain before. It never rained here—at least not in my lifetime. Rain was for when the world was angry, when its powers had been abused and the balance of life had been disrupted.

But wasn't I angry? And wasn't I connected to the planet? Didn't I understand its moods and feelings? Why wouldn't it then understand *me*? In my delirium this seemed to make sense, and the large flash of lightning that then split the sky seemed to confirm my thoughts. The flash was blinding, and I didn't have enough energy to be startled by the fact that my vision remained nothing but the same bright white light.

I shivered as cold crept into me; it didn't help that I was lying in a chilling pool of blood. The rain picked up. I was nearly soaked through, but was too weak and numb to

3

move. At least the pain was starting to slip away. I could only imagine how blue my fingertips must have looked. They felt like ice.

After the pain was gone, the fear began to fade. All the tension in my body went with it. Cold as I was, I started to feel strangely comfortable. I could feel the earth beneath me, supporting me, soft and gentle. My mom used to hold me like this.

When I realized the rage was slipping, I cried out. I wanted to keep it alive within me. I wanted to be angry and upset. I wanted to be angry because feeling an emotion—any emotion—was better than accepting death.

As the rage faded further, I thought I heard distant laughter. How could anyone be happy now? How could they laugh as I lay here, a mangled mess? It took me a minute to remember that just because the earth could feel my pain didn't mean everyone else could too—especially not the outsiders.

Their voices were getting louder and nearer. When they suddenly stopped, I heard a gasp. Mustering the last of my strength, I reached toward the voices.

"Please," I tried to say, but it came out as barely more than a groan.

"Get a doctor!" a woman's voice commanded. I felt slight vibrations through the earth as somebody ran away.

The woman who spoke came over and kneeled next to me. I wasn't too far gone to feel surprise. I imagined I was a frightening sight. I expected her to keep her distance, so my eyes widened when she took my hand in hers. She was warm, but trembling.

"What did this to you, child?" Her voice shook but was full of compassion and concern.

"Magic." I couldn't tell if I actually said the word or just thought it.

As I repeated the word over and over in my mind, the rage dissipated and the light began to dim. A part of me was upset that I'd let the rage go but I was too exhausted to call it back. I welcomed the darkness now. The woman at my side was saying something but her words made no sense to me. Far easier to hear was the heartbeat of the earth. I wanted to soothe the earth's tremors caused by the pain and fear it felt for me, but I couldn't. As my breathing slowed, memories of the past day flashed into my mind. They were of the events that led up to my death, when all this started. It seemed like a lifetime ago. Who would have known it would only be one long day that would lead me here, lying on the ground, spilling blood?

PART ONE—A DAY EARLIER

ONE

The bright sun was centered in the sky and was hot enough that I unbuttoned my shirt. I was lying on my back, face tilted toward the sun, hands and fingers weaving a comfortable pillow under my head. The small, coverless wagon only needed to be pulled by one horse and swayed back and forth beneath me in time with the regular beat of the horse's stride. A long blade of grass was between my lips. I chewed on the end of it occasionally because I hadn't eaten anything in almost twenty-four hours and the chewing motion slaked my hunger.

"Hey Edmund, aren't you supposed to be *steering*?"

I must've been close to sleep, because the sound of my name made me jump. I forced myself upright, watching a figure bound toward the wagon with a handful of alfalfa.

I wasn't alone in the wagon; the other person was my best friend Hailey and she was kind enough to answer for me.

"The horse knows where it's going, Ralph." I loved it when she used that get-over-yourself tone and rolled her eyes—except when she did it to me. Naturally, a large grin crossed my face.

Ralph, Hailey, and I had been best friends from the time we could walk. Even though all the children in our town grow up together until the age of twelve—and there were plenty of other kids our age—we had gravitated toward each other early on. Most of the adults in town treated us like siblings instead of just friends. Now that we were ten, we were each responsible for gathering food. Instead of each of us going alone, we decided it would be more fun to go together. I was responsible for blackberries, which, inconveniently, grew only in a vast forest a day's travel away from town. Ralph, of course, gathered alfalfa, which was in abundance in the stretching fields that grew for miles on the horizon. Hailey was responsible for mushrooms that were found anywhere, but grew large and earthy on the dark, damp ground sheltered by the forest.

We became accustomed to taking one day at the beginning of the moon cycle to travel to the forest, gather berries, and stuff ourselves with mushrooms. We always fell fast asleep against a wayward pine before making the journey back the following morning. On this trip the mushroom harvest had been scarce and there were hardly enough blackberries to fill the required quota for the town.

Ralph sprang over the side of the wagon and landed loudly enough that I knew he purposely tried to startle us. Hailey shrieked as the unexpected weight caused the wagon to sway, but I remained impassive to his attempt to scare us.

"Wow, Edmund. What are you daydreaming about?" his voice sounded playful. He playfully snapped his fingers in front of my face to get my attention. They buzzed with electric magic.

My gaze met his. His ragged auburn hair fell unkempt over his golden eyes. He looked at me with an odd expression of anticipation.

"What are you thinking about?" he asked.

Blackberry pie—but I wasn't about to tell him that. "Something on the horizon caught my attention," I lied.

Both he and Hailey turned their backs to peer deep toward the west. "I don't see anything," Ralph said. "What was it?"

I could tell he wasn't going to leave it alone. It was sad that the prospect of something on the horizon was enough to intrigue him, but I supposed we were all that bored. I'm sure Ralph hoped it was something shiny.

"I'm not sure," I said, shrugging. "Whatever it was is gone now."

My stomach growled and I heard Hailey snort. When she turned back to me, her face was lit with a smile that stretched so far over her teeth it must have hurt.

"Hungry, Edmund?"

"Starved. We didn't get enough mushrooms for the trip. I've been staring at the blackberries the entire time Ralph gathered alfalfa," I admitted.

"Well it's my mom's turn to cook tonight, so you know it's going to be good."

Visions of the town hall tables lined with plates piled high with vegetables, meat, tarts, and pies filled my head. Hailey's mom always worked especially hard on town feasts. My mouth watered, so I reached out and snagged another blade of grass to chew on.

"How long, do you reckon?" Ralph asked. I knew exactly what he was referring to: how long until we were home.

I stood up and gazed south as we traveled through the long stretches of fields that touched the sky. I couldn't see the slender trails of chimney smoke rising yet. Then I looked at the sun, which had traveled almost halfway between the center point of the sky and the western hills. "Two hours at best," I said, slumping back down into the wagon. "We'd better stop and let the horse eat before too long."

"I don't see why *she* should get to eat before us," Ralph complained.

Hailey shot him a disgusted look. "Because she's the one that is going to get us *home*."

Home. I saw Ralph's face fall at the word. "What did you say?" he asked, not because of misunderstanding, but because of the way the word resonated through the air, caught the wind, and floated across the grass until it echoed from somewhere behind us. It was as if the world had echoed the word.

Hailey's eyes grew large. In the pale sunlight they glowed hot ochre.

"Home," she whispered again. To our ears, the word hung in the air like the tone from a tuning fork.

They both looked at me. Ralph was the first to attempt to speak, although the words got caught in his throat and sounded more like a croak.

"Edmund, is something wrong?"

My connection to the planet was the strongest. While Ralph's abilities centered on things of the spirit and Hailey gravitated toward science and physical magic, my abilities were planet-centric and emotional. I concentrated on the blades of grass that bowed towards us to the rhythm of a new westerly wind. *Home, home, home,* was all they pulsed.

"I don't know," I finally admitted, although my head swam with a feeling that told me something was lurking, not wanting to be revealed by the wind. I couldn't ask the grass what was wrong, it was just repeating the wind. Grass didn't have deep enough roots to make a strong connection to Orenda. "I need to find something with deeper roots."

There was a line of trees just a few hills away in the direction from which the wind had come. "Feed the horse," I said. "I'll be back."

Ralph didn't say anything and hesitated only slightly before grabbing a handful of alfalfa and tossing himself over the side of the cart. Hailey sat motionless, absently stroking her arms as if the temperature had dropped. I considered saying something to comfort her but instead jumped to the ground and headed for the trees.

It didn't take long to get there at full sprint although my chest heaved with breathlessness. The muscles in my thighs ached when I finally stood among the branches. The run helped work out my tension, but the emotions didn't dissipate until I was standing grounded in the small grove. The planet had an odd effect on my emotions—

they felt heightened and overwhelming when the earth needed something from me, but when I needed to keep a cool head, I could drain them through my feet into the soil beneath me where they would be absorbed by the world around me.

When my emotions were in control, logic would assert itself and my mind could solve larger problems, problems that even the average ten-year-old mage wouldn't be able to solve.

I thanked the earth for my ability, and searched, not for anything I could see, but for something I could feel. I made my way through the thick undergrowth until I found a tree that called to me. Its bark was gnarled and split with age but its dark green leaves boasted of health and fertility. It wasn't the massive expression of the powerful and twisted limbs that struck me, it was the unconditional kindness that seemed to sprout up from deep within the trunk and through the tips of the smallest twig. The tree was inviting. Had I had a moment to spare, I would have liked nothing more than to curl underneath its shade and rest my head against its roots. Yes. This was the oldest tree here, the mother of the rest, and she was aware of my presence.

I reached out and gently stroked the rough bark. "Hello, Mother Tree," I whispered. It wasn't the words, but the feeling I needed her to hear.

A shudder went through me as the tree spoke back. *Hello, young one. Your heart is troubled and I sense you have come to make a request*, the wind hissed between her branches.

"I am from the town of Orenda." Emotion overwhelmed me as I spoke, my connection to the tree and the earth now flooding back into me. I had to fight back the tears that tried to spill from my eyes. This tree had a powerful, kind, and overwhelming spirit. "I feel there is something this land wishes me to know about my hometown. Is there a line of roots that might happen to stretch all the way there?"

My roots are deep.

"Might I use them, please, Mother Tree, to see? In return I shall grant you any favor you wish."

A favor indeed. Pluck an acorn from within my branches and take it with you on your journey home. Plant it in Orenda so that I may spread my seed across this land. If this you so promise, I will allow you to see.

I didn't have to answer. Instead, I grabbed hold of the lowest branch and swung myself up into the tree. The ripe acorns were high but I was a decent climber. It didn't take me long to reach a branch that was weighed down with large dark nuts. I plucked one gently and slid it into my pocket.

When my feet were back on the ground, I tenderly placed my hand against the trunk again. I caught my breath as emotion washed over me like an ocean, so large and deep it could have covered the entire surface of the planet. If every natural creature and element were connected to the ocean, and if I could see the beauty of the sea as it heaved and rolled, the resulting feeling that rose in me felt like someone was reaching inside my chest and holding my breastbone. That pressure, just above my heart, was where the feeling settled. That is what it felt like to be connected to the world as I was.

I surfaced somewhere in the middle of the town square, seeing through the perspective of one of the rose bushes that lined a trellis. The air around me was heavy. There was a smell I couldn't recognize because it mixed so oddly with the sweet smell of the flowers. The atmosphere was filled with fog. My eyes must have been either tainted by the color of the rose or maladjusted, because I was only able to see through a reddish hue. I couldn't make out the four walls that surrounded the square but the grass beneath me seemed normal enough.

"Who's here?" a booming voice echoed. "I *will* find you."

A cloaked man appeared beneath me. Since I was on a trellis, I was looking down at him. The cloak he was

15

wearing was familiar, but the Elder's robes were usually crisp, accented with sharp silver stitching. I had never seen an Elder looking so disheveled. The silver stitching along the seams of this robe were darkened with dirt.

"Elder!" I cried, the panic in my stomach subsiding. The man turned his face upward, and I saw a twinge in a familiar blue eye.

"Edmund?"

The sound of my name was recognizable. The man was not just an Elder but also one of my teachers.

"Joshua!" I exclaimed.

He was looking at me, a slight smile on his flushed face as understanding settled. He talked to the rose now.

"Edmund, where are you?"

"Still a few hours outside of town. We were gathering—"

"Who is with you?" His face showed concern, but his tone was impatient.

"Hailey and Ralph. We were talking about home when the wind whispered something terrible."

"Edmund, listen to me. You must return as quickly as possible."

The smell in the air that I hadn't been able to place before became evident as an orange glimmer caught the corner of my eye. The trellis to which my vessel plant was clinging was on fire. It wasn't fog that blurred my vision, it was smoke. It wasn't dirt on the silver lining of Joshua's cloak, it was soot.

"Joshua. What is going on?"

"The kingdom of men," was his response. "Quickly. The horse must run. I will take care of you when you arrive but I don't know how long I can linger. I will meet you at the gates."

The fire around me roared. I heard the flames licking at the poor plant. "What happened? Men? My father? Where is my father?"

Joshua's face fell. "There is no time. Go, Edmund. Quickly return to me."

"But—"

My vision was consumed in hot flames, my body felt like it was being stretched. The roots of the plant were failing. I felt death creep through its vines as I was ripped from the haunting images of my home by firm hands around my waist. If hitting the ground hard wasn't enough, I was forced to roll over and over again along the rocky terrain. I was disoriented and sputtering. Being rolled like that made my head swim.

"Edmund!"

The rolling stopped, but now I was being violently shaken. I opened my eyes and recognized Ralph's face, covered in dirt, just inches from my own.

"Breathe!" He shook me again.

I gasped, but the air was so thick and smoky that it made me cough.

Ralph got up quickly, holding out his hand to me. "Get up!" he commanded.

"Wha—?"

His red hair had an unnaturally fiery glow to it, and his eyes were wild. "Get up!" he shouted again.

I reached toward his hand, but balked at the sight of my own. It was black, covered in ash. I looked down at my clothes; patches of cloth were missing, singed away.

Ralph pulled me to my feet. As he steadied me, my spinning head began making sense of things. I was back at the line of trees where I had spoken to Mother Tree.

"Let's go!"

Hailey was under my arm, helping me walk. "You'll be okay, Edmund. We need to get you back to the wagon."

A loud explosion made me look back, but for the rest of my life I would wish I hadn't. My eyes grew large in horror as the rest of my body froze. Fear pushed tears to my eyes that I didn't feel coming, too quickly for me to push the emotion into the planet. I screamed, terrified, as Ralph and Hailey dragged me forward. Mother Tree, the oldest and kindest of the grove, had given her life for me.

Large flames leapt from her branches, devouring her. The explosion I heard was a large branch splitting from her body and cracking as it hit the ground. The wind carried her screams, although the roaring of the flames muffled all other sound. Her acorns, her beautiful children, exploded in a sickening symphony of percussion.

My stomach rolled and I heaved. Every muscle in my body responded by tightening, which caused Ralph and Hailey to drop me. I fell on my hands and knees. I wanted to cry out but I choked on the smoke instead. I crawled toward the tree, but before I could reach out toward her, my friends restrained me again.

"You can't save her!" Ralph pleaded. "Only fire cast by magic could have followed you back through the roots."

My body convulsed. I couldn't control the tears or the trembling. I was angry and frightened. Most of all, I was in pain.

A shower of ash and spark surrounded us. Smoke obscured the sun and coated the grove in a thick canopy of misery.

I heard Hailey whisper in my ear and I wondered how long she had been at my side. "We need to get out of here so we can find the people who did this and bring them to punishment with the Council of Elders. Please, Edmund!"

Humans. They must have done this.

The Elders. Joshua. He had asked me to return. He said he didn't know how long he could stay and wait for us. Did that mean the mages were gone? Was he our last hope of finding them?

A new emotion surged through me: hate mixed with panic. I hated the kingdom of men. Somehow, they were involved in this. Somehow, they were to blame.

I found my balance and stood. Ralph and Hailey were there to help support my weight. I still trembled but I was determined to place one foot in front of the other.

My head seemed to clear with the cool, fresh air. The farther we walked from the grove, the more stable I became. When we made it back to the wagon, I gave myself a once-over. I was covered in ash and the uncovered parts of my arms and legs didn't have any hair left. I had several burns and blisters on my legs and hands, but fortunately adrenaline still surged enough to keep the pain at bay. All that was left of my clothes were strips of charred material that clung together in patches. When I realized this, I reached for a blanket in the wagon and wrapped it tightly around me.

"I was on fire?" I asked.

Ralph and Hailey exchanged a brief look before Ralph answered with a shrug, the panic draining from his face as he found his dry sense of humor. "Only for a little while."

I grinned in spite of myself. "Is the horse rested?"

"Yes."

"Good, because she'll have to run."

TWO

I was lucky. The fact that I was on fire, at least momentarily, seemed to purge my friends' questions during the walk back to the wagon. The vibration of the cart, mixed with the rhythmic pounding of the horse's hooves on dry ground, created enough noise that Hailey, Ralph, and I couldn't talk. Although the quick-paced ride was uncomfortable, it provided an excuse not to answer any of the questions I could see burning behind their eyes. They stared at me with an expression that seemed accusatory. I knew they both realized I was purposely avoiding telling them what I saw.

I sensed their questions at the surface. I could see Ralph fighting back fear with a patience I admired. I assumed he was able to give his emotions to spirit, as I could with the planet. I knew him well enough to know when he was afraid: his eyes were growing large and the left corner of his mouth had started to turn upward in a hard line, not a smile.

Hailey looked calmer and sat taller than the rest of us. Her logic never failed her as her ebony hair tossed wildly in the high wind and her crystal blue eyes studied my face. She didn't require patience. She was piecing together meaning from my unconscious expressions.

I considered throwing the bag of mushrooms in Ralph's direction, hoping that getting something in his stomach would distract him from the thoughts he was having. Then I decided that it wasn't a smart idea. I didn't want him to think that the mushrooms wouldn't be needed for later.

As that unintentional thought crossed my mind, I felt a stab of fear. On the trellis I hadn't seen anyone except Joshua. The town square was usually bustling. Was it possible that our town was deserted?

Hailey must've seen my eyes flicker to the burlap sack. When I looked at her, her gaze drifted up to my face again. I tried to control my expression, hoping she would conclude I was merely hungry again.

The evening sun bathed the sky in crimson as the road curved to meet the base of the rolling eastern hills and the town slowly became visible in the distance. The town was nestled between the eastern hills and a large expanse of grassy plains to the west. Beyond the hills, farther east, was a forest that separated our civilization from the kingdom of men. I was always told that the forest was impenetrable and had never known someone— whether mage or human—to cross through the forest. Until now.

At first, nothing seemed out of the ordinary. Small stretches of smoke reached toward the sky from the houses just as they would if cozy fires had been started in their fireplaces.

My face slipped as I studied the town's growing silhouette against the darkening sky. When I looked back at Hailey and Ralph they were studying my face seriously, their expressions dropping to an ominous blankness I hoped didn't echo my own.

I reached out and softly touched the horse's hind end. During our brief connection, I asked her to slow. She was hot and sweaty under my touch after having run for so long, but was anxious for the stables she knew were only a few minutes away. She fought her desire to ignore my request, but it became much easier when she saw my thoughts. I felt her flinch in fear as I pulled my hand away from her, unwilling to show her the complete visions I had seen earlier.

As the horse pulled our cart closer to town, the

damage became more evident. It began with the faint smell of charred wood that mixed sickeningly with the scent of roses. The smoke that resembled comforting wisps from far away now turned to menacing billows. They weren't coming from the houses, but from somewhere near the center of town: the schoolyard, the town square, meeting places, and the parliament towers, perhaps.

Hailey looked at me incredulously. I knew the time for protecting them from what I had seen had passed. Her eyes flickered briefly to the smoke-darkened sky, then back to mine.

"Show us what you saw," she commanded.

The muscles along my jawline tightened. I drew in a deep breath in protest but held out a hand to each of them. I closed my eyes and took my memory back to what I had seen through the eyes of the rose. The warm energy from my friends' palms resting on my own began to crawl slowly up my arms. The sensation continued past my shoulders and up my neck until the warmth penetrated my head.

The vision pushed its way to the front of my mind as Hailey and Ralph pulled out the conversation with Joshua the Elder, the smoke-filled town square, the flames devouring the bush I had used for communication, and even the feeling of what it was like for that poor plant in the final moments before it couldn't support my presence.

At first they felt my fear, but then I felt theirs. Seeing into each other's minds was a two-way road. I could hear Ralph's breath quicken as if I had breathed it myself, and Hailey's logic started to fail her.

"We have to find Joshua," she said. "We need to find out what happened to our family."

By family, she meant everyone.

The horse stopped abruptly. We were at the city gates but an odd silence blanketed the town. A solid brick wall surrounded our town, the only entrance through an iron barred gate.

The entrance had never been closed to us before. Watchmen on the walls would have signaled our presence and the gates would have swung open. The town should have been alive with commotion and celebration as the dining hall was prepared.

Memories of smiles from the women and looks of pride from the men were replaced by empty silence. I realized I had no idea how we were going to get into the town.

I threw Hailey and Ralph a frustrated glance, thinking it must have startled them because they were inching toward the far side of the wagon and wore fearful expressions. It took me a few moments to realize they weren't looking at me, but *behind* me, toward a hill that was outside of the city wall. I had the strange sensation of someone watching me. I bolted over the side of the cart in terror. My quick movement was enough to justify Hailey and Ralph's fear. In an instant they were at my side on the ground, huddled behind the wagon.

"What is it?" I asked nervously.

"Someone is coming towards us," Ralph replied in a whisper.

I stole a peek over the wagon and saw a slouched, hooded figure slithering along the edge of the city wall, down the hill toward us. With its quick movements and the dim light of the setting sun, it looked like a shadow.

"Edmund," Hailey pleaded. "Edmund, what do we do?"

The figure was close enough now that we could hear the thudding of footsteps, accented occasionally by the crunching sound of a dry leaf or twig.

"Edmund, don't let it see you," Ralph said, tugging on the blanket I still held around me to hide my nakedness.

I was frozen. I had no idea what to do, but there was something about the way the figure moved that looked familiar. As the shadow got closer I could make out the shape of a man in a hooded cloak; he was almost close enough to make out his features.

The figure stopped suddenly. He stared in our direction, as though he had just noticed the wagon. His weight shifted nervously from one leg to the other before he slowly inched his way towards us.

The figure called out, but it was a cautious cry, "Ed? Edmund?"

My eyes grew wide. The next words fell out of my mouth. "It's Joshua!"

The three of us leapt from behind the cart and ran toward him. His gasp of relief was carried on the wind. When we got close enough, the same relief was obvious on his face.

"Mother Earth!" Joshua exclaimed as we drew ourselves to him. "What happened to you?"

The concern on Joshua's face immediately broke through the wall of protection that fear and tension had created for me. I looked down at my hands and saw the ash; the vision of the tree being consumed in brilliant orange flames caused my eyes to flood. "The fire followed me back," I managed to choke out between sobs. It felt good to finally let the terror I had experienced shake my body as tears rolled out of me.

Joshua pulled me into his cloak and embraced me. "That is terrible, just terrible." He got down on his knees so he could look into my eyes. "Listen to me," he said, pulling Ralph and Hailey into the folds of his cloak as well, "we don't have time for tears. I need you to be strong for a little while longer. I had hoped that you would get back faster."

He turned to all three of us and spoke louder so Hailey and Ralph could hear. "The kingdom of men has taken the town. Those who attacked us intend on inhabiting our village. They consider it secure and believe they hold the only key to the gates." He didn't need to tell us that not even magic could get us through the walls. The city was protected so a person could enter only through the gate. "These men are returning to inhabit the city with their first round of villagers."

Joshua's expression was full of sorrow. He glanced behind himself nervously. "They are just over the hill now; we don't have time to escape."

I heard Hailey let out a breath she had been holding. "What do we do? Why did we come back? You should have run and met us on the road."

Joshua reached into his robes and produced a large golden key.

"I'm searching for anyone that is left. I have a key to the city. Right now, we have to hide. Edmund, take Hailey and Ralph. Run home as quickly as you can. Clean up; get on a change of clothes. I suggest you not look around your house too carefully—these men have left their possessions everywhere. Find your clothes, get changed, and hide down in the cellar."

"Why would they do this?" I asked. "They've always stayed to themselves."

Joshua didn't answer the question. "Go. Hide down in the cellar."

It dawned on me that he wouldn't be coming with us. "Clothes? Why? Where is everyone else?"

The look on my face must have given me away, because Joshua added, "Just trust me, Edmund. Someone has to slow them down to give you time to hide. I'll come for you and we'll all leave together, but we'll need to blend in. Looking like *this* will give you away." He tousled my hair and smirked.

"If they find us, are they going to kill us?" I asked slowly.

Joshua ignored my question again. "Stay in the cellar until sunset. I will find you after dark when it's easier for me to move around undetected. Now, Hailey, Ralph, go." He handed me the key and patted me lightly on the shoulder before turning back up the hill.

On the other side, our enemies were advancing.

I stood for a moment, frozen in fear and confusion. I

watched Joshua's black cloak dance with the movement of his steady feet. Somehow focusing on something that simple and insignificant was all that my mind wanted to do. But I knew I couldn't give into the terror I felt rising from the darkness inside me. Instead, I forced myself to turn toward the city, clutching the key to the gate.

Hailey and Ralph were on each other's heels. The moment I started picking up my feet, adrenaline shot through me like a bolt of lightning. I ran fast and hard, making it to the gate a few lengths behind Ralph. The sun touched the horizon as the heavy iron bars swung open.

We were met by familiar cobblestone streets and intricate brick buildings that made up the frame of our town. There were still roses blooming along trellises and ivy clinging to the buildings. I couldn't help but feel a twinge of pain as I saw the beauty of what my people had built here.

The town was quiet and empty now. There were no people to greet us, no mothers and fathers bustling about, and no entertainers or music. The town was never quiet, but now the only sound was the slight gurgle of water that bubbled in a nearby fountain. The dark streets were covered in long shadows cast by the quickly fading sun. I felt isolated. The cobblestone looked cold. My imagination turned the shadows into nightmares.

Strong, I reminded myself. *Joshua told me to be strong. Just a little longer.*

I swallowed and pushed the fear down into my feet, allowing the warmth of the planet to ground me again.

My dwelling wasn't far from the gates, but we did have to go through the town square. Most of the damage was contained here, surrounded by pristine walls of marble. We walked briskly, but I couldn't stop myself from hesitating at the trellis in the center of the courtyard where a charred rosebush slumped lifelessly over an archway of iron. This bush, only hours ago, had roots that interconnected in a massive underground network to those of Mother Tree, a tree whose unknowing sacrifice I would not soon forget. I found myself aware of an unmarred pocket that miraculously still contained the acorn I had plucked from her. I would care for her last child until I found the perfect spot to plant it.

Ralph and Hailey hadn't gotten far from me during my few quiet moments of reflection. They had stopped in the courtyard to gawk at a smoldering building.

"Parliament?" Hailey's voice cracked.

The white marble building normally stood with a stately grandeur against the pale black sky. At night its pillars would shine bright and warm. Now, one corner was completely collapsed, embers glowing like hundreds of pairs of flaming red eyes. The smoke had stained the marble the same color as the swirling billows that filled the air.

"It's where the Elders would have been," Ralph whispered.

"Are they… dead?"

I interrupted before any of us could consider the question fully. "Joshua said he was gathering the others. He wouldn't have said that unless there were others to gather. We need to keep going. I'm sure Joshua will sort this all out for us."

"But why would he send us into the town instead of sending us to wherever the others are?" Ralph asked, his eyes still fixed on the parliament building, not looking at me.

"Maybe they already left. Maybe he's looking for the other mages who weren't in town or who ran away."

"But…"

"You trust him, don't you?"

"He's an Elder," Hailey said, her voice filled with as much conviction as she was able to muster. It wasn't much, but it was enough to get Ralph to stop asking questions.

His eyes slid to meet mine. "Okay. Let's go then."

So we continued. I picked up my pace as an inky blue

mingled with florescent pink in the sky. I didn't imagine we had much time before the sunlight was completely gone, and if Joshua was going to come for us I hoped he would come before the men got back to our town.

My house was small and simple—our people weren't used to staying long indoors. Two rooms and a cellar was all that were needed for my mother, father, and me. The dwelling was used more as a storage area for our family's possessions rather than a living space. The room we entered had an old wooden table in the center surrounded by three chairs, a sink in one corner, and a cooking pit in the other.

Ralph pumped the sink for me while I rinsed the ash from my skin. The water stung a little on the blisters that had formed. Hailey disappeared into the next room and returned with clean clothes. She had found a pair of my pants but could only find a shirt that belonged to my father and looked like it might drown me. I dressed quickly, putting the shirt on anyway and tucking it in so that I wouldn't look like I was wearing one of my mom's nightgowns.

The fresh material was harsh on my burned skin, but I found if I walked carefully the chafing was bearable.

Ralph stared out the window at the dwindling light, half of his face pulled tightly in his expression of doubt.

The other side seemed smooth but worried. When his eyes met mine, he spoke out of the doubtful side of his mouth, "To the cellar then?"

We were met by the smell of damp earth, which was heightened by the stacks of potatoes, beets, and other earth-grown edible roots stored here. The cellar was carved down and back, so it was larger than the house that sat on top of it. Even with its size, there wasn't much room. Navigating around the stacks of vegetables was something I could never do too easily.

We made our way to the back where the dim light that shined through the cracks of the wooden floor above us couldn't reach. I heard Hailey mutter a spell, followed by the same electric crackling that buzzed in Ralph's fingers when he had snapped them at me earlier this afternoon. We were bathed in light. Hailey had found one of the candles my mom had stashed down here for when she needed to go into the cellar at night.

When we reached the back wall, we could hear the pounding of horses' hooves above us. It started out as a gentle rumble but grew into a roar forceful enough to shake dust loose with the vibration. My heart beat rapidly as I realized how many men were filling our city, yet Joshua still hadn't come for us. Hailey's face looked ghostly white in the candlelight, her blank expression disheartening.

"Keep the light toward the back," I commanded in a whisper. "We don't want it shining up through the floorboards and giving us away."

Her eyes weren't full of fear. Instead they were vacant.

Ralph, on the other hand, looked furious. His eyes were large black disks and his hands were balled into fists. His red hair appeared redder against the packed clay of the wall behind him, the fiery glow of the candle emphasizing every out-of-place hair on his head. He looked disheveled and wild.

I jumped at the sound of heavy boots on the floorboards above us. I was surprised and tensed with fear. The hooves and sounds of wagons outside continued to roar, and now there was somebody in my house.

I hoped it was Joshua coming to get us but I didn't see how that could be possible with all the clamor going on outside. Did Joshua get caught?

Hailey gasped and Ralph shot her a look that cut her off in the middle of the noisy breath. She put her hands to her mouth and her gaze shot to the entrance to the cellar.

We all listened as the footsteps moved around above us. I lost all hope that it was Joshua coming to get us when they didn't head directly toward the cellar door.

I tried to keep my breath deep and regular as a second set of steps echoed across the boards.

"So this is where they are going to have us held up?" a deep voice grumbled.

The first man answered, "Just until we can rebuild some of the larger houses."

"They'll have us spread all over the city at this rate."

Hailey's reaction to the voices was to push her back against the dirt wall as far as she could. Ralph had moved so close to her that it looked like he might have been holding her to keep her from collapsing. I was paralyzed.

There was an unusual sound, like someone dropping nails on the boards above us followed by the echo of heavy breathing. I could tell it was coming from above but I had never realized how sound echoed around the cellar. Rational thought also made me think the heightened senses from the adrenaline running through my body weren't helping.

Whatever was now in my house, in addition to the two men, moved with exceptional speed.

"Ag... get down!" I heard one of the men command. "Clayton! Where can I put your mutt?"

"I think this place has a cellar."

Now it was *my* back against the wall. I had no idea what a "mutt" was, but more importantly, these men knew about the cellar. I saw Ralph and Hailey duck behind a pile of potatoes as footsteps approached the cellar door. Ralph whispered, "Apage!" and we were plunged into darkness.

My eyes didn't immediately adjust, but I could see thin strips of light shining through the floorboards above as I looked at the approximate position of the cellar door. I watched intensely and tried to keep my focus when light flooded down to the dirt floor as the cellar door was opened. I saw one heavy boot on the top step, and then a large object flashed down the stairs, through the light, and disappeared into the shadows before I could make out anything more than a black blur.

Everything was pitch black and silent when the cellar door closed. I held my breath. Hailey and Ralph did the same. They must have felt as I did—that the darkness around us had come alive. The atmosphere had an electric feel to it, making the hair on the back of my neck stand up so straight that it felt like someone was pulling it, like the darkness had hidden hands threatening to capture me.

I heard myself let out a breath and I drew in the next one with caution. I could hear Ralph and Hailey move from their hiding spots, inching toward me. As they grew closer I could hear Ralph's uneven breaths, ragged in the charged air.

"Ralph," I whispered, "be quiet."

But it wasn't the voice of a person that answered. Instead, a deep-throated growl rumbled in response. My eyes darted toward the sound as a bolt of fear raced down my spine. The eyes that met mine were glowing in the dim light, yellow and angry.

I heard a jaw lined with sharp teeth snap and I suddenly knew exactly what a "mutt" was. This dog was unlike any I had encountered. Normal dogs were friendly. I had seen this kind of reaction, but only when threatened by an outsider. Even then, a simple bit of communication would usually reassure and calm the creature. But this animal didn't seem interested in discussing who I was or what it wanted, even when I tried to communicate using expressions the dogs I had known would have understood. Instead, it practically screamed of protection, of anger, of hate.

The low rumble turned into a snarl and the animal's intentions became clear.

My feet started inching me away from the dog before my mind knew what they were doing. Logically I wasn't sure whether it was a good idea to move at all, but self-preservation asserted itself.

The animal's eyes were wild and focused on my fear-stricken face. The snarls coming from between its fangs grew louder, interrupted occasionally by an intimidating bark. The dog was forcing me toward the entrance of the cellar. Faint strips of light from between the upstairs floorboards illuminated the raised hair on the dog's back. The sinews in his giant paws tensed and I could tell he was poised to attack.

When the cellar door swung wide open, I was bathed in light. A strong voice commanded, "Calm!"

The dog sat. His bright eyes grew round and gentle. A floppy tongue fell out of one side of his mouth. The relief I felt was fleeting, however, as I now had a large man staring inquisitively in my direction.

"Sorry about the scare, kid," the man said. "He's trained to be protective. He didn't rough you up any, did he?"

The man made his way down the stairs and stood in front of me. He was easily twice my height and three times my width. He was a warrior, with big heavy boots and pieces of armor that hadn't yet been fully removed. His black hair was plastered to his forehead with sweat, his large questioning eyes had a hardness to them that could only have come from seeing too many horrors that a man shouldn't have to see.

"You all right, kid?"

I searched the man over, looking for any weapons. His hands were both clearly visible, and while he didn't have any weapon that I could see, between his muscular arms and giant hands, I knew he wouldn't need any if he wanted to kill me.

"Kid?"

I realized I hadn't answered his question, but I was too scared to speak. I fought against my tensed neck muscles to shake my head but I wasn't sure if I made enough motion for the man to notice.

His gaze softened and he let out a half-laugh, half-snort. "You must be from the orphanage. They said they were going to send someone over to take care of Max here," he motioned toward the dog. "I didn't expect them to be that quick, though. Why are you down in the cellar anyway?"

He started to walk up the stairs, no doubt expecting me to follow. I shot a quick glance to where Ralph and Hailey were last hiding but I couldn't make out their shapes in the swirling darkness.

"Just exploring, sir," I finally found my voice.

"Well, don't make a habit of it. If you are going to be working for me I can't have you constantly running off."

Working for him? I didn't think so, but I saw no choice but to pretend I was human until I had a chance to escape. I had visions of Joshua coming to my rescue and murdering these men, who no doubt had a hand in murdering my people.

When we got back to the kitchen, the two men in the house continued to pry armor off their bodies.

"We've a meeting in what's left of that parliament building so that should afford you some time to satisfy that curiosity of yours."

How did they know about the parliament building and what it was called?

"Take Max with you, though. He needs a long walk. Get to know your new town, but don't be too late. I expect us to be a few hours. I'd like something to eat when we get back."

They were going to leave me alone? That would make my escape easy. And who exactly did this man think I was, a cook? First I was supposed to work for him and now he had the audacity to treat me like his servant?

"Do you really think you should let him wander around alone?" the second man spoke for the first time. "Could be dangerous."

"The *dangers* have all been eliminated."

The inflection in his voice made me cringe.

"Just..." he seemed to consider exactly what he was going to say before finally settling on "there is no need for you to go *inside* any of the buildings. Understand, boy?"

I nodded.

"What's your name?"

"Edmund," I responded, instantly regretting giving my real name.

"I'm Clayton. Don't stay out too late."

Both men stood. They looked smaller without their armor, even thin, but they carried themselves with such a sense of pride that I still felt the need to fear them. Even after the door was latched behind them I refused to move.

I wish I could say things were quiet once the men had gone, but the rumble of wagons and clump of horses' hooves rattled my small house with a never-ending chorus of noise. I could hear people chattering and see the occasional lamplight swinging past my windows.

The oddest noise, however, was my own breathing. It wasn't frantic or ragged, but slow and calm. It sounded strange to me because I felt anything but calm. I realized how much control I had to exert over myself to keep my emotions in check. Control was something I had been taught all my life. Control ensured a complete openness to Mother Earth and all of her resources. She never lost control. She was never ruled by emotion.

My meditation was cut short when something unexpected bumped into the back of my hand. My stomach lurched so high out of fright that the rest of my body followed. On the way back down I lost my balance and fell awkwardly to the floor. When I opened my eyes, Max was towering over me, his large tongue flopping around, threatening to drip drool onto my face. *So much for emotional control*, I thought.

The dog stared at me. *I need to pee,* his expression said.

"Now you decide to talk," I snorted, pushing him aside to regain my footing.

I've never known anyone to listen, he said, trotting by my side with childlike excitement.

"Well don't get used to it." I opened the door so the dog could get outside. "Make it quick while I go find my friends, and wait for me at the door to let you back in."

Once the dog was outside I returned to the cellar. I cried out for Ralph and Hailey before I was halfway down the stairs.

"Have they gone?" Ralph responded.

"I was terrified for you. Are you okay?" Hailey added.

I ignored their questions. "I think it is obvious Joshua isn't coming for us. We need to get out of here before we're discovered."

"Where will we go?" Ralph asked, panic obvious in his tone.

"We'll head for the ancestral ruins to the north. There are caves for shelter and plenty of rivers for water and plants for food. It is far from the kingdom of men; they probably don't know it exists yet. If any of our people have survived, I'd imagine they would go there."

"Survived?" Hailey repeated.

I turned back up the stairs before I let my expression reflect my feelings to Hailey's question. I didn't answer.

"Edmund," Hailey stated in a thoughtful whisper, "it will take us weeks to get to the ruins by horse."

"Longer by foot."

"We're *walking*?" Ralph shrieked.

"We don't have a choice. I don't know why those men thought I was one of their children, but I think three kids on horses riding *out* of the city instead of *into* it would be suspicious. We are going to have a hard enough time walking out of here."

The gold flecks in Ralph's eyes caught fire in the dim light, but his face was exasperated. "And what if no one is at the ancestral ruins?"

"Then we will summon someone to us," I answered.

Hailey's face turned from fear into sour disbelief. "We aren't powerful enough to perform such a spell."

"Then we will practice until we are!"

The comment came across a little harsher than I had anticipated. Hailey's resulting grimace was enough for Ralph to take action, "It's the best plan we've got. Unless you can think of something better. We're all scared."

"What if they're *all* dead?" Hailey asked. Her question was innocent enough but it brought to the surface the fear that each of us had been trying not to think about.

"I refuse to believe that," I answered, not to reassure Ralph or Hailey, but myself. "And we can stand here all night and bicker over it until those two men that have taken over my house return, or we can gather what we can now, and leave."

It looked like it took all the resolve that he had, but Ralph started packing.

Hailey stood still for a moment, her eyes studying my own. Unexpectedly, she flung her arms around me and held me in a tight embrace.

"You don't have any better ideas, do you?" I asked honestly.

She pulled back, her eyes worried. "I just pray you are right."

THREE

Max's long black hair blended in with the town's dark cobblestone streets. He didn't appear to be much more than a shadow moving rhythmically next to me. The thick pads under his paws made his gait stealthy. His eyes, however, were bright and excited. They caught the light so intensely that the humans we encountered looked at him with fear. He was a bit too curious for my taste; he wouldn't just walk next to me, but had to swerve back and forth down the street putting his nose down as often as possible. I had to call to him a few times to stop him from venturing too far away from us.

Ralph and Hailey were a few steps behind me. We had thrown enough food into some over-the-shoulder bags to last us for a few days' travel which, as long as we weren't followed, would be enough to get us to a spot of land where we could gather more. Luckily, our people were adept at living off the land. Carrying any more in our sacks might have looked suspicious.

The city gates grew closer. I could see the lock was not in place and the bars stood slightly ajar.

Hailey's whisper from behind me was thick with concern. "They left the gates open?"

I could feel a tinge of fear center on my neck. It might seem strange for a civilization as interconnected to the environment as ours to live in a town surrounded by a large brick wall and iron barred gates. Our gates were never open at night, and with reason. I had no idea men were our enemies until tonight. They were just another species we shared our planet with, like any other animal— but we did have other enemies. Our greatest enemy was a dark species long ago subdued that would every now and again be successful in getting through the city walls to snatch one of our children. Because the kingdom of men had no magical connection to the planet, these energumen, as they were called, could prey on them without consequence.

"So what?" Ralph bantered. "We were going out there anyway."

I turned around in time to see Hailey give Ralph one of her looks. "*We* have means of protecting ourselves. The humans don't."

"So?" I said, surprised at the venom in my voice. "Let the humans suffer. I hope the energumen take them all."

Now Hailey was angry. "We don't even know what happened here."

"You're *defending* them? You saw the same thing I did," I scoffed. "I showed you the memory of Joshua. You know what he said. He never came to get us. What do you think happened to him?"

Now she was close to tears. "They can't *all* be dead."

If even one mage was dead, that was enough for me to punish all the humans—if it were my choice. So I chose to ignore Hailey. I didn't want to respond and confirm my own fear. Instead I turned and walked toward the gate.

I hadn't made it two steps before a large man emerged from between two buildings. Since I hadn't been paying attention to where I was going, I ran into his hard body with enough force that it would have made a normal man stumble over me. This man, however, was so large that I stumbled over him and tumbled onto the street.

"What are you kids doing?" he asked accusingly.

I was surprised to hear Ralph answer before I could even get back on my feet. "We're from the orphanage. We were told to take this dog for a walk."

I looked up in time to see the man's expression pucker. He pointed one long, thick finger toward the gate.

"You see those carriages approaching? They hail from the orphanage. I don't see them here just yet."

Ralph appeared to physically shrink as the color drained from his face.

"To which family do you belong, boy? Your father will no doubt want to hear about the misdeeds of the liar he shelters as a son."

"It's my fault, sir." I found myself talking before I had even thought the words. "The stories he tells get us in trouble with strangers often. Certainly you can't blame him for being scared. You are a rather," I gulped, "large man, sir."

The looming figure softened his stance enough to put down his pointing finger, but his eyes were still wary of us. "Then this is your dog, boy?"

"Yes."

"And I assume he is well trained?"

I hesitated, not sure of where this line of questioning was meant to lead me. "Yes."

"Then if you tell the truth, if he is your animal, and if he is well trained as you claim, make him do something for me."

So it was meant to be a test. "What would you like to see him do?" I asked.

The man pondered for a moment. When he asked his

question, it had a carefully contained inflection, like he was trying to hide something. "Does he hunt?"

"Yes."

The man took an ominous step forward and started pointing again, this time toward the dog. "That breed cannot hunt," he said between clenched teeth.

I had to take a step back to avoid being squashed by this man's sudden tirade. He took another violent step in my direction.

"I assure you he can!" I pleaded.

My feet were off the ground a moment later. The man grabbed me by my shirt and hoisted me up toward his face. When our noses were mere inches from each other he spoke, "Then have him hunt something for me."

The look in his eye was total victory, but he set me back down and glanced toward Max.

I need you to find something alive for me, Max. Anything will do. Some animal. Bring it back to me.

Max's expression was the dog equivalent of someone rolling their eyes. *How am I supposed to do that?*

You're the dog! Haven't you ever, you know, chased anything around?

Besides my tail? His expression was playful.

"Well?" The man grew impatient.

"Max, hunt!" I commanded in the most authoritative

voice I could muster.

The dog looked at me, obviously disgusted, but bounded for the gate.

The first carriage had just arrived, but was too large to fit through the gate. Max ducked under the carriage door as it opened, and startled the person climbing out. She sputtered profanities as she missed the last step and hit the ground with much less grace than she was obviously accustomed to expecting. Her dress was flowing and fit her wide frame with tailored precision. At the sight of her, the man who had threatened us ran to throw open the gate and greet her.

"Madam Lucacious," he said, taking her gloved hand and pressing it to his mouth.

"Hello, Frederick," she responded, acting as if having to acknowledge his presence was difficult.

We used this chance to make our way toward the gate. As soon as we were at the bars, I could see three other carriages lined up behind the first. Each was as large as the one towering above me.

"How many children?" Frederick was asking.

"61." The woman responded to Frederick's inquiries with the shortest sentences possible. As she made her way into the town, she looked down at us, her face twisted in disgust. "Uhg," she groaned. "It might be 64."

Ralph, Hailey, and I looked around at each other, trying to understand her meaning. It wasn't until the children started unloading from the carriages that we realized we looked as ragged as they did.

"This is perfect," Hailey whispered. "We can use the kids as a distraction to weave through the carriages and around the wall." She was already leading us out the gates and toward the same hill where we had met Joshua earlier that evening.

My eyes were on the children as we carefully made our way toward the open country. Each child carried a small lumpy pillowcase, no doubt filled with a few personal belongings. They huddled together, wearing weary looks on their faces as they surveyed their new surroundings.

I admit I wasn't watching where I was going. I was too busy taking pleasure in the image of these human children all being terrified of the city walls that towered above them. When I ran straight into the back of Ralph, I muttered a quick apology. I took a step back, expecting him to turn around and yell at me for not paying attention, but he stood there with his back to me. That's when I noticed his hands were balled into fists. He looked intently between the ground and Hailey, who was also frozen in place.

"Are you sure?" she asked in a quivering voice. I

realized I had missed something.

Ralph didn't answer immediately. I took a step to the side so I could see around him.

"Edmund?" Hailey's voice was pleading with me.

When I could see between them, I followed Ralph's eyes to a large snake coiled stealthily in the high grass.

"It's just a snake," I said, stating the obvious, almost questioning the reason for their rigidity.

Then Ralph muttered a word that all three of us had already thought once tonight. The word caused my stomach to ball like Ralph's fists and a surge of adrenaline caused my body to tense as rigidly as my friends': "Energumen."

"Are you sure?" I repeated Hailey's question.

This was Ralph's gift. He had the ability to see things the rest of us couldn't see; the possession of a creature, like this snake, for example. Ralph nodded his head, and we all took an instinctive step back.

Energumen weren't particularly dangerous to children of our age. The first spell we learned as soon as we could speak was the one to remove an energumen from their physical host. Energumen were spiritual creatures that had powers of their own, but could only manifest those powers if they had possession of a living body. An energumen in a physical body was definitely something to fear, but the knots in my stomach weren't because of that. The spell to exorcize the energumen was visual, and the men who made our entire magical race vanish were only a few yards away.

As if sensing our tension, the snake reared its head, its dark, hallow eyes centered on me.

How odd and how strange, we could all hear it speak, *that I would find three little mages while seeking for men.* Its voice was strangely sweet and alluring, quiet, like a whisper that sounded like a song. The creature inched toward us. We took another step back. *Perhaps I will take you back to my realm, and leave the men be. A great reward for one mage; imagine the prize for three!*

The snake lurched forward and we fell back. I felt myself hit the ground and heard Hailey and Ralph fall near my side. I tried to rebound but an unseen force pinned down my body. The world seemed to shift and I could feel the use of magic around me. My gaze was thrust into darkness, another spell cast by the energumen.

"Edmund!" Hailey called out to me, "What do we do?"

I didn't know how to answer her. If the energumen took us we would be dead, but if we used our powers to stop it the men would undoubtedly see and we would meet the same fate as our entire race. My mind, which had maintained rational much longer than I would have expected it to during this whole ordeal, was blank.

My friend, my friend! What is wrong?

This voice was familiar, but that familiarity sent another shock of fear coursing through my body—not for me—but for the owner of the voice. "Max! Stay away!" I called, but I was too late.

I heard a growl and a loud bark followed by the snapping of Max's powerful jaw. The response was a rhythmic chuckle that hissed. My mind conjured up images of Max fighting the snake, unaware of the evil contained inside. His growls were like the ones down in the cellar, when his white fangs and yellow eyes glowed viciously in the pale light. Those images, terrifying as they were, seemed playful compared to the murderous look in the empty eyes of the possessed snake.

Another snap of teeth, then a whine, and I knew it was over. I could hear Max's heavy breathing but his growls changed to high-pitched cries. The energumen would come for us.

I didn't know who cast the spell, but the sound of it was thunderous. The blindness was replaced by piercing white light. I could hear the energumen scream as it was ripped from its host. The spell was so healing that, for a few seconds, I thought myself invincible.

All that gave way when I heard the screaming.

At first it was far away, like in a dream, but as I slowly realized I was still lying on the ground, the screams grew closer and louder. I opened my eyes to see frantic children running around us as they fled up the hill. I got to my feet quickly. I thought I saw Ralph do the same, but his red hair was swept away into the crowds of screaming human children.

I only made it up the hill a few steps before two children barreled into the back of my knees, knocking me back to the ground. I sputtered as the taste of dirt filled my mouth. Movement, different than the rampage of children's feet, caught my eye. I turned my head to the left to see the snake, which was now just a snake, trying to escape the stampede. It nipped at a few heels that got too close, but with all the targets, it never got to sink its teeth into any.

A booming voice silenced all of the screaming. "Children! Sit down!" it commanded.

I whirled to see Madam Lucacious running up the hill toward us.

"Sit!" she demanded again as she lifted her dress above her ankles so her running legs could stretch for further strides.

The children began falling to the sitting position in

waves. I rolled over and got into the sitting position as well, hoping to blend in.

Madam Lucacious stopped as soon as she was close to the first line of sitting children, which was still far enough away from me for comfort. It took me a minute to take in my surroundings. I realized all of us were now far enough up the hill that I could see over the town wall.

The spell must have triggered a reaction inside the town as well. I saw the same confusion and frantic behavior inside the wall as I had seen with the children.

A cold hand touched mine and I recoiled. I spun to see Hailey sitting by my side. Her expression was fearful.

Ralph? I mouthed to her.

She shook her head, indicating she hadn't seen him, but then motioned her head sideways down the hill. I followed her gaze to where Max was lying in a motionless heap of long black fur.

My feet reacted before my mind did. Before I could consider the consequences, I bounded to Max's side. There were a few reactions from the children, and I was sure I had caught the eye of more than one adult, but I was sitting again so quickly that I must not have caused too much panic.

Max's eyes were dull, but he was breathing. I ran my hand through his fur gently, not surprised to feel thick wetness under the fleshy parts of his stomach. The energumen had been cast out, but the snake was still naturally venomous.

I'm sorry, his thoughts seemed to waft to me on the wind.

"You'll be okay," I said, a little weaker than I wanted to.

Max rested his head on my lap, closing his eyes while I stroked the fur between his ears.

When I looked back up, a large group of men had gathered at the base of the hill. Some appeared to be standing guard while others clamored excitedly, making large gestures with their hands in an attempt to visually explain to their neighbors the large flash they had seen. A quick survey revealed a few of the children mimicking their elders, clapping their hands together in an attempt to recreate the cracking noise they had heard.

I realized I was clinging to a hope that perhaps the spell would be misunderstood as a lightning bolt, but the gathering army of humans pushed that hope down to where it formed a pit in my stomach. Feelings of fear were becoming too familiar, but with that familiarity came greater control of the emotion.

I thought I was going to be able to erase any look on my face that might betray how I felt until the clamoring men grew silent. Every eye moved to the base of the hill as the air grew thick with tension. I could see some shuffling in the crowd before it parted and a man wider than the keeper at the gate stepped to the front, eyeing all of the children with contempt.

This man had an interestingly proportioned body. He was shorter than most of the humans I had seen. In that case, he was shorter than most of my people, but his thickness reminded me of a tree. The color of his skin was darker than I had ever seen, so dark that his head seemed to vanish against the black sky behind him—except for the whites of his eyes, which burned like lava.

It was Madam Lucacious who finally broke the silence. "General Dougal, your grace," she curtsied.

The man spoke out of the side of his mouth without taking his eyes off us. "Madam Lucacious, in your opinion, what took place here?"

"Nothing I have ever seen," she responded.

"Not natural then?"

"I don't see how."

I could see the muscles in the general's arms tighten at her words. "Have you been trained in these matters?"

Madam Lucacious shifted uncomfortably, hesitating before she responded. "Told, yes. But not trained."

"Did you see anyone on the hill?"

"Just my children."

Dougal's arm flew so quickly toward the man next to him that I didn't actually see him grab the man by the shirt and reposition him so closely that their eyes met. The general spoke so low to the man that I had a hard time piecing together his sentence. "Take your battalion and cut off anyone found fleeing through the forest."

The man dashed through the crowd and back into the city, a few others following him.

General Dougal turned back to Madam Lucacious. "Test them all. If any magics are found among them, kill them."

The pit in my stomach leapt, bursting through my body like pinpricks. Every hair was standing on edge.

"Okay, children!" Madam Lucacious's voice boomed, and she clapped her hands even though she already had everyone's rapt attention. "Pluck a strand of grass," she did this herself, demonstrating, "and hold it in your hand with your fingers curled around the base. Pretend your fist is a pot, with the blade sticking up."

The pit in my stomach began moving upward again. I felt nauseated. This simple test would be successful, but how the humans had learned it bewildered me. I glanced at Hailey, whose colorless face stared at Madam Lucacious with horrified intensity. She already had her blade outstretched in front of her. I saw a second blade sprout between her shaking fingers.

The one power we couldn't control was our connection to the earth. In fact, this connection wasn't even a power, but the source of our powers. Placing a broken blade of grass in our palm, with our warm fingers around it had the same effect of being planted directly into the lifeblood of Mother Earth. Rather than comparing the plants between children, these humans would be able to see the plant *growing* in our hands.

The group of men at the base of the hill moved toward us. They carefully inspected the first line of children's plants before excusing them into the town. Sixty children; probably fifteen men. The lump of fear I felt was now a physical lump in my throat. Still, I didn't dare reach for my own blade of grass.

Through the thousand pricks of fear exploded a moment of realization: we were going to be discovered and then probably killed. I thought about Ralph—if he was any lower on the hill than we were he might already be caught. It felt like a long time had passed since he pulled me from the burning tree but it had been only hours.

Only fire cast by magic could have followed you back through the roots, his words came to me, followed by the words of this awful test, *Pretend your fist is a pot, with the blade sticking up.*

If the events of this day were like dominoes stacked carefully in a line, those words were the catalyst that started them tumbling. If those dominoes fell in time, drawing the plans to a perfect scheme, their tumbling would reveal the artist behind those events.

A memory flashed through my mind, one of my happiest memories. My parents, both smiling, had taken me to a symphony a few years ago. Their faces were so excited to watch mine light up as I experienced live music combine with the songs of the planet. I found myself particularly captivated by the conductor who controlled the music. He timed the instruments with the vibrations of the planet. Without him, there could be no orchestration. My parents called him "the grand maestro."

I shuddered violently as I began to understand the awful orchestration that had unfolded here. There was only one explanation, only one reason our town could have been destroyed by magical fire, only one reason these men would know our secrets: we had been betrayed. My shuddering stopped as my vision became perfectly clear. Only one of our own could have cast the flames that followed me back through the roots of Mother Tree. Only one of our own could have taught the humans how to distinguish us from them. And there was only one of our own who was still somewhere here, lurking in the shadows of the forest, or perhaps in the town. Our betrayer, the conductor, the grand maestro of betrayal, was Joshua.

FOUR

I didn't have time for tears but they came anyway. They had threatened so many times during this ordeal that I finally couldn't fight them. I tried to push my emotion into the planet and failed. Something in me finally broke. I felt alone. Even if Joshua came for us, we wouldn't be saved. I didn't know where my people were or if any of them were still alive.

Sobs rolled through my body while hot tears ran down my face. My breath was ragged. I cried for my people. I cried for our betrayal. I cried because I didn't know what else to do.

My eyes were too blurred to notice when heavy boots were standing in front of me, but I felt someone rest their hand lightly on my head before speaking. I was too exhausted to care, so I didn't flinch. This was it. This was the moment I would be caught, but I was overcome by apathy.

"Hey, kid, you okay? What happened?"

I was startled enough by the familiarity of the voice that one of the sobs rolling through my body caught in my throat. I rubbed the tears from my eyes so I could see clearly, recognizing the face of the man who was now crouched over me. It was the man from earlier at my house, Max's owner.

It took me a minute to realize he thought my tears were for Max. I looked down at the black heap in my lap and curled my hand through the thick black hair. Max's eyes were closed, the limp body cold under my touch. Tears sprang back to my eyes, this time for a friend I'd known just long enough for him to save my life.

The man, Clayton, if memory served, had compassion in his eyes. "Come on, let's get back to the house," he said. "It isn't good for you to be out here now."

I glanced down at Max.

"Leave him," Clayton answered, his voice soft. "I'll take care of him after you are asleep."

I knew that following this man back into town would ensure my survival for at least a little while, so I stood and followed him down the hill.

I watched as the general's eyes followed us closely.

"I know the boy. He is not who we seek," Clayton

stated as we passed him. The testimony seemed to ebb any suspicion.

When we reached the town gates, I glanced back toward the hill. From this vantage point, Ralph's red hair stood out like a bush on fire. I was glad to see he had found Hailey. They were sitting together and managed to make their way up toward the tree line, putting the maximum distance between them and the small army descending upon the children. Still, I knew I had to do something to help.

Clayton noticed my hesitation. "Come on, boy. The other kids will be fine."

I wondered how much longer he would remain unsuspicious while misreading my actions. What would he do to me when he found out I wasn't the human he thought I was? Nevertheless, for the time being I was strangely grateful to this man.

I used the opportunity, the moment Clayton thought I felt concern for the children, to attempt the salvation of two of them. I knew there was no way to get Hailey and Ralph out of the situation without being caught. I had seen Hailey's plant sprout from between her fingertips and imagined that those new sprouts also had sprouts. Once her plant was seen, she would be exposed. If Ralph had been foolish enough to pluck his own blade of grass, it would be in the same condition. There was only one way I could think to disguise them. It wouldn't require a spell, just a favor—and a messenger.

I was immediately aware of the wind around me. It was calm, but fluid and cool as it brushed by my hot cheeks. I allowed myself to be encircled by it until I could almost hear where it had come from, almost see the fields and mountains it had passed through to get here, almost smell the sweet moisture it carried from faraway rivers and lakes. Then I asked it to carry a message. I added my words to the tastes, sounds, smells, and sights it already carried. *Ask them to grow*, I told it. *Ask them all to grow.* Then, for Hailey and Ralph I hastily added, *I will meet you at the ruins.*

As my words were carried off, I turned back to the town, my town, and quickened my pace. I had just stepped back onto the cobblestone street when I began to hear stifled gasps. I knew what was happening: every blade held in the hand of every child was sprouting; every one was growing. I thanked Mother Earth for honoring my request and asked her to watch over my friends.

When we got back to the house, I made Clayton some onion and potato soup from the vegetables in the cellar. Kind as this man was to me, I was still nothing more than a servant to him.

The soup was not the feast I had been hoping for in the wagon this afternoon, but it was quick to make. I set my empty bowl on the wooden table and stared intently as drops of broth fell from the well-kept hair around Clayton's chin.

"May I ask you a question?"

Clayton held out his bowl to me in response. I wasn't sure what to make of the look on his face, so I refilled the bowl and asked the question anyway.

"I heard a lot of the children tonight talking about someone named Joshua."

Clayton's eyes narrowed in response. Somehow he managed to grunt and swallow at the same time.

"They said he isn't... human."

Now he chuckled. "He's human enough. The people that lived here before us were dangerous. Conniving little gnomes they were. Joshua was one of their leaders; he helped us purge this town. No need to be afraid of him. He's a friend to us."

I took our bowls to the sink and acted like I was cleaning up so that I could turn away from him and brace for the next answer. "So the people who lived here before? They're dead?" I bit my lip.

I certainly didn't expect Clayton to laugh, but he did. "Boy, those kids in that orphanage must tell some stories.

Let me set the record straight so you don't have nightmares. The people that lived here before were sort of… magical… you know? They respond to herbs and stuff. Most could be controlled."

Most. The word was emphasized in my head, but at least there was hope. Still, I had to get him to finish the thought. "Most?" I asked. "How did the control work? What about those who couldn't be controlled?"

"Don't ask too many questions about magic. You wouldn't understand anyway."

Try me, I thought, but kept my expression inquisitive.

"And as for those who couldn't be controlled? Well kid, that wasn't my job."

He avoided my question, so I tried a different approach. "Magic? Like what happened tonight with the other kids? Do you think Joshua did that?"

Clayton visibly stiffened. "No. Joshua has been at the parliament building in meetings with us all night."

Now I stiffened. I had hoped Joshua had been killed or "controlled," too. After all, I couldn't think of any reason why the humans would still need him. But he was still alive, in the town, and I was right where he had told me to wait for him.

Clayton once again misread my expression. "Don't worry about it. Whoever cast the spell tonight will be caught. Joshua will see to that. And I'm here. You'll be sleeping just one room over."

My body was exhausted but I knew I wouldn't be able to sleep. I had to come up with another excuse to disappear.

I knew exactly where I would go. No one in town knew what my father did except him and the patriarch—the appointed leader of our people. Because of the secrecy of his work, his office was located in the parliament building, near the back, toward a far corner. The entrance was hidden. He'd shown me his office once before; I was certain I could find it again. My mind sifted through images of the partially destroyed building. I was sure my father's office was on the side that hadn't been damaged.

At this thought my heart skipped a beat. If my father had been working during the attack, or if he had escaped, he could be in his office right now waiting for me.

Clayton eyed me pensively. Again I had to push down the bubbling fear in my stomach as I worried that my face had given away my thoughts. Thankfully, this man seemed oblivious. "I know you don't want to talk about it," he said, changing the subject, "but I would like to know what happened to Max."

Sadness tugged at the corners of my mouth, an emotion that never really left me, but had been subdued in the whirlpool of others currently swirling throughout my body. Grief rose to the surface more forcefully now, making the small house we were in seem empty without Ralph and Hailey. I was afraid for their safety. That fear reminded me of the energumen. I was afraid of them. That fear, in turn, reminded me of Max. It was a vicious cycle.

"I think he was bitten by a snake," I responded, rubbing my eyes to ease the sudden headache that blurred my vision.

I heard Clayton push himself up from the table and walk two steps toward the door. "Well, I'm going to go take care of him then. You get some sleep, boy. You look tired."

My ever-sliding range of emotions wasn't helped by Clayton's civility toward me. It was hard to imagine such a man had played part in the destruction of my people. Yet the only hatred I could find for him was in imagining what he would do if he knew who I really was. Could I afford to doubt what would happen if he learned the truth? Could it be possible for him to look at me with understanding? Were humans truly a race of monsters? I had to accept that if my people consisted of both good and bad, then it was possible for humans to fall into the same ratio.

Then again, what kind of compassion would I show an energumen who pretended to be a member of my race, only to reveal to me his true form? If humans viewed me as I viewed them, then fear would win out. No matter the amount of love originally felt, it would be forgotten as soon as truth was spoken.

I waited until I could no longer hear Clayton's footsteps marching heavily along the cobblestone that twisted to the city gates. I waited a few minutes more to make sure he wouldn't return. I knew that once he had taken care of Max's body and returned to discover I was no longer in the house, any trust I might have established with him would be broken. It wouldn't take long for the entire human population to begin looking for me. There was no coming back this time.

Had I been thinking more clearly I would've packed extra food and a change of clothes instead of leaving with nothing but what I had on. The knowledge that I was waiting exactly where Joshua knew I was spurred my feet into action. I would rather face any human as the child they would mistake me for, than face Joshua as the mage he knew I was.

My feet were light and quick on the dark alleys as I made my way to the parliament building. I kept my pace slow enough that anyone watching wouldn't have reason to suspect I was up to something. I surmised that a boy running through the streets would draw too much attention, so I only allowed myself to sprint briefly through the back passages where the streetlamps' flickering glow refused to reach.

My heart thudded in my chest as the great white building rose higher the nearer I got to the center of town. I saw the beautiful lawns again. We always kept the grass maintained, but not perfectly, so that it was long enough to ripple in the wind. The trellises of white flowers lining pathways were built as homage to the chaotic yet geometric shapes we found in nature. Now most of the trellises were blackened by fire. The smell of ash was as strong here as it had been in my vision, but a light breeze carried other scents that mingled strangely into a smell that was almost euphoric, like a campfire in the mountains surrounded by evergreen and aspen trees.

A group of men were working on the northeast corner of the building repairing the masonry. Almost every window inside the building was ablaze, so they had plenty of light by which to work.

I had underestimated the number of humans here tonight. If there were enough of them to warrant using every room in parliament, plus those that were staying in the intact houses, they were more than a few clusters of peons getting the town ready for the real invasion, they were the kingdom that inherits the goods an army procures. They must have numbered in the thousands since at least that many could fit in the parliament building.

The fact that I wasn't going to be able to avoid contact with humans wasn't enough to make me change my plans, just enough to make me edit them a bit. I turned down the stone walkway and circled around to the south end of the building, facing the meager side of town. I doubted that human pride would allow them to stay in cramped quarters unless they had no other choice. This meant fewer humans to encounter. It would make for a little longer trip in the dark, but I wouldn't have to cross as many of the marble hallways once inside of the building.

I shouldn't have been surprised to see children once I got to the south side of town. I expected the orphans to be housed in the school where Ralph, Hailey, and I had lived since we were six. There was a large communal space there for teaching as well as joint dormitories. The surprise came when I discovered the children were crowded into three tiny, connected lofts that we had used for those who didn't require many resources—singles who could take care of themselves, couples with no young children, or those who couldn't prove useful to our society, like those with disabilities or the elderly who had not learned a trade that would be taught to the younger generation. I couldn't help but do the math: sixty or so children in three lofts meant there were twenty or more per loft. I was glad no one was around to see the disgusted look on my face.

My father's office was on the southeast side of the building. In order to get there—or at least to *remember* how to get there—I would have to enter the southwestern doors. When my father brought me a few years ago, we entered through the main lobby on the north. There was a large central hallway that connected to the southern wing where we turned east. I had to find that juncture again if I was going to have any luck.

The pace I set was a compromise between speed and stealth. The last thing I wanted was to draw attention to myself. I spied an empty hallway through the large glass doors. I tugged on one of them and crossed through into a sea of marble. Large, brightly lit chandeliers hung from the intricately designed and inlaid ceiling. The light reflected throughout the long white corridor, but instead of looking sterile and stark, the hallways glimmered with warmth.

I heard low murmurs like distant echoes, but the voices blended and I couldn't make out what was being said. I wasn't sure how far away the voices were from me, but the hallway I was standing in was deserted.

Evenly spaced potted trees reached toward the ceiling, lining the hallway, alternating with evenly spaced mirrors stretching from floor to ceiling. Everything in this building was ornate, from the gold crown molding to the masonry of the pots. The trees were perfectly trimmed into towering cones of leaf (some species of tree preferred to be trimmed as it made them feel more proper). I was always easily distracted when I was allowed in this building (and I was only allowed when I was accompanied by my father). There was so much to look at: the doorknobs, the framing, the swirls in the marble floor. It was all perfect.

Tonight, the only thing I examined was my reflection in the mirror. My hair was sloppy, my eyes were dark and hard, and my clothes were too big for my frame. No wonder the woman from the orphanage mistakenly confused me for one of her children. There was a bulge in my shirt pocket. I remembered the acorn I'd promised to plant in this town for Mother Tree. That was one more thing I'd have to do before leaving for the ruins tonight.

The entire survey took less than a second before I moved again. I passed a few closed doors without considering whether they were locked or if people were inside. I counted myself lucky none of them stood open, filled with humans who might see me, ask questions, or become angry. Worse, they could discover that I wasn't one of them.

I stopped to estimate my position in the building. A hallway intersected with my current corridor, but this hallway was too slender to be the main one I had walked through with my father. The second was wide enough, but angled sharply after a few hundred feet; it didn't extend all the way through the building to the northern lobby.

It wasn't until the fifth intersection that I stopped, letting out a quiet sigh. This hallway had chandeliers that were larger than the rest. Their crystal facets cast brilliant rainbows. The largest of these chandeliers was down the hall, all the way on the other side of the building, where it was centered in the main lobby. People darted back and forth from room to room underneath it. From this distance, they looked as tall as my hand, but their voices echoed down the hall loudly. Most of the conversations sounded stressed.

I didn't pause long. I continued east down the hallway, glad that my memory made the pathway familiar. My father's office was now one... two... three mirrors down.

Again I found my reflection staring back at me. My face twisted in concentration. This mirror not only marked the entrance to my father's office, but also because of the secrecy required by his position and work, it *was* the entrance. Self-doubt caused me to grimace. When father brought me here, he shattered the mirror to reveal a winding staircase behind it. He had the power to make the broken molecules lining the splintered shards piece themselves back together with seamless perfection. Even to the trained eye, the mirror appeared whole again.

My powers were not great at piecing together what was broken. That gift belonged solely to my father.

I saw the eyes in my reflection flicker with panic. I had come all this way without considering how I would get into my father's office.

I don't think you are SUPPOSED to be here! a sinister voice whispered so close to my ear that I jerked to get away from it and ended up off-balance, landing sideways onto the floor. I scrambled to regain my footing, but settled instead with my back against the opposite wall in a seated position. I wasn't sure how my feet managed to push me so quickly to the other side of the hall. I glanced around nervously for the source of the voice, but the hallway was empty.

My heart was beating so fervently in my chest that I felt the pulse shake my entire body.

You must get out before they find you!

This time the voice was to my left. In my huddled position, all I could do was snap my head toward it and push in the opposite direction with my feet. My backward slide turned into a quick-paced crab-walk until my back hit something hard enough to stop me. Again, the hall was empty.

My ragged breathing grew steady and quick as I realized that, in fact, the hall was not empty. I twitched a little as the voice returned, this time above me.

Get up! You must escape!

I looked, this time with more clarity, and saw the geometric lines of a beautiful tree. My back pressed deeply against the curvature of one of the pots.

I took a deep breath, trying to calm myself. I stood and approached the tree nearest to the mirror, the first tree that had spoken.

Is my father in there? I asked, ignoring the whispered warnings going on all around me.

In where? the tree responded, obviously playing dumb.

How about in the secret room behind the mirror! My voice bordered on hysteria.

There is no room.

Trees are notoriously bad liars. *If my father is down there, he is waiting for me. He would break the glass to get through the mirror, but my ability to repair the glass is… well… I couldn't.*

If your father is down there, couldn't he repair the glass?

So now you are admitting there is a secret room?

No answer.

I continued, *Is there another way into the room somewhere? One that wouldn't require me to break anything?*

I can only say this: your father may have broken the glass, but the patriarch would not.

Then how did he get through?

The glass became a ripple, and he would simply step through.

Understanding crossed my mind almost before the tree finished its sentence. The properties of glass were one of the oddities of science. I remembered a lesson I had a few years earlier when we discussed solids, liquids, and gasses. One of the students presented glass as an example of a solid, but the Elder told us that, in fact, glass was a liquid. The evidence was in the old windowpanes in the oldest of our buildings, where the glass at the bottom was thicker than the glass at the top. Glass had a flow, a response to gravity. It ran downhill… just like water.

I grinned devilishly. If this Elder was right, then I wouldn't have to change the physical makeup of the mirror to get through it. I would just have to make it more… liquidy.

I put my hands against the mirror, concentrating until I felt the charged building-blocks of the glass like millions of electric shocks pressing back against me. I felt them speeding up to my will, until the whole pane shuddered against my touch. Soon my hands felt as if they were sinking into thick dough. I couldn't help but feel a twinge of excitement as cool air swirled from the other side.

I pressed harder and put a foot through. My arms were up to their elbows. Then there was less resistance. I felt the glass recoil from the pressure my face and torso exerted. With one final ripple, I stepped through to the other side.

I couldn't help but laugh as I turned to see the hallway through a pane of glass. My way was *much* cleaner than my father's.

I was familiar with the solid brick landing at the top of a spiral staircase. While the parliament building had a carved and intricate flair to its architecture, once through the mirror it changed to an older dark brick. The marble floors were replaced by carefully laid cobblestone sealed with rough mortar; the giant chandeliers and gold-plated molding morphed into crude bronze gas piping that burped flames.

I was not afraid here. I knew that only my family, and the patriarch, knew how to find this staircase. I was not afraid to meet any of my people, except Joshua. But not even he should know the secret of this place.

I bounded down the stairs without hesitation, sprinting through rough hallways that twisted to dark rooms hidden well beneath the building. All I had to do now was stay in the main corridor until it ended at my father's office. My heart filled with exuberance as I rounded the last corner and saw bright light spilling out from underneath the heavy wooden door.

The word "father" ripped out of my chest like a growl as I threw myself into the room. I had only vague memories of this place, but it was obvious that a lot had been misconstrued in my younger memory or had changed. The grandeur of the office had not been understated. It was comprised of multiple rooms and an upstairs loft. The upper area was where my father's large mahogany desk sat, along with a balcony that overlooked the largest of the lower rooms.

The lower rooms were more of a library than anything else. The largest room's walls were filled with countless leather bound books. One of the smaller rooms to the right, underneath the loft, held neatly rolled scrolls and parchments. When I was younger, I wasn't allowed to look at the writings in the office, not that I could've read them anyway.

The opportunity to immerse myself in reading and learning within these rooms did not escape me, but the desire to find my father weighed heavier on my mind.

"Father?" I cried again. Only the stillness of the air answered.

Was he hiding, scared, or worried that my voice was an imitation? The thought of my father cowering in a corner was so atypical that it was almost funny. Still, I inched further into the large room so he could plainly see me from any vantage point in the office.

"Father, it's me, Edmund. Are you here?"

Lamps illuminated the entire room. This added to my hope that my father was here, but only my frantic calls and heavy breathing broke the silence.

I climbed the delicate wrought iron staircase with caution. The eerie silence bothered me, but my hope of finding a safe place, and more, of finding my father in it, outweighed any doubt or fear.

I saw the corner of the desk expand as I climbed the stairs. As I approached the top, I spied a dark figure sitting in a throne-like chair. The lighting was dimmer up here, with only one lamp illuminating the yellowed pages of a book that sat on the desk.

"Father?" I asked cautiously, inching forward, waiting for any sign of movement.

There was no response from the dark figure. My father must have worn his dress robes in to work, or perhaps he had gone home to get them so he could better hide up here in the dark. I didn't understand why he would need to hide. Concealing his identity, perhaps?

"It really is me. It's Edmund. Can you talk to me?"

I took another step closer, half bracing for the sudden

movement from the desk I was sure would happen any moment now. I didn't want it to startle me.

"I'm going to light this lamp." I made my way through a maze of books. It was so unlike him to leave things lying about.

"Are you asleep?"

I waved my hand. A spark flew from the lamp on the desk to the one beside me. As the spark caught, the filament inside burst into a hazy orange, filling the room with light. My eyes, however, saw red. Sorrow and anger overwhelmed me.

My father was there, his hand resting lightly atop a book on the desk. He wasn't wearing any robes. The dark shadows his figure cast were from charred pieces of flesh that hung loosely from his bones, blackened by fire.

My knees buckled. An ungodly howl tore through my body, starting from the tips of my toes and escaping from my mouth. My body convulsed, full of the relentless pain. I was only vaguely aware of knocking stack after stack of books to the ground and over the balcony. I writhed in agony, streams of tears gushing from my eyes. The muscles in my chest convulsed, forcing the air out of my lungs. I choked between sobs to refill them.

I coughed spit and vomit as I took out my thirst for violence by throwing book after book as hard as I could manage. I continued until I had thrown a book through every one of the lamps, plunging the rooms into total darkness. When I no longer had the strength to throw another book, I curled into a ball under my father's blackened feet and wished for death. I wanted to disappear, to sink into utter oblivion, anything to avoid the pain.

I ran out of tears before I quit sobbing. I didn't quit sobbing until my exhausted body succumbed to sleep.

***

I don't know how long I slept but it was broken by a bright light that stained my closed eyelids a burnt orange. The color reminded me of fire.

For a moment I couldn't open my eyes. They were glued together by too many tears and hours of sleep. When I finally did get them open, I was staring into a bright blue sky.

I was sure I was dreaming because I could still smell the scent of old books. As I sat up, I was surprised to discover the ceiling of my father's office looked exactly like the sky. The illusion made it appear as if there were no roof and I was sitting outside. It didn't take me long, however, to make out the crossbeams and realize that carefully placed mirrors created the amazing scene above me. *Clever dad*, I thought.

The horrors of the previous night returned with unsympathetic force. I turned to find the charred remains of my father still sitting at his desk, his hand on a book. But in the newfound light something else caught my eye. My father was holding a pen and had been writing a letter.

I got close enough to see my name on the parchment he was writing. I snatched it from the desk, shook off the ash, and revealed my father's last letter to me.

Dearest Edmund,

How I hope I get to deliver this letter in person, but I haven't much time, so I must write quickly just in case. If anything happens to me, I hope you manage to make it, somehow, to my office. It is, indeed, the safest place for you and, I'm hoping, for me.

Though you have probably already figured most of this out, my intelligent boy, Joshua has killed the patriarch and betrayed us all. It appears he has made a deal with the energumen: our eternal slavery in exchange for their service to him.

If you survive and I do not, you must know what our family does for the world. I will leave a book for you. You must read through it fully, for by understanding it you will have access to the powers of the seven levels through the seven doors, which you will need in order to fulfill your destiny and our family's legacy.

I am also leaving you my ring, which I wish for you to keep with you always. It has

I turned the parchment over, but there was no more to my father's letter. I read it again and again, to the point of committing it to memory. My father wasn't an affectionate man. His compliment in the letter made me feel pride and love. The book he spoke of must be the one still on the desk. I pried it from beneath his fingers and read the cover.

Crossing Death

I flipped through the pages, but as far as I could tell every page was blank. I added confusion to my pile of emotions.

The ring was easy to find. I knew exactly which one my father was talking about because he never took it off. When I was younger, I asked him about the ring and he told me it was a special family heirloom that would be passed to me one day. The ring was such a part of him that I soon forgot about it. But sure enough, the ring was set carefully on the desk close to the book. The fact that it wasn't on his finger seemed ominous to me, but at the same time I was grateful I wouldn't have to deal with removing it myself.

The ring had an allure that was hard to describe. It was bright silver and caught the light so completely that the red ruby at the center appeared as if it were set within a shining white flame. Surrounding the ruby was a setting that I had never studied the detail of before. The silver that surrounded the center stone was molded into three skulls. An intricate ivy design filled the hollow spaces and trailed down between the fingers. My mother once called it the death ring. The reference seemed more than fitting at this moment.

I knew that to understand the things my father said I would have to make it to the ruins as soon as possible. I realized I must have slept most of the day away because I could see the mirrored faux sky changing to a late afternoon hue of blue. I shoved the book down my shirt and folded my father's letter neatly before placing it in my shirt pocket. As I reached into that pocket, my fingers tenderly brushed the acorn that would be my last offering to my great home of Orenda. I placed the ring on my finger—surprised that it fit my small hand—stole a final glance at my father, swore under my breath that I would avenge his death, and left the office.

In that moment, something changed for me. I hadn't really considered myself to be a child at this point in my life anyway, but now I had no choice but to leave behind all childish things. I grew up. The emotion that had been my constant companion for the last day was replaced by resolve. I resolved to figure out the mystery of the book. I resolved that my father would not die in vain. I resolved that I would protect my friends until my dying breath. Most of all, I resolved that Joshua would pay for his crimes, and that I would be the one to make him pay.

FIVE

I waited on the inside of the mirror for the people in the hall to clear, but strangely, not because I was afraid of them. I waited to avoid conflict, sure, but only because I still had a conscience and didn't want to see any of them end up dead. The glass of the mirror sensed my resolve. It dissolved more easily this time and was restored with barely a thought. I marched straight out the nearest door into the late afternoon sunlight and headed for the town gates.

I avoided my house because I knew by now someone would be stationed there to keep an eye out for me. It wasn't so much that there was a missing kid that was the problem, but that there was a missing servant kid. I knew Clayton would be irritated enough by the thought of having to cook and clean for himself that he would raise some sort of commotion.

I was passing the schoolyard when the thing that I half expected to happen, did. It was simpler than I had anticipated: calmer; even kinder. It was simply a voice.

"So, dear Edmund, did you get to pay your father a visit?"

The sugary tone of the question made my blood boil. I turned slowly to see Joshua standing tall in his blackest robes, not twenty feet from me. He was not alone. A quick mental count revealed ten other men standing with him, each with unnaturally hollow, bright yellow eyes. I could hear more closing in behind me.

I knew what they were. They were humans possessed by energumen. They huddled protectively around Joshua as though he were some sort of god. The idea sickened me.

Just a day earlier I would have considered this moment my worst nightmare, but I had been wrong. Finding my father burned at his desk trumped this one.

I kept my response flat. "In fact, I did."

"I hope you found him well."

The lie in his words was meant to hurt. I felt a lurch in my emotions that resulted in a single tear beading up in the corner of my eye.

Joshua took notice. "So my fire *did* find dear old dad. Strange. No matter. Your father has—had—something I need." His words dripped with venom. "But, you see, he kept his work a secret. So much so, in fact, that his office is hidden somewhere in the parliament building, and I can't find it."

I could see where this was going. I regretted the fact that I had admitted to seeing my father.

"You see, Edmund, there's this book…"

I instinctively placed my arm to protect my stomach. The weight of the book suddenly felt heavy.

"Did he give it to you?"

I was perplexed, so my voice was not as controlled as I would have liked. "How could he have given me a book, you filthy betrayer? You killed him. You sacrificed us all for your putrid energumen!"

The accusation didn't faze Joshua at all. His face was still hard and determined. "Yet, he gave you his ring."

My hand recoiled like I'd touched a hot stove. "I took it."

Joshua inched forward. Although I inched backward at the same pace, I wondered how far the energumen behind me would let me get.

"And the book?"

"What book?"

"The book you have hidden in your shirt?"

I didn't let my expression give any response. "My

father's journals."

Joshua took one more step forward, but when I followed with my backward step I encountered strong, cold hands preventing me from going further.

"I don't believe you," Joshua said. His following step closer was meant to be menacing.

My response was cold. "What makes you think I care what you believe?"

Joshua stopped, his expression changing. He drew his eyebrows together in contemplation, took a step back, and laughed. "Edmund, Edmund," he read the expression on my face, "do you really think you could take me on?"

I knew my response could bring a death sentence, but I probably wasn't going to get out of this alive anyway. Even if I did everything Joshua asked, gave him the book, and took him to my father's secret place, he would still kill me or give me to the energumen in the end. I had the odd sensation that I didn't need to fear death as I once had. The feeling made me feel energized and foolish.

A few mumbled phrases in my head and the world around me turned blindingly white. The energumen screamed profanities as the possessing spirits were ripped from their hosts. The flash caused the humans to erupt into frantic screams again. I felt the cold hands on me falter. I pushed my way through the line that was meant to trap me.

I ran. While I ran, I asked Mother Earth to protect me. I heard the trees whisper to me in support and encouragement. With every ounce of power and respect I had for the planet, I asked them to help me escape.

The planet moved beneath me. The trees surrounding our town pulled toward me. I felt their desire to help me succeed, to grant my request. Suddenly, the roots of the giant firs and oaks broke through the ground, crumbling roads and buildings behind me, blocking the path of anyone who might try to follow. I saw the trees in the distance moving, crawling closer so that when I passed they could stand between Joshua and me. I sensed their intentions. I had never been so connected with so many of them. Their voices gave my feet power to run faster. I stole a glance behind me to view the entire path destroyed and blocked. I grinned as I felt my escape sure.

I felt the shift in the elation of the trees at the same time I ran into something hard and dark. Suddenly, I was in excruciating pain. I looked down and saw an arm thrust into my stomach, a punch so strong that it ripped all the way into my spleen. I looked up to see Joshua's cold face, his dark eyes meeting mine, a smile of victory on his face.

I coughed, and my blood splattered across his robe. "How?" I choked.

"Did you really think I would be stopped by a shrubbery?" He chuckled and pulled his hand from my stomach, taking the book with him. As he turned away from me, I heard him mutter, "It's too bad you'll never learn how much power we were capable of having."

I wasn't sure if the pain that followed was my own or an echo of the planet's pain over my defeat. I watched in disbelief as blood seeped through my fingers and dripped, thick as syrup, to the ground.

PART TWO—REBORN

SIX

My eyes flashed open. I could feel the muscles of my iris constrict in spite of the darkness. I was inundated with strange noises: heavy breathing, running water, distant chatter, a ticking clock. The smells here were awful, dust and sweat and... ugh... urine. I lifted my head from a lumpy pillow, my neck stiff and my back sore. I turned to the right and saw thin strips of light forcing their way into the room between the cracks of a closed door. A thin curtain billowed from an open window and the night breeze felt cool and sweet on my flushed face.

I swallowed hard, my mouth dry and my throat sticky. As I did, pain shot through my spine and up through my frontal lobe. *Great*, I thought, *I have a headache, too.*

I turned to the left and saw nothing but swirling blackness occasionally broken by a phantom light that came from outside the room. It illuminated another curtain, and although the light wasn't enough to see by, I could tell how wide the room was but not how long. All I could make out was a wooden paneled wall running from the lighted cracks in the doorway and burying itself into blackness.

As my memories slowly crept back into my brain, I remembered that I knew blackness well. I instinctively reached for my stomach as I remembered the cold and pain being replaced by absolute nothingness. The pain in my head surged like some kind of response to the memory. I winced and rubbed my temples.

My fingers felt like ice though the rest of my body was hot. I kicked off my blanket, tucking my hands under my arms. The coldness in my hand felt strange, almost metallic. Shocked, I held my hands close to my face to examine them. The hint of a silver skull glimmered in the dim light.

My father's ring.

The pain in my head surged again with such intensity that I grimaced. It hurt so much I forgot how to breathe. The pain grew until it overtook all my senses, roaring in my ears like an ocean and tasting prickly and bitter like dried cactus. It felt like sharp claws were raking my body. I cried out as lightning bolts filled my vision. As I collapsed, the flashes in my head brought facts and information—an entire child's lifetime of facts.

Columbus sailed the ocean blue in 1492. Two roads diverged in a yellow wood, and sorry I could not travel both. Names. Dates. $KMNO_4$. Gravity. *My Very Excellent Mother Just Sent Us Nine Pizzas.*

John 3:16—For God so loved the world that he sent his only begotten son. Peter, James, John. God, infinitely perfect and blessed in himself, in a plan of sheer goodness freely created man to make him share in his own blessed life. Our Father who art in heaven, hallowed be thy name. Thy kingdom come. Thy will be done on earth, as it is in heaven. Give us this day our daily bread, and forgive us our trespasses, as we forgive those who trespass against us, and lead us not into temptation, but deliver us from evil. Amen.

***

When I opened my eyes again, I was in a different room. Judging from the number of windows, it was less spacious. Beams of bright-colored light streamed through stained glass windows on the far wall, the colors dancing brilliantly on the hardwood floors and on my white blankets. This room smelled sterile, like bleach.

The bed I was in was much more comfortable than the one I remembered in my dim memory of the room that smelled of urine. The sheets weren't as itchy and there were enough pillows to prop me up into an inclined position, none of which were lumpy. The walls surrounding me were made of dark wood and brick, with numerous paintings of fat little children with wings and men wearing halos. I found the imagery comical and couldn't help but wonder whose imagination came up with the paintings.

I wasn't alone in the room; there were other beds like mine, some empty, and some with other children in them. Most were sleeping soundly although some of the more sickly looking ones groaned and tossed in their sleep. I realized I was in a hospital when I saw bags of clear liquid hanging over the beds. I looked up and saw I had my own clear bag, which was almost empty. A tube ran down into a needle that was plunged into my arm. My head was still achy and that told me that what I'd experienced during the night hadn't been a dream. Confused, I reached for my stomach again, lifting up my shirt. There was no scar or mark where Joshua had ripped into me. I pushed around, examining myself for any pain, but besides the dull ache in my head, there was none.

Did I manage to survive Joshua's attack? And if so, where was I now? Did the humans actually have such great healing abilities that they could repair the damage to my stomach without leaving a scar? How long had I been healing, unaware? Where was I when I woke up last night? Was it even last night? How much time had passed since I was in the dark room that smelled of urine, and how did I end up in a hospital?

The questions kept coming. It bothered me that I couldn't answer any of them. This room was like nothing I had seen before, certainly not a building in Orenda. It was too ornate to be a prison.

As I surveyed my surroundings, attempting to find a clue as to where I was or who brought me here, my gaze fell on a painting hanging above a large arched doorway that led to a decorated hallway. The painting was of thirteen men at a large wooden table. All of the men were turned toward the man in the center who wore a red and blue robe. The ring on my finger pulsed.

Jesus, I thought, *and the painting is The Last Supper.*

I wondered how I knew that, but as soon as I thought about the question my brain answered that I learned it in an art history class, taught by Sister Mary Jane. But who was Sister Mary Jane, and how did I know her? I searched my memories for a face or a voice, anything to help me put physical characteristics to the name, but I couldn't find anything. I could picture Ralph and Hailey perfectly. I could remember the Elders who taught me in school. The memory of Sister Mary Jane, her art history class, and Jesus should be just as vivid, but I couldn't remember anything about them.

I began sifting through my thoughts, looking for words that had no memory associated with them. Something called the Bible, which I knew was a book because there were verses in it I could quote. I couldn't remember ever seeing one, though. Father Michaels, a phrase that made me feel respectful when I thought about it, but I had no idea what it referred to. I drew a blank on word after word, some of which I recognized easily as common names, while others felt like ideas or objects, but not one conjured any sort of memory: church, car, boat, bus, pope, telephone…

My thoughts were interrupted when an older woman dressed in long white robes extending all the way up and around her face walked through the large archway. A younger woman pushing a metal cart filled with more bags of clear liquid followed her.

The older woman looked at my startled expression with kind eyes and a warm smile.

"Oh, Alexander. How wonderful that you are awake."

Alexander. This was another one of those words that had nothing but darkness behind it.

The younger woman was busy replacing my empty bag with a new one from her cart.

"How are you feeling, dear boy? You gave us quite a scare."

Was this woman talking to me?

She waited patiently for an answer, though I could see her eyes growing wider with concern when I didn't speak.

"Alexander? Are you all right?"

I was still confused by this "Alexander" business. She was using it like it was my name.

Ow! Headache again.

I decided I'd better say something before the already furrowed brow of this kind-looking woman folded in on itself completely. "Are you talking to me, madam?"

An expression of confusion and relief crossed her face. "Of course, son."

"Son?" I repeated. "But you are not my mother."

The expression of confusion morphed into worry. "Alexander, do you know where you are?"

I shook my head.

"Oh dear. Do you know the year?"

"No."

"Did you hit your head?"

Her hands started probed my skull, looking for damage to my head, no doubt.

"No, ma'am."

"Do you know who I am?" She was frantic now.

"A doctor of some kind?"

"My name, Alexander. Do you know my name?"

I shook my head again. "I don't think we've ever met before."

"Dear child!" the woman exclaimed, taking my hand in her own and sitting on the edge of the bed. She turned to the younger woman, who wore a similar look of worry. "Run to Father Michaels…"

There was that odd phrase again.

"… and tell him to come quickly. I need to know what happened to Alexander, how he was found. Tell him the poor boy cannot remember me. He is suffering from amnesia."

The younger woman nodded and ran for the archway while the older one looked at me intently, shaking her head, and mumbling, "Dear, dear."

I tried to remain calm, but my confusion turned into panic.

"Ma'am, my name…" No, that was going about it wrong. "Why do you call me Alexander?"

"That's what you've been called since birth. What would you rather have me call you?"

I thought it smarter to ignore her question while my mind twisted the possibilities. Maybe I had been transplanted into someone else's body… or at least my memories? That was the only thing I could come up with at the moment. Before I told anyone my real name, I had to make sure I was who I thought I was.

"Do you have a mirror?"

The woman looked at me warily, but finally crossed the room and retrieved a small mirror on a nightstand.

I took the mirror cautiously. The eyes of the old woman narrowed in suspicion as she took in my expression. I held up the mirror and tilted it until I saw my face. Two deep brown eyes stared back at me. Their color was like dark chocolate mixed with liquid gold. They were bright and clear, though a little swollen from exhaustion and pain. The hair was raven black, tousled, but definitely mine.

The muscles in my jaw and lips relaxed. I was half expecting to see a stranger's face in the mirror but was relieved to find my own. So I hadn't died? Was there another explanation for the strange facts and unfamiliar words I knew?

I handed the mirror back to the old woman, asking her name.

She was exasperated, and I knew she expected that I should already know who she was; I had gathered that much by her quickly muttered instructions to the younger nurse. She answered me slowly. "Sister Mary Rafaela."

At the sound of her name, I felt my brain play an excited game of connect the dots. Words I didn't know, like *nun, nurse, ibuprofen, injection,* and *infirmary* connected with words I knew, such as *kindness, aged, intelligent, teacher,* and *healer. Nurse* and *healer* felt somehow connected but I wondered why *nun* and *healer* didn't have the same connotation. *Nun* was connected to *Sister Mary Rafaela.* So was *nurse.* But *nun* and *nurse* didn't necessarily equate. The whole process was exhausting.

"You are a nurse," I said matter-of-factly. "This is not a hospital, but an infirmary. You are a healer."

"Yes, child." Her expression was more relaxed now. "Although I've never been called a healer before, exactly. I'm not a doctor."

In my experience, a doctor and a healer were the same. A doctor and a nurse were different. I filed away the understanding.

"And Father Michaels?" I realized the odd phrase was actually a name.

"He's our priest. Our elder in the church."

Elder was a word I knew. A word I knew all too well. I asked the next question timidly. "Does Father Michaels know Joshua?"

Sister Mary Rafaela looked puzzled. "We don't have any Joshua here, not even among the children, so I wouldn't say so."

"Is he a good elder, or a bad elder?"

"Oh, very good."

As if on cue, a man entered the room with the younger nurse. This must have been Father Michaels, but he didn't look like any elder I had seen. He wore a ceremonious robe, like my elders, but it had no covering for the head. A piece of collar was missing, revealing a bright white insert.

"Good afternoon, Alexander," the man said cordially, taking a seat on the bed next to me. The man was older too, not as old as Sister Mary Rafaela, but older than Joshua was, older than my father had been. His cheeks blushed pink in the warm afternoon sunlight. He wore a thin frame over his ears and nose that held two round circles of glass in front of his eyes. The glass was warped from my point of view and made his eyes look a little bigger than I imagined they were. "How are you feeling?"

I assessed that and answered as honestly as I could. "Confused."

"How can I help clear things up?" he asked honestly, but with a hint of a smirk.

"Well," I took in a deep breath. This was going to be a long one. "Where am I? How long was I at the hospital after Joshua almost killed me? Where are my friends, Ralph and Hailey? How did my stomach get healed so completely? Why do I know all sorts of made up words, like *Bible* and *scripture*, but can't define them? How come I know your name, but why have I never met you? What kind of name is Father Michaels, anyway? One I've never heard before. How long have I been here? What is this place? What about the war? Where is Joshua and what happened with his deal with the energumen? What was the fate of Orenda? And—" I stopped when I saw his expression empty into perfect blankness. I only had one question left. I decided to ask it anyway. "Why do you call me Alexander?"

Unexpectedly, the priest's eyes drooped and he took off his glass contraption to rub his eyes. *Glasses*, the word surfaced. I couldn't tell if he was frustrated or tired. "Alexander was a saint."

Hmm… no connection to the word *saint* yet.

"It is what we have called you for the entire twelve years you've been here."

Twelve years. But I was only ten. At least, I was only ten when I had gone home to find Orenda destroyed. Could that have been two years ago? Or even twelve years ago?

I recalled my reflection in the mirror. No, I was still young. I would have been over twenty years old if I had spent the *entire* twelve years here. My features weren't that old, but also weren't as soft as they had been in the mirror in the hallway of the parliament building.

I am twelve years old, I thought, and I accepted that because it *felt* right.

"What would you have us call you?" the priest asked.

"My name is Edmund."

Father Michaels and Sister Mary Rafaela exchanged glances. She shrugged.

Father Michaels shifted his weight uneasily. "Is Alexander in there with you?"

The younger nurse's eyes grew wide; I saw her mouth a word that I knew very well—possession.

Me? Possessed? I wondered what it would be like to have an energumen in my body, but I was certain it wouldn't feel like *this*. I was still me and, at least in the mirror, I didn't have hollow, unnaturally yellow eyes.

The priest followed up with another question. "Alex—Edmund? Do you remember your communion yesterday?"

Communion? Nope. I shook my head.

The priest stared down at my hand. "That ring," he gestured, "we found it with you when you were left on our doorstep. I gave it back to you as a gift for your communion. When we found you, your only possessions were that ring and an acorn."

I shot straight up. "The acorn. Do you still have it?"

Father Michaels looked at me in disbelief. "Um… no…"

My heart sank. I promised Mother Tree I would plant her offspring and now I had lost it.

The priest continued our conversation as if there had been no break. "When I gave you the ring yesterday you told me you found it a bit… strange. I told you I had hoped you would sell the ring and give the money to the church for the care you have received over the years."

"But this was my father's ring."

Another exchange of glances. "That's *possible* I suppose, but you can't be sure of that. You were a newly born infant when you came to us, on the verge of death. You never saw the ring until yesterday."

And suddenly I had another million questions, but I clapped my mouth shut and laid back down against the pillows.

Sister Mary Rafaela patted Father Michaels on the shoulder. "Come, let him rest. Perhaps his memory will return tomorrow."

Father Michaels took the…*glasses*… off his face again, rubbing his green eyes, this time clearly in frustration. He gave me one last exasperated glance before Sister Mary Rafaela turned him toward the door. "He was the brightest of them all," I heard him say quietly once he thought I was out of earshot.

"Do you think he's really possessed?" the nurse asked.

Father Michaels sighed. "I don't know. If he is, at least we know what the demon calls itself. Edmund. I'll have to look into that name."

"Edmund was a saint, Father."

"Indeed. Perhaps it's mocking us. Strange coincidence, this one. The day after his communion. I do suppose if the devil wanted to claim a soul it would be such a one as Alexander's. He is so pure, so good. If he's possessed by some evil thing, you can rest assured, Sister, that I will not rest until the mighty power of God exorcises it back to the Hell it came from."

More words I knew but didn't understand. Exorcism I got.

I had every intention of resting, or at least lying back in hopes of figuring things out, but I had to know that this was a safe place to stay for a while. I needed to know where I was. I turned to the young nurse in the room.

"Are you a Sister too?"

Her eyes rested on me momentarily before she turned back to changing clear liquid bags above some of the other beds, but she did answer me.

"No. Not yet, anyway." Her voice was heavily

accented, something I had never heard before. The sound of it almost made me chuckle.

"Can you tell me, please, where I am? What is this place?"

The question made her stop. She smoothed her already wrinkle-free dress and I started to worry I wasn't supposed to know, or at least that she wasn't going to give an answer.

"Saint Vincent's orphanage," she paused before continuing, a look on her face that told me she was hoping I would understand, or at least recognize what she was saying. "In Los Angeles, California."

Her voice rose a few pitches on the last syllable, like it was a question. The strange thing was I *did* recognize what she was saying; the words just had no meaning.

She stood, anticipating my response. I didn't know what to give her, so I smiled gently and nodded a thank you.

Whatever this place was, it was certainly unfamiliar to me. I could now say with certainty that these people believed, beyond a doubt, that I had lived here with them for the past twelve years as a young boy named Alexander. But I knew that I had lived for ten years in Orenda with my mage community, with Hailey and Ralph, and my mother and father. As if my father's ring wasn't proof enough of that, I could feel my connection to the planet screaming inside of me. The feeling was different than it had been before. The planet seemed to be in more turmoil now, but it was the same inner spirit, the same magical fire, the same Mother Earth that I knew so intimately.

I had no idea how I was going to sort out the two separate lives I was supposed to be living. I decided to go with what I knew: I had come from Orenda. I had lived there before. Now, I was here in Saint Vincent's orphanage, in Los Angeles, California. I would try my best to fit in, and hopefully find a way to the ruins where I knew my *real* family would be waiting for me.

SEVEN

I had to spend one more night in the infirmary before Sister Mary Rafaela promised to release me back to my dormitory. I hadn't been sleeping well in the infirmary, even with the better beds. The other patients kept me awake with all their whimpering. My thoughts probably would have kept me up anyway.

To distract myself, I found a book tucked away in a bedside drawer and started to read absently. The title caught my attention briefly, enough for me to connect the title with a word I had been hearing. I opened the leather bound book with the imprint *Holy Bible* on the cover. As I read, it was like being reminded of something I already learned years earlier. Adam and Eve were two names I remembered instantly and I was grateful to finally have a memory to connect to the names, even if that memory was only plain black-and-white text. Sister Mary Rafaela had left my lamp on when she found me reading, but suggested I sleep.

She sent me back to the dormitory when the sun was spilled pink into the sky. I had just gotten to where some guy named Moses hit a rock and made water come out. What a strange book. I wondered about the physical limitations of such a story but perhaps it wouldn't be too far-fetched for someone who could alter an object's molecular structure, like my father. I determined to try this trick for myself eventually.

My dormitory was not impressive. It had a smell that was already familiar to me in this life. No doubt this was the room I had been in when I first opened my eyes to this strange new world. It was light enough to see rows and rows of cots just like mine, and the room was more of a large hall with doors at both ends. Almost all of the cots were occupied but all the bodies that rested on them were still asleep. Sister Mary Rafaela told me that another nun would be along soon to wake them. I was to sleep and rest until the next morning. Then I would be expected to resume my classes. I didn't have trouble following the instructions. As soon as I hit the cot with the lumpy pillow, I fell asleep from exhaustion.

My dreams were disconnected, sometimes bursting into scenes of bright colors with Hailey and Ralph, other times dark and silent with words and meanings piecing together without the help of memories to aid them. I was growing more and more unsettled, and even in sleep could feel my muscles tense. My mind flashed between black and red, sometimes red like blood, sometimes red like fire.

When I woke, the sun was slanting sideways through the windows with a late-afternoon haze. My head felt clearer, but my muscles were still tired from the constant tension they had held for the last few hours. I managed to kick my sheets into twists and I was damp and sticky with sweat. My stomach growled, trying to get my attention away from my parched throat. I desperately craved a hot bath. But I had even more pressing needs. Two days being pumped full of fluids without a visit to a restroom was taking a toll on my bladder.

The clothes I wore were old and dingy grey, and desperately needed washing, but I couldn't remember where any extras were. I hobbled out of bed and made my way, barefoot, to the nearest door. This was, in fact, the only way I knew how to go, as it was the reversal of the way Sister Mary Rafaela had led me from the infirmary. I didn't remember passing a bathroom on the way, but I did remember seeing the entrance to a chapel. I figured, with the chapel being so large, that religious services must be held there sometimes. As such, patrons might need facilities.

Religion. What a funny notion! I was pleasantly surprised to find that I didn't balk at the blankness that surrounded the word in my head. I had even just used it in a sentence to convey a coherent thought. Intriguing.

Through the doorway was another massive hall. Everything from top to bottom was fashioned in dark mahogany, not that I could see much of it under the tapestries, paintings, and carvings that decorated almost every inch of this place. Any leftover space was crowded with tables, vases, or shrines (did I know this word?).

As I approached the chapel, I heard melancholic singing. I cracked open the door, the same one that had been standing open on my trip back to the dormitory. I caught a glimpse of a children's choir rehearsing.

I knew what a choir was. We had choirs in Orenda and would sometimes sing for our parents.

One of the nuns was directing and I knew I would be interrupting, but I was determined to ask her to point me in the direction of the bathroom.

The children's voices dropped off when I entered the chapel, their song replaced by excited chatter. The nun turned and looked at me angrily but her expression softened at the sight of me.

"Ah, Alexander. So good to see you up and about,"

she chimed.

I stared into her dark eyes and almost wet myself. For some reason, having the attention of all of the other children, as well as this woman, felt uncomfortable. Too bad I hadn't thought about that before interrupting the choir.

"I'm sorry, Sister." I didn't bother continuing with the rest of her name. I didn't know it. "I was hoping you could point me to the bathroom. And maybe a place where I could get something to eat?"

The nun smiled wryly. "No memory yet?"

I shook my head, although honestly didn't know if doing so was telling the truth or not. I had a memory—just not the one they wanted me to have.

She turned to the group of children, who were intently peering at me. "Nicholas! You are a friend of Alexander?"

"Oh yes, Sister Mary Chantale," a small boy answered with more volume than I would have expected. He reminded me a bit of Ralph, though his features were all wrong.

"Would you reintroduce him to the church grounds and answer his questions… em… carefully. Meet us for dinner in the mess hall?"

"Oh yes, Sister."

"And me too, Sister Mary Chantale?" a high soprano voice rang hopefully.

"No, Ruth, you can see your friend at dinner. There is no reason as to why a young lady such as yourself would need to escort young Alexander to the restroom."

A giggle escaped from the group.

I had warm feelings toward Sister Mary Chantale. I didn't know why, but the way she interacted with the children, the way she had them laughing while at the same time commanding respect, was kind and gentle and inspiring.

Nicholas tugged on my sleeve and led the way out of the chapel as the children began singing again. The melody was familiar. I concentrated and was able to make out the words to "Our Father."

"Did I sing this song?" I asked Nicholas as we passed through the corridor back toward the dormitory. Guess that meant I had walked right passed the bathrooms.

"Of course. Don't you remember it?" Nicholas asked, quickening his pace.

I matched his gait. "Actually, I do—sort of."

"That's good. We'll be singing it in two days for the families."

"Families?"

A look of hope brightened Nicholas's grey eyes,

"Yeah! All the families who are looking for children are coming. Wouldn't it be so cool if you and I got adopted together and became real brothers?"

I didn't have time to respond before he continued.

"Clean clothes are in the cupboards along the far wall. Try to hurry. Maybe we can go down to the river."

I didn't realize the room around me had changed, mostly because the walls were still the same mahogany. The only difference in this room was that the walls were lined with cabinets that ran from the floor halfway up the wall, and there were benches interrupting the smooth wooden floors. We had a room similar to this in Orenda near the fields where people would play sports.

"This is the locker room," Nicholas prompted when he saw the confused expression on my face. "The showers are that way," he pointed, "and the toilets too. They weren't joking about you having hit your head or something, were they?"

I shook my head in response.

He shrugged and walked over to one of the cabinets. He opened it, revealing clothing similar to what I had on, but the ones in the cabinet weren't stained with sweat. "Well, we're the same size," he said taking two pairs of pants and two shirts from the shelf. "Underwear and socks are by you."

121

I took out two pairs of everything and handed them to him warily.

Nicholas grinned. "Well I'm not going to waste the time. If I shower now I don't have to do it with all the other guys tonight. I can use the time to try to jog your memory or something."

"Okay," I responded, following him toward a big tiled room with showerheads protruding from the walls.

"Toilets are that way," he motioned again. "But let's hurry. Dinner is in less than an hour."

It felt good to be clean again, even if my shower was a bit rushed. Nicholas chattered on and on about subjects I found fascinating: the other children in the orphanage, our classes, the nuns, the river behind the chapel, and how he liked to get dirty playing on the bank. He reminded me a lot of Ralph, and Ruth sounded a lot like Hailey. I couldn't help wonder about the possibility of them actually being my lost friends. I contained my excitement at this thought, even though it brought a smile to my face, and reminded myself that Nicholas and Ruth just had similar dispositions.

I didn't stop myself from feeling excited to meet Ruth, or reacquaint myself with her as the case may be. That seemed like a good emotional compromise—more realistic.

Nicholas had no interest in showing me the cavernous building we called our home, opting instead to pull me out back into the expansive grounds. It became apparent that his aptitudes didn't lie in books and schoolwork, but in nature and athletics. His energy surprised me as he bounded across an expansive lawn toward a row of trees in the distance. I had to remind him I had just spent the last few days recovering from dehydration in an infirmary. He slowed his pace, albeit reluctantly.

We reached the row of trees just as the sun was setting behind them. I followed Nicholas to a makeshift shelter fashioned out of long pieces of wood leaning up against a large tree.

"You helped me build this," Nicholas said, carefully watching me survey my surroundings. He sat on a tree stump and motioned for me to sit on another. "And that over there," he pointed, "was where Simon died."

I followed his finger to a large white rock interrupting the flow of water at the river's edge, and cringed. "He drowned?" I asked.

Nicholas nodded slowly. "Do you remember?"

I shook my head as the name *Simon* connected to the word *drown* in my memory.

"That was a hard day for all of us."

"They still let us come out here?" I asked, surprised that the adults would permit Nicholas and I to be out here alone.

A sheepish grin crossed his face. "If we get caught I'll just tell them I was trying to help you remember. You should have some pretty strong memories here."

"Why's that?"

"Well, Simon, for one. And you spend a lot of time here whenever you can. You and I sneak out here pretty often. It's a good place to think, to get some fresh air, and play. When they told me you were in the infirmary, I honestly thought you were playing some sort of joke to get out of classes so you could get out here."

"Would I normally fake an illness to get out of class?" I asked, amazed. That didn't sound like me at all.

Nicholas chuckled a bit. "Are you kidding? You are the *best* at getting out of class. I always get caught. But I think that's just because the nuns like you more."

His grin was contagious and I couldn't help but smile.

Nicholas's eyes glazed over a bit, his smile fading. When he looked at me again, I could tell there was something he was trying to say, but didn't know how to form the words. "You really don't remember Simon?" he finally choked out.

The question caught me off guard. I thought we were

done with this subject. "No," I answered. "Why?"

Nicholas kicked the dirt, not looking at me.

"What?" I prodded.

"Nothing," he answered, blinking back hurt in his eye. "You'll remember soon enough."

My eyes narrowed—a gesture that he didn't miss, but ignored.

"Come on, we'd better head back for dinner."

"Okay," I agreed reluctantly, stealing another glance at the large white rock in the river.

It wasn't until I was almost back to the church that I had an idea. In fact, it wasn't an idea at all—just a realization. As I walked back toward the stone edifice, with its windows now lit against the murky sky, I thought I could hear a murmuring coming from inside. It wasn't until I got closer and the murmur seemed farther away that I realized what I was hearing. It was the trees near the river that were talking to each other.

I couldn't remember if I had heard them down by the river or if I had just started hearing them now, but even if they had been talking to each other while I was sitting with Nicholas in our makeshift fort, I probably wouldn't have noticed. The sound was so familiar to me that it wouldn't have been something I would have picked up on immediately. That thought gave me an odd sense of comfort. The fact that something as simple as the whispers of the trees could be familiar in this unfamiliar world was exactly what I needed to start unraveling my current existence. I resolved to ask the trees about my time here—surely they were older than I—in hopes of determining not only how long I had been in this place, but how I got here.

EIGHT

I met Ruth that night at dinner, as well as a few of the other children that claimed to be in my classes. I probably would have met more had I remembered I was supposed to answer to the name "Alexander." It was easy when people were looking right at me when they called me that name, but I had a hard time responding when it was shouted across the room while I wasn't paying attention. I found the food incredible and the environment in which we ate wasn't that far off from what I remembered in Orenda; everyone ate together in a large cafeteria, and we all ate the same thing. There were choices in drinks and desserts, and the nuns ate at separate tables instead of with the children. I didn't see Father Michaels at dinner and couldn't help but wonder why he wouldn't join us for what would have been considered a joyful community meal in Orenda.

I was right in my assumptions about Ruth. She was smart, articulate, full of wit, and had a short fuse, just like Hailey. I was quickly convinced, however, that Nicholas and Ruth were not, in fact, Ralph and Hailey in the same way that I was both Alexander and Edmund. There were differences in their personalities that extended beyond the simple physical. Hailey was both warm and inviting while Ruth was slightly distant. This was a trait found among most of the children, and I decided that it was because they were all alone in the world. All of the children seemed to have one similar hope: to find a family to adopt them and to love them.

I was different. I had a family that loved me. I had no desire for another family. I only wanted mine. And if I couldn't have my mother and father, I still wanted my larger family—my people, the mages—my town. I began to realize that family, by definition here, was a close group of a few people who were biologically related. The idea of adoption was both foreign and common to me, as everyone in Orenda was "adopted" by all of society. The ability to adopt a single child into an already formed biological family was the part that was unfamiliar. Immediate family, extended family, and the human family all had different meanings here. I was more comfortable with "the human family" because it was communal.

I didn't sleep well that night, in spite of being tired. The dormitory slept all of the boys and there was more movement and noise than I was used to. To top it off, the night air sometimes grew hot and thick. My dreams translated my discomfort into nightmares with dark creatures that breathed hot, wet air into my face while pinning me down so I couldn't move. I woke up more than once, sticky with sweat (this was becoming all too common), my finger with my father's ring the only cool part of my body.

The morning brought with it the promise of new experiences. A nun I did not recognize woke us, but at least I was now starting to get familiar with the unfamiliarity of my life in this orphanage. Unfamiliar faces were so common that I anticipated hearing a name or a word that would connect facts in my brain together with the newly impressed image of the face. After just one day of experiencing this pattern, I realized I had grown to expect it. This unknown nun became 'Sister Mary Elizabeth' as soon as I heard the other boys acknowledge her name. I knew she came to our convent three years ago and was one of just two nuns who were assigned specifically to our care. She was the closest thing any of us had to a mother, but I felt *disconnected* from her. The emotions that connected back to her name were emotions of indifference, not emotions of love. I didn't dislike Sister Mary Elizabeth. I just didn't trust her.

Nicholas was by my side almost immediately. He yawned and stretched before wishing me a good morning. "Today is Saturday," he told me with as much excitement as his just-waking body could muster. "We only have Sister Mary Elizabeth's class, and choir. Then we are free to do what we want."

This thought excited me. I couldn't wait to get back outside, hopefully alone, to talk to the trees. I asked myself if I should have felt guilty for wanting to ditch Nicholas, but quickly decided that any guilt I had was overshadowed by the importance of having a moment with the trees to get my questions answered.

I followed the large group of boys into the locker room where we washed our faces and made our hair look somewhat presentable. I had to give up on a few strands that refused to do anything but stick straight out from the side of my head, but flattened the rest down over my forehead to where it fell just above my eyes.

Breakfast consisted of a bran muffin that tasted like salt and a small carton of orange juice.

Nicholas and I met up with Ruth at breakfast. She seemed eager and full of energy today.

"Between classes, would you like to play chess with

me?" she asked excitedly.

Nicholas made a face while I searched for the word *chess* in my mind. "What's chess?" I finally asked after finding the word, but not being able to connect it with anything else.

Ruth looked disappointed and surprised. "Our favorite board game."

I shrugged and responded to her expression with an apologetic look. "You're going to have to remind me how to play."

A calculating grin pursed her lips, "Hmm," she sighed, "I guess that means you're not going to have any chance of winning."

"Just remind me how to play," I grinned.

"Alexander will beat you even *if* he doesn't remember how to play!" Nicholas interrupted.

Ruth responded with a roll of her eyes. "Oh Nikki," her voice trilled, "if you only had a brain."

"Don't call me Nikki."

Ruth winked at me, ignoring Nicholas's clenched teeth. "See you after class, Alexander."

She bounded away, leaving Nicholas fuming.

I chuckled. "She likes you, you know."

I didn't think Nicholas's eyes could get any wider, but they did. "What?" he screeched.

I laughed again. "You two remind me of Hailey and Ralph. Hailey is always giving Ralph a hard time, and—" I stopped, catching myself.

Nicholas didn't miss a beat. "Who are Hailey and Ralph?"

I floundered, trying to come up with an appropriate response, finally deciding to keep my mouth shut this time. "Oh, never mind," I said, grateful when Nicholas shrugged his shoulders and started walking toward our class.

"I'm kind of excited for class today," Nicholas changed the subject. "We're supposed to start talking about the Council of Trent and the Catechism before the Catechism of Pius the Fifth."

He might as well have been speaking a different language. *Council*, I understood, and *catechism* was at least one of those black words, but the rest was just rambling.

"I'm really fascinated by the doctrine of four hells. Aren't you?"

I stared at him blankly as we entered a large classroom. I recognized Sister Mary Elizabeth from this morning, standing in the front of the room. She was watching the clock with more zeal than she had for watching the students, obviously waiting for the proper time to start the lecture.

"Oh come on, Alexander," Nicholas continued.

"We've been talking about this for days!"

I was about to mouth some sort of apology or reminder about my lack of memory, but Sister Mary Elizabeth hurled a piece of chalk at Nicholas with such force that it bounced off his head in more than one piece.

"Sit down you two—you're late," she boomed. "And you, Alexander, are lucky your head is already damaged."

She feigned throwing another piece of chalk in my direction. At least I now understood why my feelings for this woman were unpleasant: her presence was entirely overbearing and rude.

I sank into my seat.

"Now, the Council of Trent was the 19th Ecumenical Council of the church, and convened in Trent between December 13th, 1545, and December 4th, 1563. There wasn't another council until the First Vatican Council which took place in what year?"

Nicholas raised his hand excitedly. "1869," he answered when called upon.

I found myself re-evaluating my prior thought that Nicholas wasn't book smart.

"Correct. Now the Council of Trent was extremely important in the wake of one Martin Luther, who taught the doctrine of justification by faith alone. This is just one of the doctrines of the Protestant faith that the Council of

133

Trent helped to solidify as false. In addition the relationship between faith and works as it relates to salvation was clearly defined."

I was already bored.

Nicholas, however, was paying rapt attention. When he caught me looking at him he nodded his head excitedly at me, like some sort of encouragement for me to agree with him that this was the most fascinating thing I had ever learned. I yawned.

The trees outside the window swayed back and forth gently in a light breeze and were more entertaining to watch. I strained to hear their conversation but the walls of the building and the ornate stained-glass windows were too thick to allow me to hear anything.

It didn't take long for the gentle swaying of the trees to have me hypnotized and I watched their methodic dance as I slipped in and out of the moments before sleep. I could still hear Sister Mary Elizabeth droning on in my subconscious, but was only half aware as the words she said made connections to past events in my head. She discussed the concept of Christ before and after the Council of Trent, as well as the church's teachings on prophets of the Old Testament, the idea of the sacrament and transubstantiation, of celibacy, and sainthood, and the challenges the church faced regarding Saint Mary (which helped me understand why all of the nuns took the name Mary).

But it wasn't until the talk of purgatory, and the pre- and post-council beliefs in limbo, that she said something that caught my attention.

"… and so," she was saying, "it could be said that in Medieval times, most theologians described Hell as divided into four distinct levels; the hell of the damned, purgatory, limbo of the fathers, and limbo of the infants."

This last sentence was said in summation, and I was disappointed I had missed the discussion of what these four levels represented. I wondered if they had any representation in the "seven levels" I had seen in my father's letter.

I must have flinched at the thought, because Sister Mary Elizabeth, who noticed the movement, glared at me. "Nice of you to join us again, Alexander. Did you have a question?"

Actually, yes, but I didn't know how to ask it without revealing my underlying purpose. I searched my mind quickly for something, and was surprised to find all of my new connections. Heaven and Hell were succinctly related somehow, so I chose this connection in hopes of forming a coherent question. "If there are four hells, how many heavens are there?"

"There are not four hells," Sister Mary Elizabeth said harshly. "Limbo is simply an idea, a *possibility*, not doctrine. Remember, a lot of time has passed since the Council of Trent."

Having thought she made me feel stupid, she turned back to the chalkboard and had her mouth half open to start on another topic when I interrupted, "How many heavens are there, *possibly*?"

The chalk fell from her hand, her face twisted in annoyance. After letting out a sigh, she turned to her desk and picked up a book. She leaned against the desk and flipped through the pages—the entire class silent. I wasn't sure if she was going to answer my question or not, but finally she found what she was looking for, stood, walked quickly over to where I was sitting, and dropped the book on my lap.

"Second Corinthians, chapter twelve, verse two. Would you kindly read that passage for the class?"

I found the resulting scripture and read aloud, "I knew a man in Christ above fourteen years ago, (whether in the body, I cannot tell; or whether out of the body, I cannot tell: God knoweth;) such as one caught up to the third heaven."

I closed the book and put it into her waiting hand. "Now that you have wasted our time, we can add that time to the end of the class."

A groan echoed throughout the room, but I wasn't about to let the subject go. Three plus four equaled seven. My heart thudded.

"If the four hells are the hell of the damned, purgatory, limbo of the fathers, and limbo of the infants, what are the three heavens?"

The entire class was staring, dumbfounded, in my direction now.

Sister Mary Elizabeth grinned at me. "More time after class, then. There are some theologians that believe the three heavens are literal, but our doctrine states they are the atmosphere, space, and the kingdom where our Holy Father resides."

"What do the other theologians call them? The ones who believe the three heavens are literal?"

"You'll have to ask the Mormons that question," she sniped. "They are the only ones who believe that verse literally. But doing so will put in jeopardy your salvation!"

"Who wrote that passage?" I asked.

Sister Mary Elizabeth rolled her eyes, "If I had known your amnesia would have proved so difficult, I would have told Father Michaels that you were not welcome in my class."

Nicholas suddenly interrupted, trying to get me to

shut up. "Alexander, you have a chess game with Ruth after this class. You don't want to miss it and make her angry, do you?"

I ignored him, and continued to address Sister Mary Elizabeth. "Can I speak to the person who wrote this passage?"

Now the class erupted into laughter. Sister Mary Elizabeth responded, "Paul is the author of that verse, and he has been dead now for about two thousand years."

"Did Paul write that entire book? May I borrow it?"

"The book is the Bible," Sister Mary Elizabeth responded in unbelief, "and many prophets wrote it."

The Bible. The infirmary had one of those I was sure I could borrow. Now the stories I read while recovering became much more interesting and real.

Sister Mary Elizabeth continued, anticipating my next question, "Prophets like Moses and Noah and apostles like Peter, James, and John. They wrote it so we would have a record of Jesus Christ, the Son of God. You've been taught this, Alexander, since you could understand plain English."

Her face was turning red, but I couldn't let the chance pass to understand where I was, who I was, and what the seven levels were. I recognized one of the names: Moses. I had read about him. "Did all of these men perform supernatural acts like Moses?"

"Yes. They all had the power of God." The poor nun was getting exasperated now, but I was grateful she continued to answer my questions. "And the greatest of them all was Jesus Christ, who performed many miracles, such as changing water into wine, healing the sick, and raising the dead. It's thanks to Him that you can be resolved from your sins and go to paradise when you die."

Paradise? When I die? That couldn't be true. I had already died once, and this place definitely wasn't paradise.

"Am I a Jesus?" I asked subdued, half wondering aloud to myself.

Sister Mary Elizabeth heard the question, and her body started to shake with anger as her face burned a bright crimson. Her words came out in a spitting accusation, "You... are... not... like... the... perfect... Holy... Son... of... God!"

The children in the class were now all pressed against their seats, straining to be as far away from Sister Mary Elizabeth as possible. I was so involved in my own thought processes that I was oblivious to her anger.

"Then Jesus, Peter, Paul, and Moses. They were all like me?"

Sister Mary Elizabeth lashed out, striking my face with the open palm of her hand. She hit me so hard that I flew out of my chair. I caught myself only momentarily before my hands instinctively covered my stinging cheek.

My blood boiled. Why didn't anyone understand that the people who had written the Bible were *my* family? I was one of them. How could I make them see? Should I make them see? I couldn't just coddle my cheek doing nothing. If these people worshiped those like me, perhaps I could get them to help me find the survivors of my people. I stood slowly. Sister Mary Elizabeth glared at me venomously, still huffing in rage.

"I'll prove it," I whispered.

I knew she didn't answer because she didn't know what to say.

Her desk was made of wood, just like everything in this place, and had a thick stone slab as its desktop. The stone called out to me as the words of Moses echoed in my head. It told me how Moses did it—how Moses simply had to ask. I walked to the desk cautiously, and once I was standing over it, punched down with all the strength the anger within me allowed. I hit the desktop hard, but I felt it give way to my request. At first, nothing happened. Then slowly, the entire surface of the desk began to sweat as the whole room sat in stunned silence.

It started as slow drops forming like dew over the surface, but quickly turned into a puddle, like someone spilling a cup of water on the desk. Then, the water began to run, and soon, to flow. The water dripped over the edges, faster and faster until it poured.

I heard a thud somewhere in the classroom and looked up to see Sister Mary Elizabeth unconscious on the floor. The children looked at her, then at me, and started to scream.

NINE

I found myself in Father Michaels' office. Sister Mary Elizabeth had just finished telling him what had happened in her class and now sat in the corner of the room, breathing heavily, almost hyperventilating. She clutched her chest with one hand while clutching an ornately carved rosary with the other.

Father Michaels stared at me with vacant eyes. I could tell he was thinking about something, but he sat staring at me so long that I started to think he was being rude. He could have been mistaken for a statue with how still he was sitting, and, unlike the hyperventilating Sister, I couldn't tell when he drew a breath.

There were three sounds in the room. Two came from Sister Mary Elizabeth: the whoosh of her frantic inhalations, and the soft, puppy-like whimper of her exhalations. The third sound came from a large wooden clock hanging behind Father Michaels' head: the ticking broke the silence with a regular and constant beat.

The only word to describe how I was feeling was 'smug.' I had a hard time keeping my lips from curling at the edges, so I pressed them into a thin line while I waited.

Oh, good, I thought. *He blinked. At least he isn't dead.*

Any minute now he would stare at me with envy, anticipating my next prophetic move. Then he would lead me to the prophets living today and I would have found my family. I had to press my lips harder together in order to stifle a grin.

Finally he rubbed his temples. With his eyes still closed, he said, "I want you to stay in the infirmary again tonight."

My excitement fell.

"I don't even want to hear whatever your side of this ridiculous story is. For God's sake, Alexander, you are a baptized, confirmed, God-fearing member of the Catholic community now. Whatever is affecting you needs to stop. I'll have Sister Mary Chantale come visit you later to remind you of your part in the choir tomorrow. Tell Sister Mary Rafaela to keep an eye on you until Sister Mary Chantale arrives.

"But I'm warning you," he continued, "I am in no mood for this kind of behavior this week, do you

143

understand?"

I didn't answer; I just stared at his still-closed eyes. He couldn't even look at me.

"But he is a child of the devil!" Sister Mary Elizabeth screeched.

Father Michaels sighed. "He was baptized, confirmed, and his communion was less than a week ago. Tell me, how could it be possible that what you say is true?"

"What about the boy, the name, the other you discussed with us. This Edmund?"

The venom with which she said my name caught my attention. I clenched my fists.

"The children are your responsibility," Father Michaels said. "Why don't you tell me?"

"It is the name of the spirit in possession of his body. That is the only explanation."

"I'm not possessed!" I yelled frantically. Possession required an energumen, and I had already ruled out that option. Besides, I had yet to see a yellow tint to my eyes. Were these people oblivious? They spouted off about possession like it was something they expected to happen to everyone in their little *religion*.

Now everyone was standing and speaking in elevated voices and Father Michaels' eyes were finally trained on me. Sister Mary Elizabeth's robe flew wildly as she repeatedly pointed in my direction.

"It is a possibility," Father Michaels admitted. The confession was followed by a brief silence before he added, "But not one I'm willing to accept at this point."

I was appalled. Did they really have no concept of what possession entailed?

"To the infirmary, Edmund."

I was surprised he didn't realize his slip, but the fact that he used my real name calmed me down a bit.

"And you," he addressed Sister Mary Elizabeth, "gather the Sisters. I would like to discuss this further, without the boy."

The look he gave me told me I had overstayed my welcome, so I turned out of his office and headed toward the infirmary. I had been there enough now that I knew where it was without thinking.

I was so livid that I didn't notice most of the glares the other children gave me as I passed them in the hallways. Although a few were curious, most were fearful.

Sister Mary Rafaela met me at the door with a concerned look on her face. "You're back?" she asked politely. "But why?"

"I'm sure Sister Mary Elizabeth and Father Michaels will explain it to you soon enough."

I could tell from her expression that my answer was

not what she had hoped, but I didn't elaborate.

"Where would you like me?" I asked.

She motioned to an empty bed.

"I was *instructed* to have you watch me until one of the other nuns can take your place while you are informed of the situation." My voice was filled with venom.

"What situation?" she asked, concerned.

I, again, didn't answer the question. Instead I huffed myself onto the medical bed, propped myself up against the pillows, folded my arms, and turned my head away from Sister Mary Rafaela's questioning eyes.

"Are you ill, child?"

"No!"

She sat on the foot of my bed, and I could feel her looking at me, but I didn't meet her stare. Instead, I studied everything I could about the room. My eyes settled on the face of a young girl I had seen the last time I was here just a few days before. At the same time, they started to brim with tears.

"What's wrong with her?" I asked, purposely derailing the subject from me.

"She's sick and the doctors don't know why. She sleeps all day and all night, is barely awake long enough to eat, and when she is awake, just lies there with an empty look in her eye. If I don't get her out of bed soon, she'll have to be taken to the hospital."

I couldn't help but notice the giant winged human in the painting above her head. What were those things called? Angels. I found the painting oddly soothing and hoped the girl, when awake, felt the same.

I allowed my frustration to overwhelm me and found myself grieving, yet again, for the loss of my former life. I clenched my teeth and pursed my lips in an attempt to hold back tears, but a single drop managed to escape from the corner of my eye. I wiped it away angrily as soon as I felt it start to roll down my face.

Sister Mary Rafaela's presence wasn't helping. I wished she would just go away but at least her patience afforded her silence.

I don't know how long we sat there but it was long enough for me to run out of irrational thoughts, which included the many ways I could think of to murder Sister Mary Elizabeth. I only *slightly* understood the meaning of blasphemy but I was quite sure it applied to that particular train of thought. Still, it made me feel better.

"Sister Rafaela," a high, soprano voice sang more than said, "Father Michaels would like to see you and the other Sisters in the chapel."

To see Sister Mary Chantale standing in the doorway was like seeing the first signs of dawn after a long winter's night. I needed her beam of hope, love, and kindness—she was the type of person that resulted from overcoming a horrific past—the hope, love, and kindness of a changed heart.

There was a difference I could see between someone who had always been good because they were expected to be good, and someone who had been confronted with evil but chose good anyway; I settled on *humility* to define the difference. Sister Mary Elizabeth had been good for so long that her haughtiness and assurance of righteousness before God was unbearable. Sister Mary Chantale, however, was good because she didn't want to be anything else.

I sighed in relief as I met her eyes, which were as hopeful and bright as ever. There was no judgment in them.

Sister Mary Rafaela bustled out the door as Sister Mary Chantale sat down at the foot of my bed. She gave my leg a little squeeze.

"You know, Alexander," she said softly, "you and I have always been pretty open with each other. I've always trusted you. I've never doubted your love for God or your fellow man. I can't remember you having ever lied."

I knew where this was going.

"Won't you tell me what's going on?"

The question was asked so quietly that I almost didn't believe it was the same voice I had heard earlier directing the choir class. Even still, somehow I knew she had a marvelous singing voice.

"Sister," I answered, "I cannot tell you what I don't know."

"Have you really lost your memory?"

"Not exactly, but it is hard to explain. I remember facts, words, even scripture. I could sing you the songs you have taught me, but the memory of learning all those things is missing."

"Tell me what you do know."

This woman was sincere but I swallowed back any words I was about to say. I was afraid. I didn't know where to start.

"Alexander, please tell me. Whatever it is, I'll be on your side."

I bit my lower lip, raising my eyes to meet hers. "First of all," I said, "my name isn't Alexander."

From there, the recounting of my life as Edmund burst out of me. I told her about my home, Orenda, Hailey, and Ralph. I told her about Joshua, the betrayal, and finding my father dead in his study. She listened without interruption while I stumbled over the parts of my story that didn't make sense, like the fact that I

149

experienced death, the seven levels of *something* that were important to my father, and his ring, which was the only physical representation that I currently had to validate my story.

When I finished, Sister Mary Chantale looked at me intently. She had only one question: "What of your mother?"

The response brought a tear to my eye. "I don't know."

The nun then did something I did not expect; she hugged me.

She smelled like wild eucalyptus. The smell and the embrace caused me to feel a sense of relief. Instead of letting go, my arms clung to her while I cried into the folds of her black habit. She stroked her fingers through my hair and rocked me gently until I pulled myself together.

When I sat back up, Sister Mary Chantale held her hand out to me. "Come with me."

"Where?"

"You taught me something valuable a few years ago," she said. "You and a friend of yours showed me a place you liked to go to think down by the river. I would like to sit there with you for a moment so that I might ponder your circumstances. Perhaps the Lord will be kind to us there if we pray before we go."

I took her hand and we kneeled at the side of the bed while she offered a prayer of supplication, asking that I be delivered from whatever challenges I was facing. The only thing she asked for herself was that she might have understanding.

We both remained silent as we walked across the large grassy grounds toward the river. It felt good to get outside again and the evening breeze was just cool enough to be refreshing. The air outside was light and crisp, not like the heavy and foreboding atmosphere found inside the cathedral.

The trees were alive and buzzing in the evening glow, the sound of their gentle whispers calming my nerves until I was at a point of relaxation.

Sister Mary Chantale and I sat down together on a log along the river near Nicholas's makeshift shelter.

"You know, Edmund," she started, "I've often sat in this spot and pondered on my life."

As soon as she started talking, something odd happened; the trees went suddenly silent, as if they were listening to her.

"I'll sit in this spot and have conversations with myself about what my life could have been like, and ask myself whether or not I am happy where I am." She paused. "See, I have had some struggles of my own. Not with my faith, or my calling, but just with life."

The trees roared at this statement. All around me I could hear them whisper, *Simon, Simon, Simon*.

My eyes widened. "Simon!" I echoed.

Sister Mary Chantale jumped at the name. "What did you say, boy?"

"Simon," I repeated. "How did you struggle with him?"

For a moment, she just stared at me blankly. Finally she said, "Oh, Simon was a wonderful young man. He had great spiritual potential, just like you…"

But I was no longer listening to Sister Chantale; the trees were answering my question too.

The melodic tone of Sister Chantale's voice set the tempo for the story the trees were telling me, like the undertow of a perfectly synchronized river of thought.

The story was so vivid that I could see it take place as the words formed in my mind. I could see Sister Chantale, much younger at a church similar to this one. She stood outside, alone, with her back to a heavy wooden door while her damp eyes gazed reverently into the night sky. It was cold but her discomfort came from within. Her hand reached toward her swollen belly.

The heavy wooden door opened, spilling bright light onto the icy, concrete pavement. Father Michaels appeared in the doorway but quickly stepped out and shut the door behind him.

"Your ride is almost here," he whispered hoarsely. "After you have the child, I will have you transferred to an orphanage in Los Angeles. I will meet you there as soon as I can so that I can oversee your penance."

"And the child?" Sister Chantale asked.

"He is not your child. You are to give him to God as repentance for your immorality."

His words felt like a physical attack to Sister Mary Chantale.

"Now, until I arrive, how is it that you will behave?"

"I will spend my days in prayer and fasting," came her response.

"And the rosary?"

"Only at night, while no one is watching, so that they might not know of my... sin." She hesitated on the last word.

"Ten times," Father Michaels said as though he were repeating himself.

Sister Mary Chantale nodded her head.

A soft honk echoed in the distance.

"There is your ride. Go."

"Thank you, Father."

The rest of the story came in fragments. I saw Sister

Mary Chantale arriving at Saint Vincent's with a child in her arms. I saw Father Michaels arrive and take over the duties as Father at the orphanage. I saw the child grow and play while Sister Mary Chantale hovered longingly in the background. I even saw myself as a young child, interacting with the boy.

"Simon was your son!" I exclaimed aloud.

I didn't know what Sister Chantale was talking about, but whatever it was, she stopped her story mid-sentence. Then, just as if you could remove the undertow from a current, the thoughts of the trees fell silent and my vision closed.

Pain. That is the only word to describe the look on Sister Chantale's face. "Who told you that?" she snapped.

I recoiled at the tone, fumbling across my words. After stuttering for a response, I finally shook my head. "How did he die?"

I didn't know what Sister Chantale was going to say, but she opened her mouth as if to respond. When she did, I held up my hand and gave her a quick "Shh." The question was not meant for her.

The trees suddenly sprung back into conversation and I could see Nicholas, Simon, Ruth, and I playing in the river with a group of other children. I could almost feel the hot summer air on my damp skin as we jumped and splashed each other. Simon sat lazily on the large white rock Nicholas had shown to me earlier, while the rest of us wrestled to keep ourselves upright in the current. I was a good swimmer, I could remember, so I didn't fear the swift moving water. Simon, although not possibly older than eleven, looked so large and strong that I was sure he didn't have any fear of the river either.

Then, as I watched the trees tell the story, I saw a large black figure emerge from beyond the river. His yellow eyes swept over the playing children and fell on me, filled with venom. Though the figure had the shape of a man, it was clearly something else—something that I had never seen before—but whose eyes definitely flashed like those of an energumen.

Why didn't I see this creature? Why didn't Simon or the other children see him?

Because this demon has no body of flesh and blood, the trees responded in their fluid whisper. *Human eyes cannot see them.*

I watched as the creature charged hungrily after me. His movements made no sound and the water flowed through him as if he weren't there. The current didn't seem to slow him down as he barreled toward me.

I watched as his ghost-like hand pushed me under the water. I struggled against the unknown force and kicked my legs in hopes of gaining another breath. I thrashed

155

about as the other children looked on with horror and surprise.

"Cut it out, Alexander," I heard Ruth scream.

"This isn't funny!" Nicholas added.

Simon's eyes just grew large. "Guys! I don't think he's joking."

"What?" I heard Nicholas cry as Simon threw himself off the rock into the quick moving water. He allowed himself to be carried by the current until he was near me. He then stroked hard to get his body in line with mine.

By this time my thrashing had slowed and I was growing weak. Simon grabbed my body and pulled me toward the bank of the river.

The dark figure's eyes pulsed with unnatural power, a power I had never seen. He turned his wrath toward Simon. I listened to the trees in horror as they told me how this dark creature used that unnatural power to rip Simon's soul from his body, leaving his limp remains to be swept away by the river.

I was so startled when Sister Mary Chantale placed her hand on my knee that I flipped backwards off of the log. I saw her worried face appear over mine as she shook me violently.

"Breathe!" she demanded.

I had been so paralyzed by the story the trees had

been telling me, and so horrified by the vision, that I hadn't dared to breathe. I took a loud gulping breath so Sister Mary Chantale could hear.

It must have worked because she stopped shaking me. Instead, she pulled me to my feet.

"Dear child!" she exclaimed. "What is wrong with you?"

The fear I had felt was not subsiding, and adrenaline still pumped through my veins. "It was horrible!" I sputtered, gasping.

"What did I say?"

"Not you! Them."

My fear started to spread to the kind eyes of the Sister and she quickly scanned the area around us for signs of anyone who could have startled me. "Who?"

The deep breathing was calming my nerves and I was able to answer her a bit more steadily. "The trees."

Sister Mary Chantale had already heard my story about my experience with the Mother Tree on my way home to Orenda, so her expression quickly changed from confusion to understanding. "You can hear them now?"

I nodded my head. "They told me about…" I hesitated, "… Simon."

Now her look was worried. "What about him?"

"How he died."

"But we know how he died," the pitch of her voice slid upward. "He drowned."

I could see the swift moving water of the river behind her. I made a quick decision that believing her son drowned would be for the best. Drowning would be a much better fate, less painful, and more *final* than what I saw.

I shivered.

"Come, Edmund," Sister Mary Chantale said, saying my name carefully. She placed her hand on my shoulder with a bit of pressure. "Let's go back inside. Just the fact that you knew Simon was my son is enough for me to believe you. Something must have told you that. Only Father Michaels and I know about my transgression. I am certain you didn't hear anything from either one of us on the subject."

I started walking with her. Before we had managed to take more than a few steps, I took her hand in my own. "Sister Mary Chantale, I am sorry for your loss. It must have been very painful."

"Thank you, Edmund. Your condolences are greatly appreciated."

I didn't see anyone else that evening before I fell asleep. Sister Mary Chantale and I made our way back to the infirmary as quickly as we could. By the time we entered the cathedral, the sun had set and the lights in the infirmary were low. There was now only one other child in the beds—that poor girl who had not been able to eat. Her skin was pale in the dim light and I could see her shivering under heavy blankets.

Sister Mary Chantale took a seat in the chair near the entrance of the room. It wasn't long before her eyes closed and her breathing was heavy. I tried to read some more of the Bible in the nightstand next to my bed but the lack of light made the words difficult to read. My eyes quickly grew tired.

I was having the best dreamless sleep of my life, swimming through the swirling waters of oblivion, when an overwhelming heat caused my subconscious mind to push off my blanket. The fact that my body did not respond caused my eyes to flutter as my conscious mind attempted to regain control. At first I balked at the awakening, trying to force myself back into sleep. The fact that I couldn't move nagged at my brain until I opened my eyes.

The room was hot and heavy, blackness swirling around me with such completeness that I wasn't even sure I had opened my eyes. I tried again to push my blanket off my body but my arms were pinned to the bed.

My breathing increased as I struggled to move, but

the harder I struggled, the harder something tried to keep me held down.

I screamed as two bright yellow eyes appeared above me.

"Alexander!" I heard a voice cry out in the darkness, though it sounded distant.

I started chanting the spell I learned as a boy, the one that was used on the energumen in the snake, and willed the world to cast away this being.

As the room around me turned a stunning white in response to my spell, I saw the full creature pinning me down. He was literally kneeling on my body, but not in a body of his own. This creature was reminiscent of the horrible monster that killed Simon, just a human-shaped black mass with penetrating yellow eyes.

I willed my spell to completion. Like a bolt of lightning, the creature was gone.

For a moment, everything was absolutely silent. Then, slowly, I heard a whimper from the girl in the bed a few paces away from me.

I bolted upright and turned toward her. I could see her pale skin in the dim light, but my eyes were still adjusting to the room. I was dizzy from sitting up so quickly. It took me a few seconds to see her clearly. Her face was turned upright, her back arched, and she looked like she was in pain as her eyes glared at the picture of the angel in the painting above her bed.

I followed her eyes to see another black figure standing in the frame.

I gasped audibly enough for the creature to hear me. His eyes turned toward me.

I began my spell again, but before I could get out the first few words I felt a tingling sensation in my throat. I reached up and felt nothing, only to have the sensation tighten violently.

The creature looked at me with defiance and victory in his yellow eyes. With a burning intensity, I was thrown back onto the bed.

I choked against the pressure on my throat and gasped for breath as I clawed at the invisible hand closing off my airway.

I flinched at the screams of agony that came from the ill girl. I turned my face toward her and kicked my legs as furiously as I could in an attempt to free myself from my unknown assailant. The energumen ran his dark hands over the girl's pale skin, causing deep scratch marks that filled instantly with blood.

He was taunting her.

I felt anger overpower my fear as I reached out toward her but I couldn't get myself out of bed.

The eyes are the window to the soul, I heard him say menacingly, and I knew the words were meant for me. He liked the fact that I was watching him maim this poor girl. He was *explaining* his actions to me!

"No," I managed to choke out. I had seen this already once today. The trees had shown me the horror.

The air around me charged with pure evil. I tried to look away or close my eyes, but the energumen liked having an audience. His mystic power somehow forced me to watch as his fingers dug into the eye sockets of the girl.

The screaming grew unbearable and every muscle in my body hardened in horror. The girl was in such pain that her back arched almost to the point of bending in half. I could see the creature, his hands now buried in her skull, manipulating her body like a puppet. Her back arched harder and harder. Finally, with his other hand, the energumen pushed on the lower half of her body and she completely bent in two.

There was a sickening snap. Her screams trailed to silence.

But the snap was not the worst sound of the experience. I watched helplessly as the energumen ripped the soul of the girl from her body. The trees had not been able to adequately describe that sound.

I suddenly had three pairs of hands on me and was

sprayed with water.

"God, whose nature is ever merciful and forgiving, accept our prayer that this servant of yours, bound by the fetters of sin, may be pardoned by your loving kindness," Father Michaels was chanting, while drawing a wet cross on my forehead.

"Strike terror, Lord, into the beast now lying waste in your vineyard. Fill your servants with courage to fight manfully against that reprobate dragon, lest he despise those who put their trust in you, and say with Pharaoh of old: 'I know not God, nor will I set Israel free.' Let your mighty hand cast him out of your servant, Alexander, so he may no longer hold captive this person whom it pleased you to make in your image, and to redeem through your Son; who lives and reigns with you, in the unity of the Holy Spirit, God, forever and ever."

The energumen was about to leave with his hard-earned soul, but at the words of the Father, turned toward us.

"No, no!" I cried. Father Michaels was getting the attention of the beast. He needed to stop but must have misinterpreted my protests as a sign that his words were having some affect on *me*, because he continued even louder.

I found my hands and legs were now free and the

sensation of the hand around my neck had subsided. I sat up and sputtered out a warning to the Father, only to have Sister Mary Rafaela and Sister Mary Chantale push my back down against the bed.

"Stop!" I pleaded. "You don't understand!"

"I command you, unclean spirit, whoever you are, along with all your minions now attacking this servant of God, by the mysteries of the incarnation, passion, resurrection, and ascension of our Lord Jesus Christ, by the descent of the Holy Spirit, by the coming of our Lord for judgment, that you tell me by some sign your name, and the day and hour of your departure. I command you, moreover, to obey me to the letter, I who am a minister of God despite my unworthiness; nor shall you be emboldened to harm in any way this creature of God, or the bystanders, or any of their possessions."

The energumen, to my surprise, responded. "We are legion, for we are many."

"It mocks us!" Sister Mary Rafaela cried.

"Let us pray."

Then all three chanted together, "Almighty Lord, Word of God the Father, Jesus Christ, God and Lord of all creation; who gave to your holy apostles the power to tramp underfoot serpents and scorpions; who along with the other mandates to work miracles was pleased to grant them the authority to say: 'Depart, you devils!' and by whose might Satan was made to fall from heaven like lightning; I humbly call on your holy name in fear and trembling, asking that you grant me, your unworthy servant, pardon for all my sins, steadfast faith, and the power—supported by your mighty arm—to confront with confidence and resolution this cruel demon. I ask this through you, Jesus Christ, our Lord and God, who are coming to judge both the living and the dead and the world by fire."

The energumen was behind them now as I cowered on the bed.

"This is wrong," I warned. "You aren't doing it right. It isn't *inside* of me!"

The Father continued his chanting after putting his right hand on my head.

"Maybe he's right. We should listen to the boy," Sister Chantale said, frantic over the look on my face.

I couldn't take my eyes off the pair of yellow eyes that weaved unseen through the three physical bodies.

"God and Father of our Lord Jesus Christ, I appeal to your holy name, humbly begging your kindness, that you graciously grant me help against this and every unclean spirit now tormenting this creature of yours; through Christ our Lord."

I cast my own exorcism, but the blinding white light seemed to only aggravate Father Michaels more, and to my dismay, did not dismiss the bright yellow eyes.

The energumen was playing with us now. I could see his eyes smiling darkly at me when my spell failed. "I'm not in a body," I heard him whisper. "You don't know the ways to send me back to Hell, and neither does he!"

His laughter was so loud that even the nuns heard it echo off the walls of the room. Sister Mary Chantale took a step backwards and crossed herself.

I locked my eyes on hers and pleaded with her to run.

"I adjure you, ancient serpent, by the judge of the living and the dead, by your Creator, by the Creator of the whole universe, by Him who has the power to consign you to…"

Mid-sentence, Father Michaels fell silent. His hand was authoritatively raised above his head, his face red from the strain of shouting. His eyes bulged and he drew in a staggered breath.

"God almighty!" he exclaimed, falling limp to the floor.

Sister Mary Rafaela shrieked as the air around me charged again.

I looked into the worried eyes of Sister Mary Chantale. "Run," I groaned. "For the love of God, run."

But it was too late. The two nuns didn't even have time to draw in another breath before the energumen sprayed me with their blood.

PART THREE—RECOVERY

TEN

I found the sound of the rain pelting the windowpane to be rather relaxing. The overcast day was a nice change to the usual sunny weather that prevailed year round in San Diego, California.

Nicholas was nonchalantly playing with the plastic cap at the end of the cord that adjusted the blinds, bouncing it off of the glass as he stared out at the rain. I paid no attention, although the sound of the cap pelting the windowpane was not as soothing as the sounds of the storm.

I heard his mouth drop open before he said anything. "You're doing it again."

I blinked away from my computer screen, and stared at him. "What?"

"You're zoning."

169

"Sorry," I lied.

"So what is it this time? Fire, flood, or little crickets eating the wheat destined to be shipped off to the children of Cambodia?"

When I didn't laugh, Nicholas became more somber.

I didn't know exactly what to tell him. It had been nine years since that day in the orphanage. We never spoke about it, but now I was staring at an online version of an article in a Grand Junction, Colorado newspaper that I knew I couldn't *not* talk about with him.

"It's Ruth," I started.

The name only caused him to flinch a little.

"She died last week."

I couldn't meet his gaze. This was a subject Nicholas wanted nothing to do with. Not only did he doubt his own memories of the events leading up to our last day in Saint Vincent's Orphanage, but also he hadn't been in contact with anyone from the orphanage until he and I happened to bump into each other at a Starbucks near the UCSD campus. We were both in our senior year of high school at the time, had been accepted into UCSD, and were there for a campus tour and scholarship interviews.

"How?" he finally asked, though I could see in his expression he only wanted an answer to his question, not a dissertation on the past.

I debated telling him something about how she was devoured by man eating crickets that grew abnormally large after eating flour on a boat headed to Cambodia—my morbid sense of humor still perfectly intact—but decided that this subject was one that required a bit more sensitivity.

"Suicide," I answered. "It says she hung herself in her dorm room, but the details are sketchy."

"Is there an obituary?"

"Yeah," I pulled it up with a few mouse clicks.

Nicholas stepped forward and peered at the screen where the black-and-white thumbnail of a beautiful young woman with easily recognizable facial features peered back at us. "Yup, you should have boned her," he jeered, taking a small Nerf ball off my desk and tossing it into the air.

Obviously I had overestimated his sensitivity to the issue. "We were twelve!"

A greedy grin exposed his white teeth, which contrasted with his tan skin. "Never too early, right?"

I just rolled my eyes.

"Edmund, Edmund, Edmund," he sighed. "You need to get out more. What is it about these newspaper articles that interest you so much anyway?"

"You really want to know?" I already knew his answer.

"Not really."

So I made something up as I got up from my desk and turned to face him, "I just like to keep informed." I stole the ball as it fell from his most recent toss.

Nicholas may have been stronger, darker, taller, and better looking than I was, but I was faster. Over the years his Native American blood had asserted itself, turning his brown hair and grey eyes into almost equal shades of black. He had grown proportionately up and out and obviously took great pride in maintaining his muscular physique.

I hadn't gotten any wider at all, just taller. My black hair was still unruly, but I had become rather fond of my honey colored eyes and the strength and determination with which they sparked. Sure, Nicholas could win a physical fight with me, but it would never come to that; he would have to get past my eyes first.

We had never really argued, but I always got my way. I got the bed I wanted and the desk I wanted, all because of how determined I looked when I wanted something badly enough. This was a tool I often used to my advantage.

"I'm bored. I want to go surfing," Nicholas said, but I knew that he was thinking about Ruth, about his time in the orphanage. He often changed the subject rapidly when the conversation was drifting toward a place he didn't want it to go.

I didn't push it. I never did. Instead, I just pointed toward the window. "It's raining."

"I'm going to get wet anyway!"

"It rains maybe two or three days a year and you can't think of *anything* better to do?" I jested.

"Well, it *is* the perfect kind of day to cuddle with someone in bed. What are you and Quon doing tonight?"

He didn't mean to run the two sentences together, and didn't realize how funny his question sounded. I laughed anyway.

Quon was our other roommate; a student from Japan.

"I was just planning on registering for next semester tonight. Nothing exciting. I don't know what Quon's plans are."

Nicholas rolled his eyes. "Your big plan on a rainy *Saturday* night is to register for next semester?"

I grinned.

"Fine. I'll bite. At least tell me what classes you are going to sign up for."

"Probably another literature class," I hesitated before adding, "and a few theology courses. Strangely enough, there is a class on the history and meaning of color in the interior design department I think might be kind of interesting."

"And what, exactly, are you majoring in again? I mean, come on Edmund, history of color?"

Nicholas had gotten used to my rather odd taste in… well… everything, but he still enjoyed giving me a hard time about it. Currently my desk was littered with as many translations of the Bible as I could get my hands on, as well as a few scattered newspaper clippings and a couple of journals—not exactly your average college student's reading materials.

"Color," Nicholas scoffed when I didn't answer. "Whatever. I'm going to the gym."

I made a few more mouse clicks while he gathered his gym bag and headed toward the door. He paused just before pulling the handle closed behind him.

"Hey Edmund, how did you hear about Ruth's death anyway?"

The fact that Nicholas had returned to this subject was nothing short of shocking. "I was looking for her." I said carefully.

"Hmm," he responded, and closed the door behind him.

***

I lied to Nicholas; I did have plans that evening. I had

called the Catholic Community Center and had set an appointment with Father Paul. I had never met this man, and, in fact, had not stepped into a Catholic church since my foster parents grew tired of the weekly struggle to get me to attend mass. Father Paul seemed soft spoken on the phone and I found comfort in the fact that the Catholic Community Center of UCSD actually met in a rented space in a nearby *Episcopal* church.

I was ushered into a small office by a kindly woman with fiery red hair and an abnormally large mouth. When she spoke to me it was always with her lips pulled far over her teeth. A few days ago, on campus, I was witness to an event where the participating students were required to see how many Twinkies they could shove in their mouth without chewing. The winner fit nine. I was suddenly filled with the desire to start stuffing the little cream filled cakes into this woman.

"I'm Kathy, if you need anything," she said after seating me in front of a large, but underused desk. "I'll be just outside in the administrative office. Father Paul will be with you shortly."

I idly twisted the ruby ring on my finger while I waited. This office, though much more plain than Father Michaels' back at Saint Vincent's, was all too familiar... and creepy. A large picture of Christ hung behind the desk and it seemed to me that every artist who decided to paint Jesus focused too much on making me feel like I was being watched. I supposed it made some people feel comfortable, believing that a great God was watching over them. It probably made some people feel guilty; I was sure that helped a great deal when it came to terrifying people into avoiding sin. I just found it spooky: all the idols, the candles, the images of a man's torture and death on a cross, the holy saints portrayed in various positions of judgment; the whole idea of religion seemed to me to be based more on a fear of (rather than a love of) an omnipotent, caring creator. But I sort of assumed I felt that way because of the few days that had been seared into my memory at Saint Vincent's orphanage. If people wanted to worship out of love, I had no issue with that, but when they did it out of fear—fear of death, fear of punishment—that was something I just refused to understand.

"You must be Edmund."

The voice behind me was stronger than the one on the phone. I jumped.

"Sorry if I startled you. I'm Father Paul," he said, walking around me and taking a seat at his desk. "I have to admit, I'm really rather excited to talk to you. You told Kathy you were at Saint Vincent's as a child?"

I nodded my head, "For about twelve years."

"Were you there during the…" he hesitated, "… incident?"

I nodded again, not mentioning that I *was* the incident.

"Well that is just fascinating. I have to admit though, when we got your call and you mentioned to Kathy that Saint Vincent's was your last parish, I tried to look you up…"

I interrupted. "I changed my name and asked that those records be sealed."

"So you never attended a Catholic parish under your current name?"

"No."

The priest pursed his lips. "It's been a long time since your last confession then."

I grinned, "Indeed."

Based on his scowl, that wasn't the response he was expecting. "Well, if you came for a confession, this isn't the usual way to go about it, but we have the confessional open…"

"I didn't come for a confession."

"So you do not intend to return to the faith?"

"Sorry, Father, but no."

He crossed his arms and I saw his eyes turn

defensive. "Then what can I do for you today?"

"I was hoping you could provide me a list of the names of the children, workers, nuns, and priests that survived at Saint Vincent's, and, if it is possible, where those children were sent, and where the workers and staff were reassigned."

His jaw dropped. "For what purpose?"

"My reasons, " I paused, "are personal."

"I'm sorry, Edmund, but you are going to have to do better than that. Church records are private, probably not even available to a member of the church, and certainly not to a heathen."

This was going to be harder than I thought. "Well, then, perhaps you could inquire as to the whereabouts of Father Michaels' journals?"

Father Paul sighed. "Actually, Edmund, after your call I became a bit fascinated by the Saint Vincent massacre. I called the diocese and told them I might have one of the children from that incident in my congregation. They sent me a copy of the journals."

Now we were getting somewhere. "Can you tell me if there was anything in them that stood out to you?"

Father Paul chuckled. "Just a part about a boy named Alexander claiming to actually be named Edmund, but I'm certain you already know all about that."

My stomach muscles tightened reflexively, just like someone had punched me.

"Are you that boy? If you answer truthfully we may be able to have a more honest discussion."

Father Paul emphasized the word *honest* in such a way as to make me believe he wasn't being honest at all.

But still, I considered, and then nodded.

"More interesting than the journals of Father Michaels, whose entries obviously end just a few days after he makes reference to the 'Edmund conundrum,' are the journals of a Sister Mary Elizabeth. I was only able to read a few months past the time of the death of Father Michaels, Sister Mary Chantale, and Sister Mary Rafaela, but Sister Mary Elizabeth has been kind enough to agree to send me the remainder of her writings on the subject."

"Sister Mary Elizabeth is still alive?" I asked in amazement before thinking of the consequences of my question.

"She is."

"Where?"

"I'd rather not say. She didn't trust you much, at least not after your communion. Before that she thought you were very special. She blames you for the deaths in the orphanage. Her formal report to the Vatican was that Father Michaels was performing an exorcism on you at the time of his death. I must admit I find that rather shocking. Are her report of the events true?"

"I don't know, I haven't read them."

"Would you like to?"

I knew there had to be a catch to this question, but I narrowed my eyes and nodded.

Father Paul pulled open a lower drawer on his desk, and took out a file folder. "Here is a copy of Sister Mary Elizabeth's statement to the Vatican," he tossed the folder toward me. "As I said, I find this story fascinating, and since I am the first church representative to have contact with you since your... disappearance, I must admit I am looking forward to our future conversations."

"So your intentions, then, are to help me as long as I answer your questions?" I asked, feeling like Father Paul was more interested in the story inside of my head than in me as a person, as a human, or as a Catholic.

He smiled. "Perhaps you could start by telling me about what happened after you left the orphanage. How did you escape the massacre when everyone else in the room was killed? You were placed with a foster family, were you not? Tell me about them."

I balked. "Why don't you just ask my foster parents? They have already asked me those questions. Surely, you know who they are."

"They're dead."

Any emotion I was feeling at that moment was washed away with a sense of surprise at the amount of loss that swept through me. My foster parents were disgusting role models, but I found myself now being unable to focus on anything but their redeeming qualities.

"You didn't know?" Father Paul was legitimately taken aback.

I pressed my lips together in a tight line in an attempt to control my emotions, and shook my head. "How long ago?"

"Six weeks. Your mother three days after your father." Father Paul's voice was now filled with genuine concern.

"Heart attacks?"

Father Paul blinked in surprise, his answering tone reflected that emotion. "Yes."

"Father Paul," I stood and put my hands on his desk so that he could see the pleading in my eyes. "I really need that list. I know of nine deaths that occurred after the massacre at the orphanage, the most recent a friend of mine named Ruth. All of them had heart related injuries. In Ruth's case the coroner guessed that as she hung herself, her own fear of death caused heart failure, killing her before either asphyxiation or the breaking of the spinal column. Does that sound possible to you?"

Father Paul's eyes lit with understanding, "The deaths in the orphanage all had heart related problems as well?"

I nodded slowly.

"You think… but… the deaths in the orphanage were ruled homicide."

"Homicide, suicide, natural causes, it doesn't matter. The injury is the same."

"You want this list because you think someone is trying to kill everyone who survived?"

"I don't know."

"According to Sister Mary Elizabeth, *you* were the reason all those people died," Father Paul said with a slight amount of fear in his expression.

"Sister Mary Elizabeth believed I was possessed."

"Were you?"

"Father Michaels performed the exorcism didn't he? And I'm still Edmund, aren't I?"

"I don't know, did he? Are you?"

"I'm sorry Father Paul, but these are questions with answers that I don't have any explanations for. Perhaps you need to find those answers yourself. Can you at least tell me how many people survived?"

"Thirty-four children, nineteen staff members, and six nuns."

"Please, Father, check that list and find out how many are still alive."

"Why would anyone still want these people dead?"

"I don't know, Father, but that is what I am trying to find out."

ELEVEN

It is just over a seven hour drive from San Diego to Prescott, Arizona, and although it was a few minutes faster to go up I-15 and catch I-10 across the desert, I always preferred to take Interstate 8 up through Yuma. My chosen path might have been less populated all together, but the population was more widespread, making me feel like I wasn't in the middle of nowhere, at least until I had to start going north on 95.

I remembered Prescott being a big town when I was a child, but that is when I thought twenty thousand people all trying to get rodeo tickets was the defining characteristic of a big city. Even though the population had now close to doubled that, there was still no comparison to the millions of people in San Diego. Not only did the city feel small to me now, but sort of reminded me of the kind of town in a horror film.

My foster parents owned a square cut, three bedroom, southwestern cottage with barely 1,000 square feet, but the lot that the house sat on was large enough to comfortably fit one of the larger UCSD buildings. There were no cars in the driveway when I parked my beat up Toyota Tacoma against the curb but the horses were in their stalls and hadn't been taken care of. I glanced at my watch and deduced from the hour that if my older sister hadn't been staying in the house and had to work or something, then she probably wouldn't have made it over to let the horses out into a shared pasture that was tucked behind our property line.

It had been two years since I had done any work in the stables but I was still quick at it. I led the horses to the pasture and had the stalls raked (which, I might add, obviously had not been done regularly) in just under an hour. Then, since I didn't have a key to the house, I climbed a large willow tree that grew at the end of the pasture and watched the horses nibble on the grass.

This tree was familiar to me. I had spent hours amongst its branches as a child. Even now, I could feel the warmth of its life force cradle me as I curled up between the junctures of its trunk. Yet the tree remained silent.

Trees, I had discovered, did not have the best of memories—at least not individually. Their consciousness was somewhat collective, and as such, the collective thought patterns of the grove become the forefront concern. Everything else would be forgotten until the trees agreed on a new item to ponder. Unfortunately, this willow was part of a grove whose roots intertwined halfway across the desert. Although I had had many conversations with this tree in the past, it was always hard to garner the attention of the grove.

The horses also were not very chatty, they were just angry. Their regular schedule had been interrupted since the death of my foster parents. My sister was obviously not as meticulous as my foster father had been at ensuring their care. On top of that, they were upset that I hadn't come to ride them, to discuss their needs, or to spend time with them over the past two years. Horses, unfortunately, had a phenomenal memory—and they knew how to hold a grudge.

"Well now, this is a surprise. What are you doing here? Come to see what they left you in their will?"

The voice came from below me, but it was familiar enough to be instantly recognizable. I grinned down between the branches to where my foster sister, Jane, was standing at the base of the tree.

"I didn't even hear your car pull in," I yelled down at her.

Jane's face was pale with exhaustion. She didn't seem overly happy to see me, but I half expected that. There was a persistent warmth in her hazel eyes though, warmth that I realized I missed. "You always did get lost in your own little world up there. Let's go inside where it is a bit warmer," she chirped. "I'll make us some lunch."

The small house had not changed much. It still smelled of sugar and dust and cleanliness was forgotten among shelf after shelf of religious trinkets. The only difference now was that it felt colder. Jane must have thought the same thing, because the first thing she did was turn up the thermostat.

"It's supposed to snow this afternoon. Just an inch or two but we should keep an eye on the roads." She tugged the door to the fridge open but stopped to look at me as I walked into the kitchen. "I'm assuming you aren't staying long."

"Sorry," I stated. "I've got classes tomorrow."

"Do you have any plans for Christmas?"

Wow. Christmas. I had almost forgotten it was less than six weeks away. I glanced over toward the calendar on the wall—November 6th. "No, not really," I answered.

Jane cracked an egg into a flour mixture she was preparing. Pancakes, from the look of it.

"Look, Jane. I'm sorry I didn't come. I didn't know."

187

She hesitated for just a moment while tucking a stray strand of strawberry blonde hair behind her ear. "I know. I tried to call…"

"I changed my number."

"Did you really hate us that much?"

"Hate?" I had to search my emotions here. "No. I never…"

I stopped as I saw tears well up in her eyes. She covered well, turning quickly to the refrigerator to get out the milk, only lingering a bit longer than necessary, like she couldn't remember where she put it. I knew she was composing herself.

"Well, it was…" she started blinking rapidly, "… hard without you. You know how they got."

"It didn't get any better when I left?"

Jane added a cup of milk to the batter and started stirring. "A little, honestly. A few days after you were gone, when they were sure you weren't coming back, they went through your room."

I hadn't expected less.

"After they burned everything you left behind, they tore up the carpet, and painted the entire room white, the floors, the ceilings, the walls. They were so convinced the symbols you had everywhere would bring evil into the house."

None of this was news to me. The reason I left so abruptly was because they had accused me of being a worshipper of Satan. Our arguments had escalated when the trees started to hear rumors that concerned me, rumors of energumen. I insisted on protecting myself the only way I knew how but protective symbols from my life in Orenda weren't exactly welcomed in a Catholic household.

I had been accused of being in league with the devil once, and that ended in the massacre of dozens. I wasn't about to stay in a place where I was accused of the same thing. As little as I loved my foster parents, I didn't want them dead.

Jane chuckled. "It's funny, though. Since Mom and Dad died, your room is the only place I can sleep at night in this house. Even though it is so cold, hard, and stanch white now. Everything else in this place just seems dark."

A gust of wind rattled the windows; the sky was turning from a light grey to a smoky black.

"Storm's rolling in," Jane commented while she poured the batter onto the griddle.

Most of Jane's story so far was what I had been expecting but there was one piece that bothered me.

"Jane," I asked gently, "why would you be afraid of this place? With all the pictures of Christ, the shrines to Catholic saints, the candles, it seems like this is the last place you would feel evil. You always took such great comfort in the Catholic faith."

"I'm assuming, since you haven't asked, that you know how Mom and Dad died?"

I wasn't sure how the question was significant, but I answered truthfully. "Yes. Heart failure. I went to see Father Paul at my local diocese. He told me." I said the last few sentences as easily as possible to make it sound like Father Paul and I were better acquainted.

"Do you remember when we were kids and I asked you what happened in the orphanage? You used to tell me elaborate stories, about demons in possession of human bodies with yellow eyes. I always believed Mom when she told me that those stories were just your way of coping with what happened to you. I never thought…"

My heart jumped into my throat. "Where are you going with this, Jane?" The question came out more forcefully than I expected.

Jane pulled the pancakes off the griddle and handed me a plate, which I took, but didn't move. Instead I glared at her, willing her to answer my question.

"It's nothing, really. Just a strange chain of events. I'm sure it's nothing."

"Tell me."

Jane let out a sigh. "Well, a few days before Mom and

Dad died, a young man came to the house looking for you."

I tried to hide my reaction, which was somewhere between disgust and anger.

"He told Dad that he had been speaking with Sister Mary Elizabeth from the orphanage about how you and he used to be friends."

Two things bothered me about this part of the story. One, just the name Sister Mary Elizabeth was enough to turn my face red. Two, I had no idea what male friend this could have been. The only two I could even remember were Simon and Nicholas, one of whom was dead, and the second would be snoring right now in our dorm room at UCSD.

"Do you remember this person's name?"

Jane shook her head. "I only met him briefly, and not the day he came. After he discovered we didn't know where you were, he told dad he had come a long way and wondered if he might do some work to earn enough money to travel back. Dad told him we didn't have much but let him work with the horses for a few days."

"I'm still not sure where this is going."

"Well, there was something about him I didn't like. That first night was when Dad started having pains in his chest. I couldn't help but think this man did something to him."

"I admit, the timing is a bit strange, but I really don't see how…" my attempted words of reassurance and comfort cut short when Jane looked at me with pleading in her eyes. I remembered that feeling and recognized the look. I knew exactly what it was like to plead with someone to believe something that you knew to be absolute truth but made no logical sense. "Why do you think he…?" I couldn't get the rest of the question out.

"I know it seems stupid," Jane said, "but I…"

Her voice cut off and she began breathing heavily. I watched as her hands started shaking so badly that she had to put down her own plate.

"Jane, are you afraid?"

"Edmund, I've had dreams of this man. They are always of him…"

"Go on, Jane."

"It's embarrassing."

"I need to know."

Jane sat down at the table and started drumming her fingers nervously. "In my dreams this man is on top of me… naked. But it isn't normal. It hurts. I can't move, and it's dark. I hear screaming in the distance, and then I realize it's my own voice screaming. But at the same time, I can't speak, I can't scream. It hurts to even open my mouth. I don't know where I am or how I'm screaming in the distance. The only thing I can do is watch this man take advantage of me. Sometimes, when I wake up, I have bruises. Two nights ago, I woke up bleeding. I went into the bathroom to clean up. When I got back to my room I looked out the window and thought I saw him standing across the pasture, just inside of the trees, peering at me with eerie yellow eyes.

"I didn't know what to do. I just stood there, frozen. I know you don't believe me Edmund, but I was so scared I just stood there watching him, frightened that if I looked away for even a moment he would disappear and I wouldn't know where he went. I felt safer because at least I knew where he was and knew he was far away from me. Then, a horse ran in front of the window. I didn't know why the horses would be out of the barn, but in the time it took for the horse to run past the window, the man was gone.

"I was so terrified I ran room to room, checking to make sure he hadn't somehow gotten into the house. I hesitated in your room. I could still see one of the symbols you had drawn on the floor through the paint, glowing in the moonlight. It dawned on me that this symbol would have been right underneath your bed. I curled up in the middle of the symbol, and felt such peace and warmth that

I completely forgot about the man in the woods and fell asleep."

Every muscle in my body tensed as I listened to Jane's story. I was so lost in my own thoughts that I almost forgot Jane was sitting at the table. I jumped when she touched my hand.

"Edmund?"

"I believe you, Jane." I said quietly. "But I need to ask you some questions."

She nodded.

"Did you have these dreams the nights Mom and Dad died?"

She shook her head. "They started after."

"When was the last time you saw this man?"

"Last night."

"And where did you stay last night?"

Jane blinked in disbelief. "Here."

My stomach lurched like I had been kicked. "Jane, when I got here there were no cars in the driveway."

"Of course there were. I sold Mom and Dad's last week, but mine has been there." She pointed out the living room window, where her black Chevy Cavalier was plainly visible.

I shook my head. "And this man, Dad had him caring for the horses?"

She didn't have to answer. As soon as I asked the question a bolt of lightning struck my brain. I could literally feel the synapses shooting electric currents, connecting Jane's story to the death of my parents. This stranger had been looking for me, had asked for me by name. He was put to work with the horses, to which I had told my most intimate secrets. If this person could communicate with animals as I could, he would now know more about me than any person on the planet. If he were an energumen, a full-fledged, in-possession-of-an-actual-body, energumen, his power could be...

Terror struck next. If this man had gained the trust of Sister Mary Elizabeth, he could feasibly learn the names of all the children who had survived the incident at the orphanage. And if the horses had been angry with me, but trusted him, they could—"Jane!" I exclaimed, bolting out of my chair, "Are you *sure* this man said he had learned this address from Sister Mary Elizabeth?"

My sudden reaction caused Jane to get out of her chair too. "Yes. Why?"

"You can't stay here." I grabbed her hand and led her toward the front door.

"Edmund, what's going on?"

I turned toward Jane and locked onto her fear-filled hazel eyes. "The story I told you about the orphanage is true, just as your story is true. He is one of *them*."

I didn't think it would have been possible for Jane to go any whiter, but she did. Her reaction told me she understood and remembered the part of my story with the demons with yellow eyes.

I pulled her through the front door and out to where my truck was parked at the curb. I heaved the door open as the first flakes of snow started to fall.

"Edmund?"

"Do you know anyone?" My question came out incoherent as I rummaged through a toolbox underneath my back seat.

"What?"

"Do you know anyone new? Do you have any friends who have never…" I paused; this was going to sound stupid, "… met the horses?"

"What?" Jane echoed, but then answered, "Yes, I've got a few friends I've met online."

"Far from here?" I was still searching.

"Yes, in…"

"Don't say it!"

Finally, I found what I was looking for. I handed her a piece of iron suspended from a thin strip of leather. "I know it's a bit manly," I joked as the wind picked up again.

She took the necklace from me, and peered at the

word *occulo* carved deeply into the metal. "What is this?"

"It's Latin." I answered, "It means 'hidden.' It will keep you safe."

"Safe?"

I rolled my eyes at her and pulled her to her car. She opened the door and got in. "You can't come back here until I say it's okay. Is your phone number still the same?"

She nodded.

"I'll text you my number. Call me when you get where you are going. I'll call you when—*if*—you can come back here."

I took my key out of my pocket and dropped to my knees. Jane eyed me warily as I carved the same Latin word into the paint along the side of her door jam.

As if on cue, the wind shifted, and an immense feeling of cold blew over us.

"He's coming," I said before thinking it over clearly. "Go!"

Jane's breathing was frantic and her eyes pleaded with me.

"I'll be fine. Hurry!" I closed her door and watched as she backed out of the driveway. I saw her glance in the rearview mirror at me for a moment before her foot floored the gas and her car lurched away.

I didn't have much time. The energumen would be

here any moment. The feeling of having one so close was sickening and all too familiar. I could hear the whispers of the trees on the wind, realizing why they had been so silent. They weren't saying good things, but they were talking about me. He had tasked them with alerting him should I return.

I was angry, especially at the horses for betraying my confidence. I was angry at the trees, which had always been my friends, for heeding the call of a demon. My hands tingled at the thought of a fight with a demon (for so they were called in this world), but I knew nothing of him, and I knew that he knew too much about me. As angry as I was, I knew I wasn't in the best tactical position for a fight.

I made a quick decision and jumped into my truck. I turned the key and the engine roared to life as a dark cloud descended on the pasture.

TWELVE

Three hours into the drive back to San Diego, I received a text message from Jane letting me know she had arrived at her destination. A cold shudder rippled down my spine and I hoped three hours would be enough distance to keep the demon from finding her. I knew that as long as she wore the necklace I gave her she would be relatively safe. I responded with a text containing further instructions: salt drawn in a circle around the house she was staying at, and sage or red cedar at the doors and windows of her room.

I spent the majority of the drive listening to the soothing roar of the engine and contemplating the sequence of events that occurred at the house. Perhaps the most startling realization was that the trees had betrayed my family and me to a demon. I found myself wishing I had a greater understanding of the natural, interconnected consciousness of the planet. I, no doubt, had friends among the trees—there were plenty on campus, and the small line of trees at Saint Vincent's orphanage had certainly sided with me—but what I didn't know was whether or not it were possible for a tree to keep a secret, at least from the other trees. Which begged the question: if I was betrayed by the trees surrounding the pasture behind my foster parent's home, why didn't the other trees on campus warn me?

I had to have permission to tap into the collective consciousness of a tree. One of them had to share that connection with me. Was it the same for them? When I skipped across the roots in my childhood, when Mother Tree allowed me to see the courtyard of Orenda, did every plant along the way have to agree to allow me to see?

With how much I knew about them and their forms of communication, I still knew so little.

I reached over and turned on the windshield wipers as a light rain started leaving smatterings on my windshield. The desert road was far from dark, illuminated by moonlight that reflected off large stretches of sand, but the road was mostly deserted. I pressed on the accelerator as the only other pair of lights I could see disappeared in my rearview mirror.

The solitary feeling of being the lone car traveling on

a highway through a large stretch of desert at night while it was raining was enough to make anyone feel isolated, and perhaps a bit frightened. I enjoyed the silence. Unfortunately, it didn't last long.

My phone buzzed with a text message from Nicholas: *Where r u?*

I responded: *Driving.*

Quon's cousin is visiting; we want to set you up. She's hot.

I rolled my eyes. *What? You don't you want to take her out?*

Lol. U know she's not my type. Got a date anyway.

Tomorrow.

She's very much YOUR type.

"My type?" I wondered aloud, before echoing my sentiments into the response. Too bad I couldn't somehow emote the way I had said it.

Earthy. Pagan. Loves spirituality. She's a girl. You'll have lots in common.

Nicholas' double entendres were always lost on him. *Now I know why you don't want to date her.*

Lol.

I was considering my response when a sudden flurry of colorful lights exploded across the desert sand. The unexpected flashing excited my already frayed nerves and I swerved instinctively.

"Stupid, stupid, stupid!" I exclaimed after regaining control and glancing in my rearview mirror to discover the source of the lights. I glanced down at my speedometer; even after the swerve I was doing ninety-eight. This was going to be one expensive ticket.

I applied even pressure to the brakes, hoping somehow the officer would see that I was perfectly capable of driving safely, and pulled over onto the soft shoulder. In the swerve, my phone skidded under the passenger seat. I didn't want the officer to think I was reaching for a gun and shoot me, so I made a quick decision to forgo retrieving it until after I spoke to the officer.

I sat staring at the circling red and blue lights for what seemed like an eternity. It must have been somewhere close to 11 p.m., which would put me just under three hours from home. As I sat there watching the lights, the mesmerizing effect made me feel more tired and a little disoriented. I was pulled over; what was taking the officer so long?

The rain picked up slightly, but the culminating clouds blocking the moonlight drew extreme attention to the black sky. Any light reflecting off the sand now was alternating blue and red on a backdrop of inky blackness.

After my nerves settled, I gathered my license and registration and yawned. A dark figure finally emerged from the police cruiser.

I saw the beam of his flashlight as he casually walked up to my driver's side window. He rapped rudely on the glass with the tail of the flashlight before turning the bright beam on my face. My vision was flooded with white light.

I inched the window down. "Officer, do you mind not shining that thing in my eyes?"

"I need you to step out of the truck, please."

I balked. "What? No. Look, I haven't been drinking or anything. The swerve was just because you startled me. I know I was speeding, but I'm trying to get back to San Diego at a reasonable time. I've got classes in the morning and—"

"Step out of the truck, please."

The tone in his voice caused me to close my mouth immediately. It was harsher than I expected. Oddly familiar. Sinister.

My body flushed ice cold.

"Officer," I chose my next words carefully. "Would you mind calling for backup or following me to a more populated area or something? I'm not really comfortable—"

Without warning, my window shattered, spraying my face with glass. My reaction was immediate—I jumped over into the passenger's seat, and cursed under my breath.

The flashlight reappeared inches from my face, but there was another colder metallic object for me to see as well. My body tensed as I realized I was looking down the barrel of a shotgun.

"Get out!" the voice commanded. "Get out or I'll shoot you."

My hand scrambled for the door handle, as I tried to say, "Okay," but that wasn't what came out. "No you won't," I said instead. "That isn't your style."

Why did I say that?

I closed my eyes and braced for the sound of an internal explosion, followed by the pressure of thousands of tiny metal balls burrowing through my flesh. I had no doubt that a shot at this distance would not only kill me, but that parts of my head would be found scattered around the desert for miles. At least death would be fast.

But no explosion came. When I dared open my eyes again, I found the scene exactly as I had left it. I was still partially blinded by the bright light held on my face, and could still see the menacing glimmer of the barrel of the gun. Certainly the time to shoot had passed, hadn't it?

The cop's answer was a low, throaty laugh followed by the retreat of the barrel.

"Edmund, my dear dear Edmund, you're right."

The flashlight dropped, and a pair of yellow eyes

confronted me.

I would have preferred to have been shot. A ripple of fear caused the smell of bile to flood upward into my sinuses. I kicked my feet frantically, bracing myself against the passenger door, as far as I could retreat from the yellow gaze.

"How did you find me?" I said breathlessly.

The demon's smile pulled back over two rows of perfectly white teeth. The body he possessed was strong and muscled, every inch well kept.

He inhaled deeply. "I followed your smell from the house," he finished with a moan. "You are so deliciously... human."

To say I was disgusted would be an understatement.

"I've been looking for you for a long time. Ever since you exorcized me all those years ago."

My mind flipped through the demons I had crossed paths with in the orphanage. None of them had this voice. None of them were quite as evil.

"Oh no no," he whispered. "Not *this* life."

In my memory I was in a confrontation with Joshua. Surrounding him were so many energumen. I remembered being sure I would die, but defying Joshua anyway. A voice, a voice in the group of energumen stood out as they clamored for Joshua's victory. That was the voice I was hearing now.

"How did you come to be here?" I asked in amazement. Though fear had taken complete control of my body, I could not let this opportunity pass. This demon was the first assured connection I had to Orenda since my father's ring. Nothing else—nothing even hinted to the supposed existence of Orenda. This demon knew who I was, *and* where I had come from.

"I crawled my way back from Hell, thanks to you. And you?"

"I don't know."

The creature laughed. "I'm sure Joshua would find that answer interesting. I'll have to tell him I found you."

Then came the pain. Strangely, it wasn't excruciating, just paralyzing. My limbs fell limp and I found myself unable to speak.

"I know your thoughts, Edmund. No. I will not let you exorcize me again. You will be in Hell before I am. You have built yourself quite a safe place inside of this truck of yours. Your symbols and protections indeed will keep me from physically entering, but Edmund—there is so much you don't understand! This truck exists in so many different worlds, and you cannot protect it in all of them unless you know where they are. So, bravo. My power can still get to you—I just have to use one of the worlds you know nothing about."

Levels, I thought. *He's talking about levels.*

The demon grinned. "Whatever you want to call them."

My body would have frozen in shock had my brain been able to communicate anything to my limbs.

"Oh yes, Edmund. I can read your thoughts. That is how I am going to get the information I need from you. I am going to ask you questions, and you are going to think about the answer. Perhaps, together, we can figure out the one thing our dear friend Joshua has not been able to figure out. How did you get here, Edmund? How did your physical presence cross from Orenda into this world?"

How did you get here? I asked myself, wondering why the answer wasn't one in the same.

"Oh, we energumen have a great gift. We can cross into whatever world we choose. We are spirits, but it is only in physical form that we can express our greatest powers. We can possess the weak and the willing, but Joshua is a physical being already—as are you. How did your physical presence cross from there to here?"

The end of his question sounded angry or exasperated. I couldn't tell which. Luckily, I had no idea how I got here, so his question would remain unanswered.

But there was a hint of something in the back of my

mind, something that the demon caught onto.

He smirked. "What did you bring with you?"

My mind instantly settled on my father's ring.

"Interesting," the creature paused. "That ring also exists in another world, but not as it does here. It is unattainable there, yet physical here, much like a spirit to a body."

I could see his eyes coveting the ring as they fell upon my finger.

"Pity I cannot come inside and snatch it away from you."

I snorted. It was the only physical response I could give him.

"What is the purpose of the ring?"

I did not know.

"Does it have power?"

As far as I knew.

"What is that power?"

I did not know, all I had been able to figure out was that I didn't remember my life in Orenda until the day in the orphanage when Father Michaels gave the ring to me, and after that, I couldn't remember the twelve years I had lived on Earth.

The demon looked a bit confused, which was good, because even I wasn't sure how, exactly, I was able to live two places at once, either.

"Is the ring responsible for your ability to cross into this world?"

I didn't know. I wasn't alive when I had crossed into this world, at least, as far as I knew. I had been dead.

"Impossible."

Perhaps you have an explanation then! You were there. Joshua killed me, I thought angrily.

"Give me the ring."

No.

I could see the demon's frustration start to boil. It caused his hold on the human body to slip, which caused his hold over me to slip. I wiggled my finger.

"Give it to me and I will let you live."

I still couldn't speak. *Liar*, I thought.

He screamed. At first I thought his scream sounded metallic, but then the bed of the truck ripped away from the cab, completely severing the truck in two. I saw the bed fly hundreds of feet into the air and disappear somewhere in the desert.

"I *will* kill you."

You can't get into the cab.

A look of exasperation crossed his face momentarily and he started stomping his feet in frustration. Honestly, it was a bit amusing to see a grown male figure throwing a temper tantrum like a five year old.

"I can't," he growled at me. He spun my head around toward the oncoming traffic, "but *that* can."

The demon used his power to force my head around to where I could see a large oil tanker as it wound its way unsuspectingly toward us. I could now move my entire hand and was able to see back through the pathway the demon was using to control me. The path went into places I had never before seen, so it was difficult to trace back directly to the mind of the demon.

I did, however, know his intentions. His intentions were to cause that truck to barrel into me and explode. With any luck, the symbols and protections I had used would incinerate with me, and he could then take the ring and give it to Joshua.

I had hoped to live long enough to sort out the details I had just learned. This demon knew about levels and said he knew more of them than I did. He called them worlds, and I couldn't help but wonder if they were more like alternate realities, like I had read about in sci-fi novels. He had confirmed that Orenda was a place—that it did exist—and that I had been there, physically, as I was here now. He could not explain my death, which led me to believe he could not explain the twelve years I had spent on this planet without memory of my past life, or how I could not remember those twelve years once I did. He didn't know about the ring, at least not that it was somehow important—I wondered how my ring could exist on my finger and in another place at the same time.

I knew the demon could sense my thoughts, but I also didn't care—and neither did he. He was too busy controlling the truck, which was gaining speed at an alarming rate. The truck was close enough that I could see the driver flailing about in the cab. No doubt he had no idea why his truck was behaving so erratically.

Maybe if I could break the demon's control over the diesel I could survive, but every power, level, world, doorway, whatever it was that I knew, everything physical needed to be spoken—while the demon was in a body every spell had to be physical. I couldn't cast him out but I had to do something!

The red and blue flashing was now reflecting off the large tank full of oil. I didn't have much time. I closed my eyes and followed the trail of power the demon was using to grasp my mind, looking for anything familiar.

It was like following a silver strand of light through a wormhole to an unknown universe. There were so many distractions, things I had never seen before, but every time I started to get distracted by one of the oddities I found, I lost the silver trail and had to start over.

I told myself to focus and to move quickly. As I followed the trail I found a doorway, not symbolic or imaginary, but quite literal. It was open far enough for the tiny strand to fit through. I pushed, it swung wider, and I fell through it. Then there were yellow eyes all around me, watching me. I could hear their anger as they shouted curses at me, trying to get me to forget about the silver string and fall into the unknown.

The strangest thing about this place was that it was cold. Freezing. My mind started to fight with me. I tried to get it to push forward, but everything was so sluggish here. My vision was hazy, my thoughts blurred, but I could see another door just a few feet in front of me.

Then familiar yellow eyes confronted me and spoke:

"You are too late, Edmund. In just moments, you will be dead. Then, I will take whatever soul you might possess and bring you back here. Do you really think you can pass through my world freely? Do you think you can use *my* powers? *My* doors? *My* worlds? Stupid, stupid boy. Without the path I laid out, how will you find your way back?"

Then it was gone. Everything. The silver line, the doorway, everything went black.

I had no idea where I was, or what ethereal state I was in, but it took me a long time to realize I was falling. It wasn't that everything was black, but there was so much space between the few quick flashes of color that I wasn't sure if I was imagining them. I felt like I was gaining velocity as I tumbled over and over myself.

The demon was right. I had no idea where I was or how to get out. I felt like I had fallen for an eternity when in reality it could have only been a few moments—because I was still alive—the truck hadn't hit me yet.

Then everything stopped. I looked around me and discovered seven ancient-looking doors. There were many that were strange, but three that I recognized. I had seen them before, although only in my mind, like I could see them now.

One in particular caught my attention. It was the only one I knew would help me at the moment. Although I knew how this door worked, I had never used it without knowing where I was starting from or how to get to where I wanted to go. I would undoubtedly pass through worlds, levels (whatever they were) that I knew nothing about— but anything was better than death, right?

I remembered what it was like to die—the pain, the fear, the doubt, and the unknown. Somehow I had cheated death once. Now I was about to try again.

I drew in a breath, a real breath, and walked through the door.

The sensation was familiar, like having my whole body sucked through a vacuum tube at the bank, but so much was unknown to me that I almost missed the path back to my body. Thankfully, the glimmering red and blue reflecting off a large silver tank as the tanker buckled my front bumper was enough to catch my attention. I snatched my body away from the destruction and fell headfirst into the unknown.

Teleportation had been something I had tried in the past, but never with my own body. Small objects, like pens, screws, maybe a nickel or two. I had been able to move these objects from one end of the room to another, but I had never been able to track their exact path through the space in between spaces, and sometimes I failed to make them reappear.

I opened my eyes and hoped to be back in California or anywhere far away from demons. I found myself again passing through strange places and universes. I realized I had no idea how to get home. Unexpectedly, I had the strangest desire to go on that date with Quon's cousin.

Something was happening to me. The tips of my fingers were tingling and when I looked at them they appeared to be imploding on themselves. As I tried to stretch them out, my hand stretched into eternity instead. The harder I tried to uncurl them, the longer and longer they appeared.

But what was unnerving was that this sensation seemed to be spreading. It wasn't long until my whole arm appeared two-dimensional and I couldn't feel my fingers at all.

I didn't panic until my chest collapsed and I couldn't breathe. I gasped until I no longer had a throat to do it with. I didn't feel like I was holding my breath—it was more like I had no lungs.

I felt darkness creep over me and reach toward my eyes. I fought as they dimmed slowly, first from the outside, then inward.

As my eyes went dark, everything went cold, a familiar cold. There were no words to describe the sensations that coursed through my body—or what was left of my body. Perhaps the demon had been right. Perhaps I couldn't navigate the worlds he knew so much better than I. He was more powerful, and now he had won.

My consciousness was sufficient to feel a dim glimmer of pain as my molecules lost cohesion. I consigned myself to a second death as I felt my body rip apart.

THIRTEEN

The most amazing thing about feeling myself enter a state of oblivion is that I still *felt*. When I realized that I could still feel, I became almost nauseatingly familiar with my surroundings. I was exceptionally cold and the smell of sweaty socks filled my nostrils, but most obvious was the intense screaming.

"What the... Edmund? Someone hand me that blanket."

The voices were frantic.

"Is that blood?"

I didn't recognize that one. It was too high-pitched.

"Call the campus nurse. Edmund? Can you hear me?"

I could feel hands on me but I couldn't respond.

"He's cold as ice. Quon, stop staring and help me get him under some blankets."

"Is it hypothermia?"

"I don't know. Get under here with me, we need to get him warm."

Moments later it felt like two giant fireballs were lying on either side of me. Their heat was enough to make me recoil.

"He's freezing!" I heard Quon exclaim.

"I don't know the number," the unknown voice returned.

"Just dial zero!"

Ouch… just how close was Nicholas when he yelled that into my ear?

"Hurry up so you can get in here with us."

"Where did he come from?"

"Just dial the damned nurse!"

"Jesus, I think he's bleeding!"

Thick heavy accent: yup, that was Quon. "Jesus" in a Japanese accent sounded funny.

"At least he's thawing. Put a little more pressure on that if it starts to bleed too much."

The fireballs were ebbing down into a comfortable blaze. The voices I heard before I drifted off to sleep were calmer.

"Is the nurse on her way?"

"Yes. She said to give her a few minutes to gather some gear. I didn't exactly know what to tell her was wrong, so she didn't want to leave anything she might need behind."

"What did you tell her?"

"That I guessed hypothermia, and a couple of bad gashes."

"You didn't tell her…"

"What? That he appeared out of thin air. No. I really didn't know how to go about saying that."

"We're going to have to figure out a way to cover for the hypothermia."

"You could always tell her he got caught outside in the rain."

"I guess that's as good of an excuse as any. By the time she gets here at least the ice should be melted."

***

The next time I woke was because someone was calling my name.

"Edmund?" then to someone else, "That is his name, Edmund?"

"Yes. That's his name."

I opened my eyes to see a round, carefully made-up face hovering over me. I stiffened as the light from a nearby window caught her teal colored eyes and made them momentarily flash yellow.

"You're okay. You're in your room, in bed."

I peered into her eyes, searching for any sort of demon presence but there wasn't one.

"How are you feeling?"

"Fine," I lied, my throat scratchy. I swallowed harshly.

"You have some very dedicated friends. They probably saved your life."

I rolled over to find Nicholas lying next to me in bed.

"Hiya, Edmund," he smirked.

I chortled drowsily. "Where are your clothes?"

"I could ask you the same thing. I took *mine* off at the insistence of this kind nurse. *You* arrived without yours."

"Arrived?" the nurse questioned.

"When I found him," Nicholas covered.

The nurse seemed to accept that answer and instead focused on me. "Edmund, how did you get the cuts on your chest?"

But I wasn't paying attention. I was still caught off guard by the realization that I was naked.

"Huh?" I responded.

"The cuts."

"I... I don't remember." My hand prodded at the bandages strapped tightly to my chest. I was bundled so tightly into the covers that I could hardly move. Nicholas gave me a dirty look when my hand grazed his leg.

"Well, you were lucky. The scratches are bleeding but they aren't too deep. I don't see any reason why you need to go to the hospital if you don't have insurance," the nurse continued. "Just stay in bed for a few hours until your body temperature returns to normal and make sure you change the bandages every day. Drink lots of warm liquids, but not too hot, and you," she pointed to Nicholas, "stay there with him for another hour or two."

I could practically feel his scowl as the nurse grinned, making fun.

"Get plenty of sleep, Edmund, and call me if you need anything. In the future, a better story might help. Getting caught in the rain in southern California? I'd try something a little more creative. Maybe include the cafeteria's freezer."

The nurse smirked, but made her way to the door, closing it softly behind her.

"You… owe… me… big… time," Nicholas enunciated through a clenched jaw.

I couldn't do anything but laugh in response. I was so happy. Teleportation! It had worked. Granted, it was more painful than I would have imagined. I didn't realize my entire molecular structure would have to break down to make it work, and I didn't know much about how I came out looking on the other side, but I had escaped. I was back in California, in my room, hundreds of miles from where I started. And I was alive.

"What's so funny?"

"You don't want to know," I answered.

Nicholas grunted in response. "Your boss says if you ever decide you want to show up for work again, you can do it at minimum wage."

"What? Why? What time is it? What *day* is it?"

"Thursday."

"I was gone for *four* days?"

"Three and a half. You've been laying here like a popsicle for ten hours. You're lucky I got the ice off you before the nurse came in. Xia thought you stood her up and Quon and I were worried sick when you didn't answer your phone."

"Ice? Xia?"

"Where have you been?"

"I don't know. Ice?"

I could see Nicholas get that look on his face, the one where we were breaching a subject he didn't want to discuss.

"I don't want to talk about it," he said.

"You're the one who started asking *me* questions. Ice?"

Nicholas balked, but I knew he was going to answer my question. My eyes were pleading with him.

"Look," he snorted, "we were worried about you. You never showed up after our text conversation, and I tried and tried to get you to pick up your phone, but you never answered. Then a few days ago I get this call from the Nevada department of... of... transportation-something-or-another telling us your truck had been involved in some kind of accident with an oil tanker? But that they weren't even sure if you were *in* the truck. Then this morning you appear out of thin air, blue as death, naked, frozen solid, ice literally covering your body, with five giant bleeding gashes on your chest."

He paused, his eyes now pleading with mine.

"Does this have something to do with..." the words caught in his throat, "... the orphanage."

Bingo. He had finally cracked. I nodded.

"Never mind. I don't want to know."

And just like that, Humpty Dumpty was put back together again.

"Oh, here. You'd better call Quon. He got a little freaked out when the nurse told everyone to take off their clothes and get into bed with you," Nicholas winked, "so he took Xia shopping. He'll want to know you're awake."

"The nurse asked everyone to take off their clothes,

huh?" I laughed, taking my phone from Nicholas's hand. "She probably just wanted to see you naked."

"She did leave her phone number."

I gave Nicholas my rehearsed disappointed-in-him look.

"Don't look at me. She left it for you!" he grinned back.

I couldn't help but chuckle as I pressed the contacts button on my phone and scrolled down to Quon's name. I was about to hit dial when an eerie feeling came over me. "Wait," I said turning the phone over, scrutinizing its very existence. "Where did you get this?" The last time I saw the phone had been in the truck.

"I was wondering when you were going to ask. Some cop came over and said he was driving by after the accident. He stopped to help and found your phone by some miracle. Luckily, he was already on his way to California, so he dropped it off. He made it sound like he was pretty sure you weren't in the truck, so that was somewhat comforting…"

"What did he look like?" I asked, very alarmed.

"Dude, chill. Just a regular cop."

"But what did he look like? What color was his hair, his uniform," I gulped, "his eyes?"

"Why are you freaking out? He came by, dropped off

the phone, and left. It's not like I went out for a night on the town with him. I don't remember."

I kept my eyes on him while I hit the dial button and waited, rather impatiently, for Quon's voice to answer on the other end. "Hi Quon, I'm just fine. Hey, do you think you could come back to the room for a minute. We need to talk."

Nicholas's eyes grew large at the "we need to talk" line, and after I hung up he had little to say except, "No. No, no, *no*, no, no."

He was suddenly out of bed, pulling on his favorite pair of button fly jeans. He looked up at me once more as he pulled a shirt on over his head. "No."

I didn't know what to say in response, but I also jumped out of bed. I didn't realize how cold it was going to be until I was standing outside of the warm blankets. The fact that I was nude surely didn't help. "Look," I reached for a pair of pants myself, "we just need to talk. All of us."

"I don't *want* to know. I don't want to be *dragged* back into this again. One cop was enough! I don't want to have to deal with more investigations or answer any more questions when the people around you get murdered again. And I swear if I have to hear one more shrink tell me I have some warped *aversion* to religion, or some other *aversion* to this, or another *aversion* to that, I'm going to hurt somebody."

"You went through therapy?"

"We *all* did, Edmund. Every last child survivor was required to submit to psychoanalysis. You freaked everyone out. I thought maybe people made up the things they said about you, but this thing, whatever it is, follows you around. Whatever you did in that class that made water come out of solid granite, whatever happened in that room with the nuns during your exorcism, it is still following you."

"It isn't following me, it *is* me. Part of me. I can explain everything, I can even *show* you, but I need you to stay. I need to talk this out with you. You need to know what happened in the orphanage."

"No, I don't. I buried that. It's dead."

"No it isn't. I'm here. I'm your friend. And honestly, I need your help."

"I'm sorry, Edmund. I'll help in any way I can. I'll be your friend. I'll help you in school. I'll help you get laid. I'll hold your head when you are drunk and vomiting. I'll even get naked in bed with you when you show up as an ice ball, but I cannot, will not, help you with *this*."

Nicholas gave me an emotional "good luck" look and started rubbing his hands together nervously. It almost looked like he was going to say something else, but instead he pressed his lips into a hard line and turned toward the door.

"Wait." I almost whispered. "This isn't all about me."

He froze with his back to me. "Then who is it about, Edmund?"

"You."

"And how does *this* have *anything* to do with me?"

"It concerns you, because it's your life that's in danger too."

"What do you mean?"

"Ruth," I paused as his muscles tensed in response. "And some of the other orphans, the orphans that got away…" I couldn't continue.

"What about them?" His teeth were clenched again.

"I think they were killed because of what happened. I think they are being targeted because something is going after everyone who survived."

"Targeted by what?"

"That's what we need to talk about."

Nicholas shut the door, and turned to look at me. "I don't believe in the supernatural," he lied. I found it particularly idiotic in light of the circumstances—ice ball and such.

"You're going to have to," I responded.

He walked to the bed and sat down, his shoulders slumping forward. "I don't want to."

"I know."

Nicholas tensed as my phone buzzed to life.

"Hello?" I answered.

"Hi, Edmund? It's Father Paul. Do you have a second?"

"Not a good time, Father."

I heard Nicholas grunt when he realized I was speaking to a priest. Today was not a good day for him.

"I checked on those names, the survivors…" he trailed off, baiting me.

"And?" I was impatient.

"Well, this is a little strange. Do you remember a nun by the name of Mary Chantale?"

How could I forget. My voice cracked as I responded. "Of course."

"It seems that all the orphans that survived the massacre and died recently had something in common: they were all in the same music class, Sister Chantale's music class. Anyone not attached to her seems to be doing just fine."

"How many are dead?"

"I can't really tell you that."

"How many are still alive?"

227

"Look, Edmund, I'm only telling you this because I want you to do something for me."

"Father?"

"Only three children that had a music class with Sister Chantale are still alive. You, Nicholas, and Simon."

"Well, Nicholas is here with me, but Simon?"

"Well, that is the weird one…"

My heart almost stopped. "Father, I know of only one Simon at the orphanage, and he…" I didn't finish my sentence.

I could feel Nicholas look up at me when I said the name, and could tell he was angry. First, the supernatural, then a Catholic priest, and now the name of our childhood friend who died mysteriously at, as only I knew, the hand of a demon. I was a little shocked he hadn't stormed out of the room yet.

"Well, his last listed address is the same as the ex-Sister Mary Elizabeth."

"Sister Mary Elizabeth? Ex?" I had to swallow hard just to get the name out.

"I'm going to give you the address, Edmund; but I'm also going to call ahead and let her know you are coming," Father Paul added quickly. "Do you have a pen?"

I grabbed one off my desk, and then nodded even though Father Paul couldn't see me.

"She lives in Los Angeles still, so it shouldn't be too far a drive."

I jotted down the address on the cover of my American history book. Father Paul said a quick goodbye, but then followed it with a low mutter about how I should ensure I treated Mary Elizabeth with some dignity. I assured him I would, and hung up the phone just as Quon walked through the front door with Xia in tow.

Quon's dark eyes were filled with concern, but they softened when they saw I was out of bed.

"The color came back," he said in his Japanese accent. "I'm glad you're okay."

I had never actually seen Xia before, but I recognized her voice as the high-pitched voice I had heard when I first arrived in the room half-conscious and almost frozen. "I'm glad to see you're... clothed," she said.

As angry as he was, Nicholas couldn't help but snicker.

"She's just angry because you missed your date," Quon winked at me. "She was very much looking forward to going out with you."

"Well, we skipped the date, but you did get to see me naked," I jested.

"That's the perfect date in my mind," Nicholas guffawed.

Xia didn't seem fazed at all by our exchange. She just glared at me from behind two beautiful, chocolate-brown eyes. I could go on and on about her amazingly shiny black hair that fell in carefully constructed ringlets around her soft skin, or how her long legs and netted stockings made her look almost as tall as her cousin Quon, or how she dressed just provocatively enough in a short skirt and baby doll tee to pique a man's imagination without giving too much away, but it was her aura that really screamed beauty. She was literally on fire with radiant orange colors radiating from her. It was a wonder that no one else in the room could see it.

An aura like that meant that she was aware of it and worked on it, like a body builder works on his muscles. I had no doubt that Xia had her own sort of connection to the supernatural. Though not quite flawless, her aura undoubtedly spoke of hours of concentration and communion with doorways she probably didn't even know existed. Nicholas was right when he said I would be interested. What did he call her? Earthy? But it was much more than that.

I'm sure she noticed the way I was staring at her, but her reaction was more reserved that it would have been had she caught someone staring at her body.

"Blue," she finally said.

"Huh?"

"You are blue; electric almost; very bright. When I first saw you, I thought it was because of the ice. I was wrong. The blue, as strong as your aura was then, is even bluer now." Xia shivered, the hair on her arm standing on end. "Glacial," she whispered.

"Orange," I said, "Like a sunset; almost flawless."

"Almost?" she mused.

Out of the corner of my eye I saw Quon and Nicholas exchange a confused look. "What'd I tell you?" Quon laughed.

"Oh brother. What have you done?" Nicholas chided in both exasperation and playfulness.

"I'm Edmund," I said.

"Nice to meet you... finally." She stepped around Quon and extended her hand. I must have felt like ice to her incredibly warm skin. I realized I still didn't have my body temperature back up to normal.

"Well, Quon, Xia, please sit down. I'm afraid I have some things to tell you, and whether you like it or not, you are a part of it."

Xia's face almost exploded in delight. "See, I told you!" she jabbered at Quon. "This has something to do with that man that showed up with your phone doesn't it, and the fact that you appeared out of thin air. Quon told me you were into some sort of witchcraft or something. Are you Wiccan? How long have you been practicing? You must be really strong to…"

"Uh, no. Nothing like that. Not exactly," I interrupted before she could get carried away. "I don't really practice any belief system. They're all standard sets of rules that have access to some truth while attempting to explain a bigger picture no one understands. To me, Wicca is just another religion."

Xia looked offended, but stopped talking.

"But yes," I continued. "This does have to do with all of that. There are beings that some could consider demons, and I'd assume, angels, but not in the way any religion prescribes. The definitions aren't that easy."

"So all religions are wrong," Nicholas stated, beaming. He jumped to a simple conclusion that fit him.

"No, Nicholas. It's more like... well..." I was having a hard time phrasing what I wanted to say. "What if all religions were stories, and all stories were true?"

I watched as three expressions tried to grasp what I was saying. All I got was confusion.

"Let me give you an example," I said. "In Mormon theology, there are seven degrees of existence. They believe we existed before we came here, that's one, and then we are here now, that's two. After we die we go to something they call the spirit world that is divided into two sections, paradise and prison, that is three and four. Then, after the judgment and resurrection, we go to one of the three heavens Paul talked about. Remember that scripture we discussed in Sister Mary Elizabeth's class, Nicholas? Three heavens. That makes five, six, and seven. Seven levels.

"It is the same with the Catholics, at least before the Council of Trent. Four levels of hell, three levels of heaven. Seven."

"Christians believe only in three," Nicholas stated matter-of-factly. "This existence, then heaven and hell."

"An oversimplification," I stated. "The Christian bible says *three* heavens, just like any other."

"Buddhists believe in ten planes of existence," Quon added.

"Perhaps a complication of the truth. But even in those religions we see a seed of consistency. Reincarnation, for example. Every major religion believes in an eternal soul that will come back somehow. Sometimes on another level of existence; sometimes on the same one. Whether we come back as a spirit, as a resurrected or perfected being, or a cow, or a blade of grass, or as nothing more than intelligence—there is a thread of commonality."

"I think we get that you are saying that in these

commonalities is where we find the real truth, Edmund," Nicholas said, rolling his eyes. "So what?"

"So what if those levels weren't actual worlds, separate and distinct, but instead existed right here, right now, stacked on top of each other, with doorways between the worlds that allowed access to the gifts and abilities of that world. What if that is what ghosts are? Echoes from the other worlds. What if that is what magic is? A simple opening of the door to allow the abilities of another world into our own, maybe like a place where the laws of physics can be different."

"Sounds complicated," Quon said.

"Simpler than most religions," Xia responded.

"So what?" Nicholas reiterated.

"So, Nicholas. The story I told you about in the orphanage is true."

"You were somehow reincarnated here, with some amazing gift to remember your past life?"

"Not exactly. I'm not sure. Somehow this ring came with me," I said, holding up my hand. "I don't know exactly how the doorways work, or how the levels are interconnected, but what I do know is that demons are spiritual creatures from another level, a bloodthirsty and power-hungry level. I met one on my way home from Arizona. He destroyed my truck, and tried to kill me in the process. He told me that Joshua is trying to find a way into the other levels. I don't know why, but it can't be good."

"Now you've gone over my head," Xia said sharply. "Who are you talking about?"

"That's why I needed you all to come together," I responded. "I need to tell you my story. Hopefully, together, we can figure out what is going on. We need to do this. If we don't, we won't be able to save Nicholas's life."

FOURTEEN

Although he looked uncomfortable, Nicholas sat quietly with a dazed look on his face while I recounted my story. I started at the beginning, discussing briefly what I remembered about growing up in Orenda, which, sadly, wasn't much anymore. I supposed I could blame that on the years I had lived since, and the fact that my existence there, I believed, wasn't even an existence on this level. My memories as a child had grown fractured and dreamlike, but I was able to tell Quon, Xia, and Nicholas about my father, mother, Ralph, and Hailey.

The exception was the two days before my death. Those memories were still just as vivid as they were on the first day I woke up in the orphanage. I recounted the details quickly but effectively, including the grass-growing test on the hillside right after Max's encounter with the demon snake, the strange events surrounding my father's death, and the book that Joshua stole from me.

Xia interrupted there. "Wait. You actually died?"

"I think so."

Her puzzled eyes were filled with excitement. "Then how did you end up here?"

Nicholas scoffed. "You're really buying into all of this, aren't you?"

"I don't know exactly what to think, but I do know what I saw, Nicholas," Xia chided. "Do I need to remind you that he dropped out of thin air?"

Her retort caught Nicholas a bit off guard and I saw a moment of anger flash across his face. He wasn't used to being challenged.

I started talking before either of them could say anything else. "I don't know how I got here," I stated bluntly.

As soon as I started talking again, Xia returned to hanging on every word and Nicholas went back to staring out the window. I slowed my story down as I talked about my few days at the orphanage. Nicholas didn't have to feign interest as soon as I started talking about Sister Chantale and her son Simon. As soon as I said the names, his ears pricked up and he was sitting taller.

I told them about how Sister Chantale was actually Simon's mother. This was part of the story Nicholas had not previously heard. I told them about our conversation by the river and how the trees had shown me the story of Sister Chantale before she came to serve at the orphanage. When I recounted the events of Simon's death, Nicholas turned green and finally looked at me. I paused when he looked like he was about to vomit.

"Are you okay?" I asked sincerely.

I could tell by his face that he was struggling with whether or not he wanted to answer my question. I had never seen him look so strained.

"I saw that," he finally blurted out.

My mind whirled to the subject of Simon's death as I tried to comprehend what he obviously thought was a great revelation.

"I know you saw it," I said, "I know you were there when Simon died. It must have been a horrific experience for you."

"No," Nicholas said, "I saw the shadow people."

"Shadow people?"

And in that moment I understood: Nicholas had seen the disembodied energumen who had killed Simon.

"You could see them?"

Nicholas just nodded.

"How long has it been since you've seen one of them?"

Nicholas swallowed hard. "It *had* been a while, a year or two, until…"

"Until what?"

"Until you disappeared."

"So you've seen them recently?"

"Every day this week, at least one."

"Where?"

"On campus, in the dorms, at the mall…"

"In this room?"

Nicholas shook his head.

"Then they are close. Do you know if they know you can see them?"

"Come on, Edmund," Nicholas's demeanor changed and he was suddenly back to his old sarcastic self, "it's just my eyes catching a moving shadow or something. Don't make it a big deal."

I glanced at Xia, who was positively glowing with anticipation. Quon just yawned. "What's the big deal about shadows anyway?" he asked wryly. "Everyone's got one."

I ignored Quon completely. "Nicholas, I need you to stay with me here. Please stay with me. Do they know who you are?"

I could see the wheels spinning in his head again as he shifted uncomfortably. He was debating about whether to tell me the truth or not.

"The truth," I demanded.

"I only thought so once. They've always ignored me, always just been shadows."

"Except once," I repeated.

"Not recently. When I was little... it freaked me out."

"When?"

"Right after I got adopted."

"Tell me about it."

"Come on, Edmund! What does it matter? I was a kid. I probably imagined the whole thing. We all know everything you are saying isn't possible anyway. There is no such thing as magic *or* the supernatural *or* levels *or* demons *or* heaven *or* hell. It's *all* make-believe. Intelligent people don't need it."

"Did you miss the mysterious appearing ice-ball boy?" Xia asked sharply. "You were *here* for that."

I saw ire flash in Nicholas's eyes as he answered. "Who says there isn't a *scientific* explanation for what we experienced? You are just so willing to accept whatever he tells you."

"And you aren't? He's your friend, isn't he?"

"My best friend, but that doesn't exclude him from fault."

Xia harrumphed and her voice went up in pitch, "So you think he is lying or making up his story? What about his experiences in Orenda?"

"Guys," Quon weighed in, but his lack of mastery of the English language didn't allow him to express himself fully. He muttered something in Japanese and Xia's eyes flashed at him briefly before they calmed a bit. This was the first time I realized that Xia spoke better English than Quon.

Whatever Quon said to her must have worked because her voice was a bit calmer when she continued.

"I'm just saying we shouldn't dismiss something simply because science can't prove it. Just look at the bumblebee. Until September of 2000, no one could prove that the two dimensional hovering motion of the bumblebee's wings could generate enough lift to carry the bee, but the bee flew anyway. Science is always evolving."

"Fine." Nicholas said through clenched teeth before turning to me. "Go ahead then, Edmund. Prove it."

"Prove what?"

"Anything. Prove that what you say is true."

I wasn't sure if he was being serious or facetious. "How?"

Nicholas just shrugged his shoulders. "Defy the laws of physics."

That one would be easy, but at his request my mind immediately returned to that day in the orphanage when

Sister Mary Elizabeth slapped me, and in retaliation I made water spring out of the stone topped desk in a recreation of what I had remembered reading in the Bible when Moses smote the rock. For some reason, the feeling in the air was similar now. The last thing I wanted was to cause hysteria. Maybe I shouldn't have trusted Xia or Quon with my secrets, maybe I should have just dismissed my mysterious appearance (even if I wasn't sure how), but my biggest fear was that by simply knowing me they were in danger. If the demons were actually after the survivors from the orphanage, then my friends, undoubtedly, *were* in danger.

But this was not what I expected. Perhaps they would have been better off not knowing. Too late now.

Nicholas grew smug when I didn't act. No doubt he translated the worried look on my face as my inability to fulfill his request, but my true nervousness was not lost on Xia.

"It's okay, Edmund. Go ahead. Show us something."

Her interest was genuine but, I felt, sadly misplaced. She wasn't excited for truth. She was excited to see someone more advanced than she was show her a magic trick.

Still, I could see no other alternative.

"If I do this," I finally spoke, staring intently at

Nicholas, "will you tell me about your encounter with the shadow people, leaving out no details?"

The smug smile faded as he nodded.

It wasn't until this break in the conversation that I realized how we had ended up situated. The three of them—Nicholas, Xia, and Quon—sat on the edge of my twin bed while I stood over them, dominating. As I peered down at Nicholas's upturned eyes, I couldn't help but see a flash of uncertainty.

I had to stop and think for a few moments to come up with a plan that would have sufficient shock effect without driving the three of them out of the room in terror. I didn't think I had enough grasp of the teleportation power to repeat the recent events, nor was I looking forward to feeling that cold again. No, I wouldn't do that to myself. I still wasn't sure exactly how I came back together after the mind splitting experience.

But it wouldn't be too frightening if I were to try with an object. After all, the worst that could happen would be my inability to rematerialize it.

Then I got an idea that would be sure to impress. It would require strength on my part, as well as kindness in my pleading with all of the earth's elements in regard to the laws I would have to bend, but I knew it could be done—I would take inspiration from my father.

I went to my closet and threw a pile of clothes that I didn't remember putting on the shelf—all of which were probably dirty—in order to get to my small, metal toolbox.

I pulled out the hammer and held it lightly in my hands. The head was made of dark, heavy steel, and the handle of a light wood. I had only used it occasionally, once to put a bookcase together when I first arrived, and another few times when a friend needed to borrow it for a project. I focused on its shape, on the weight, on the coolness of the metal and the smoothness of the wood. I needed to know these things. I needed to have a connection to this object that belonged to me, a connection I didn't have because I hadn't used it enough. I needed to feel the elements of this hammer and how they affected the world.

The existence of this hammer had a ripple effect that extended beyond the tree that was cut down to fashion the handle, or the steel that was heated and shaped to make the head. It put together my bookcase, which was now weighted with books. That weight had to be supported by the planet as well. All of this was tied together.

I handed the hammer to Nicholas.

"This is a moment of trust, my friend. I will require the strength of your trust to make this work. You must trust me to do what I am going to ask you to do. I must trust you as well. If I don't, then the circle of that trust will be broken and the power will fail. I want us to have this trust in each other so that you can tell me your story without fear."

I took a few steps back and glanced over my right shoulder to ensure my alignment was correct.

"And what am I supposed to do with the hammer?" Nicholas asked.

I half grinned. "Throw it at me."

His face contorted into an expression that said he hoped he misunderstood what I asked.

"As hard as you can," I continued. "Trust."

I saw the switch flip in his understanding. It told him that in order to trust me, he had to throw the hammer and trust that I wouldn't get hurt. I had to trust him, and trust that he trusted me enough to actually throw the hammer. Still, I could see his hesitation.

Xia and Quon looked at him with stern expectation and disbelief. I almost expected Quon to wrestle the hammer away from Nicholas, his face was so shocked when Nicholas's finally showed some resolve.

"You'd better get ready to call the nurse again, I think," Quon whispered to Xia.

"As hard as you can," I said in a voice that was barely audible.

Things moved in slow motion as soon as Nicholas wound up for the throw. I heard Xia gasp at one point but the hammer had already left Nicholas's hand. I watched it turn over and over as it approached.

I had already opened the door in my mind and now just had to physically extend it around the hammer. I pushed my thoughts outward, a sensation that felt like stretching a large piece of plastic wrap. I could feel a space between levels just at the threshold of the door. My mind pushed the hammer into this space, and then the hammer, which was catapulting toward me, disappeared.

I didn't want it to go too far. If I pushed it completely out of our world and into another, I would probably have no way of finding it without going in after it myself. I found it invigorating, knowing that I had experienced this sensation myself. It was much easier to monitor the hammer in the space between spaces having experienced these limits and boundaries myself.

My mind accompanied the hammer into the space between levels. Once there, I was able to change the direction of the hammer. This was not done by moving the hammer itself, but by changing the angle by which it reentered the door in my mind.

The hammer reappeared just two inches away from my nose. It was so close that all I could see was a dizzying blur. I felt the air on my face that the steel head displaced.

Now came the hard part. The hammer had changed directions almost a perfect ninety degrees. My alignment had been off just a degree or two, but would still suffice.

Nicholas made a noise that resembled a groan as he realized the hammer was now headed straight for the glass window. I heard everyone draw in a nervous breath as the hammer shattered the glass so effortlessly that it barely slowed in momentum.

I stretched my arms and hands out toward the window. The sound of the breaking glass was distinct and violent, but what no one else knew or understood was that I had learned the secret that had plagued me since childhood—how my father could break the glass into his secret chamber in the parliament building of Orenda.

Xia let her voice squeak slightly when she realized the shattered particles of glass were not responding to the law of gravity. Instead, they were suspended in the air, spinning on multiple invisible axes, reflecting light like a disco ball. It wasn't exactly that the pieces of glass were defying the laws of gravity, just that they currently existed in a pocket between our world and one where the law of gravity didn't exist.

The secret to my father's glass doorway wasn't that the glass was reconstructed by some unknown magic that repaired broken molecules, as I had originally thought. Instead, the actual magic was done before the glass was broken. My father simply asked the molecules to align themselves in such a way that the breaks would occur between them—the space within the elements was not what was broken, just the bindings between the elements themselves.

And since glass is technically a liquid, not a solid, the molecules themselves could eventually piece themselves back together anyway, just like broken water doesn't stay broken once it is poured into a shape. Glass has the same properties. I just had to speed up the process.

I waited until the spinning splinters of glass had stopped, then asked them to realign themselves the same way they had been before they were broken. None of the pieces had any reason to ignore the request, and it wasn't more than a few seconds before I was ready to pull them all back.

Molecules all want something. They want each other. I assume they are much like humans in that regard. They exist to create something, to fulfill a higher purpose beyond their own capability. When asked to reform this plate of glass, some became so excited that their atoms began moving faster and faster. Once hot, they pair up with the molecule next to them. Understanding the science is what allowed the magic.

I pulled the millions of tiny pieces back together. It was difficult to keep track of them all, but their excitement to come back together, with not a single one actually damaged, helped the process. The cracks sealed themselves as the smaller components rebounded on a level almost incomprehensible to the human mind.

My head was now swimming and every muscle in my body felt at the brink of breakdown. I could feel cold sweat beading on my forehead as my breathing grew labored. I forced myself to complete the glass pane just as a trickle of blood began to flow from my nose.

My knees buckled and I collapsed. It felt good to let the floor support me as I fell into a heap.

I heard everyone call my name in worry and I instantly had three pairs of hands shaking me.

"I'm fine," I responded unwillingly. Just talking seemed like it took too much effort. "Trust, remember?"

The shaking stopped, but they all stayed kneeling over me, their wide eyes filled with shock and concern.

"Just let me rest for a minute," I continued. "Nicholas, you can start your story."

It was a long time before Nicholas's smooth voice filled the room with something other than the sounds of breathing. The sun had just finished staining the sky a ferocious red, and the first stars were beginning to appear. I pulled a blanket down from the bed, and curled up inside it, cursing myself for using my abilities so soon after being so cold. I could feel the coldness seeping in again.

"Well…" Nicholas started, much more calmly than I had expected, "I know you and I haven't really discussed our adopted parents, Edmund. Mostly, we've avoided talking about our childhoods all together."

I grunted in agreement.

"My parents joined the Catholic church with the specific expectation of adopting someone from Saint Vincent's. After years of trying to get through the catechism classes, they almost gave up. Then, when…"

"…*it* happened…" I continued for him.

"Yeah. When it happened, the orphanage had to either adopt us out or ship us off to another orphanage. They relaxed their restrictions a bit. My parents were not Catholic at the time of the adoption. They were allowed to adopt me under the assumption that they had a legitimate interest in the church, which wasn't true. In fact, they practiced a pretty scary form of witchcraft."

"Did they just want you for a sacrifice or something?" Quon jested.

Xia backhanded him. "Shut up."

But Nicholas didn't seem to be affected by the

comment. In fact, he continued as if nothing were said. "Things often got a little scary for a kid but I wasn't involved in most of the heavy stuff. My new parents cared about me a great deal. They took good care of me and gave me everything I wanted. They really did just want a child. Every time they got pregnant they would hold a ceremony in celebration and thank the gods and goddesses for blessing their union. Then my mom would miscarry.

"When I was fourteen, my parents were again expecting. My mom didn't want to have another ceremony, because she had started to believe they were causing the miscarriages. My father insisted.

"I snuck down into the basement during the ritual. I had never been allowed to watch this particular ceremony, even though I had been involved in prayer circles, séances, and other rituals. I don't remember much, but I do remember seeing my mother, naked, in the center of a large pentagram painted onto the cement floor. She was surrounded by the coven that had become my second family. The coven was a mixture of men and women, and as the ritual began they disrobed. Though I didn't understand the sexual component of the ritual, as a young boy just starting to experience sexuality on my own, I did understand sex and realized the reasoning behind my father's insistence on my mother complying with this bizarre séance. He wanted the sex, and he wanted it with the other members of the coven.

"I watched my mother cry, lying alone in the circle while the coven did what they did around her. At one time, she looked up and saw me sitting on the stairs. Her eyes didn't beg me to help her, but for the understanding of why she didn't want to be there. I could tell she wished I were older. She wanted me to be a man strong enough to rescue her from my father. She wanted me to run away, to not watch, but at the same time couldn't ask me to leave. She wanted me to stay and give her strength. Her eyes told me so much—like we were having a conversation.

"When she miscarried again, my father left. My mother, although very earthy and drawn to Wiccan beliefs—"

"Whoa!" Xia interrupted. "That ritual definitely wasn't Wiccan. Don't get me wrong, it sounds sort of like the Great Rite, but that's a very specific ceremony held during Beltane. What you're describing wasn't right."

"I know," Nicholas responded. "It was my father's bastardization of the rituals. He convinced my mother, the whole coven, that his ways were more powerful, better than the traditional rites. When my mother learned the truth she turned her back on them because of what my father had put her though. She sought for answers as to why she couldn't have children in medicine, in Christianity, in Islam, and in Scientology. The drastic religious changes I experienced in my life were so jarring and instant, that I began to believe in none of them."

"Well that explains why you are such a horn-dog. Like father like son, right?" Quon chided.

I felt an instant rush of panic, and rightfully so. As I bolted into an upright position I saw Nicholas's eyes ignite in fury. His hands balled into fists.

"Quon! You insensitive idiot!" I bellowed. *Oh, please let my reprimand settle Nicholas down*, I thought to myself.

It did, but only slightly. "Sex for the fun of sex is one thing," Nicholas contended through a clenched jaw. "I think we all know about *that*! My father was a bastard who used it to control and demean. I wouldn't have cared if my father had been a swinger. I could even understand him having an affair or a whore on the side, but he humiliated my mother in front of his coven *on purpose*. He got off on the fact that she cried while he went to town on another woman in front of her. The whole situation was just... depraved. Not to mention that as it turned out, my father was giving the spirits of my mother's unborn children to a demon. That is why she always miscarried."

Nicholas's face was red and hard, daring Quon to say another word. He didn't.

"Okay, okay," I said, positioning myself on the bed between them. "Tell us what happened with the demon. What does this all have to do with your experience?"

"I was getting to that part," Nicholas said shortly, glaring right past me. Then he huffed. "One Sunday my mom and I pulled off the side of the road into the parking lot of a church we had never seen before. It was one of those holy-roller churches, ya know? The sermon was on demons—the servants of Satan. The preacher talked about possession and stuff, and about how there are certain *worldly* religions that used the powers of the devil and of these demons. The preacher said that these demons could be powerful if we gave them control over us, powerful enough to hurt us. It hit a little close to home, I think.

"When my mom and I left, and she was so so quiet, I assumed it was because she had realized what she and my father had been doing was considered a sin to the majority of the world. By now I had given up on the doctrine of Catholicism, but I still remembered being taught in Catholic school that all types of occult spiritualism were wrong. I figured my mom and I were just going to return to Catholicism.

"But I was wrong. Something that the preacher said had given my mom the idea that if she could find the demon that was causing her miscarriages, if she had somehow been possessed by it, then all she would have had to do was somehow get rid of it."

I could now see where this was going.

"When we got home my mom took me down to the basement and uncovered the pentagram. 'A coven requires thirteen, but today two will have to do,' she said, handing me an old robe. 'I need your help now.'

"I don't really remember what happened next," Nicholas said, his voice almost a whimper.

I had never heard him this weak before.

"I remember it getting really dark and smelling like rotten eggs. Then, inside of the pentagram, a figure appeared. I could hear my mom screaming at it, asking it questions, but every time it spoke back all I could hear was the sound of wind, like I was standing in the middle of a tornado.

"Strangely, I wasn't scared through any of this. Not until I heard my mom say 'Yes, I do have a child, but I will not trade his soul for another.' She looked at me briefly. I could tell from the tone of her voice and the look in her eye that she had considered trading me to this thing for a biological child of her own. I think that is what made me the most afraid—that I wasn't loved like I thought I was— that perhaps my mother wanted something more than I could give her. She then went on, telling the shadow that if it was claiming the souls of her unborn children, and if that was why she constantly miscarried, then she would simply stop trying to have children.

"That made the demon angry. Mom kept screaming at it to tell her how it was summoned, or who summoned it, or whether my father had anything to do with his ability to steal the souls of their unborn children, but by this time it was just screaming.

"When it got angry, it came after me. As it turned to look at me the strangest thing happened—I could understand him. He didn't speak in words vocally—he could only wail like the wind—but as he looked into my eyes I could hear his thoughts. If she would deny him more souls, he would deny her mine.

"Then, the only thing I thought about, besides my fear, was you, Edmund. I don't know why, but I found myself wishing you had been there in that room with me. The thought of you in that room gave me comfort. Even though I've always been curious as to why I thought of you in this moment, I never really wanted to know. I had a feeling the answer to that question would have been scarier than even the shadow creature in front of me."

I opened my mouth to answer his question, but he quickly echoed, "I don't want to know."

Nicholas continued, "I guess the demon could read

my thoughts just like I could his because as soon as I thought your name, a certain level of curiosity was piqued. I heard him take note of my name and my family and then he seemed to pull information from my memory. Strange, I know, and I'm not sure how to explain it, but I found myself experiencing memories of the people I knew in the orphanage. Even people I had forgotten about appeared in flashes of remembrance. Because of this, I became extremely important to the demon. He thought of somebody... somebody who he had to take these memories to... somebody more powerful than he was... somebody he was afraid of."

"Who?" I asked, but I already knew the answer.

"Joshua," Nicholas said, meeting my eyes. "The name was said so hurriedly, like the demon didn't want me to hear it. Then, he reached out and touched me briefly before vanishing."

"He touched you?" I asked.

"Actually, I think he attacked me."

"What makes you say that?"

"He left marks."

"Marks?"

Nicholas's eyes fell to my chest.

I reached up and touched my shirt, where blood had started to stain. I had almost forgotten all about the cuts

257

and bandages; I hadn't even looked at them after the nurse had left. They must have still been bleeding, because the bandages were soaked through.

"Where," I asked almost incoherently, but Nicholas understood. He reached up and touched his right cheek.

"He cut all the way through. It took seven surgeries to fix it. Luckily I was still young enough that the scar stretched and faded as I grew."

"You said that you have recently seen one of these figures again?"

"The other morning when I went to the gym," he nodded. "I was in the steam room after my workout. I thought someone else had come into the room, because it got cold, like someone had left the door open. I could see a figure through the steam, but couldn't make it out. It just stood there staring at me. I made some comment like, 'Hey buddy, stop staring at me.' The response was familiar, recognizable."

"How so?"

"It sounded like wind."

FIFTEEN

Two days later was Monday, which meant I had to go to classes I neither cared about nor could focus on. For so many years I had been at a dead end when it came to my past: Orenda, the orphanage, and most importantly, demons. I now had two leads—Sister Mary Elizabeth and Nicholas's mother.

Xia followed me to my classes, insisting that she had nothing better to do since Quon was too wrapped up in a project he was working on in computer architecture to be much of a conversationalist, but now, as she sat next to me in American history, I couldn't help but notice that the longer the professor droned on the more her head bobbed. It was kind of adorable, watching her teeter on the edge of sleep.

Although I was excited at the prospect of no longer being at a dead end in my search for the truth of where I came from, I was worried as well. If I was no longer at a dead end, thanks to a demon that set off a series of events that led me to people who might have some answers, that meant the demons were no longer at a dead end either. I wondered if the murders of the orphaned children had helped them arrive at the same two people I was now going to visit. I sincerely hoped not.

"Edmund?"

Great. The professor had caught me not paying attention… again.

"Yes, sir?"

"Did you hear the question?"

"We were talking about national policy in the 1920's." At least, I hoped we were still on that subject.

"Specifically we were talking about the Kellog-Briand Pact of 1928."

"The one that the United States co-authored that outlawed war as an instrument of national policy?"

The professor looked a bit taken aback by my statement. "Sufficient recovery, Mr. Gavel."

I supposed that I had somehow answered his question, although I was still unaware what that question was.

I turned to Xia and caught her smiling at me as the professor assigned the next chunk of reading that would be covered in the following class period. Commotion ensued as my fellow classmates and I put away books and notepaper and started filing out the door.

Xia spoke before I got out of the classroom, "Difficult time concentrating," she said, her inflection halfway between a statement and a question.

I pulled my bag over my shoulder. "You looked pretty bored yourself."

"I enjoy history," she stated matter-of-factly. "Just not American history."

I grinned, not quite certain myself whether I was trying to imply my agreement, sympathy, or understanding. I was distracted. She was so intoxicating in that skirt. My eyes couldn't get enough of her.

"So what's the plan?"

When I looked back into her eyes, they darted in an I-noticed-you-noticing-me way. I felt color rush to my cheeks when I realized her question wasn't just for conversational purposes, but to pull me out of my momentary trip into manhood.

Recovery from manhood idiotic question number one: "Well, are you going to keep following me around all day?"

She eyed me quizzically, inviting me to try again. It was awfully kind of her to forgive the lack of blood flow to my brain, but that embarrassed me even further.

"What I mean is, I'm not sure I'm going to the rest of my classes today. I'm having a bit of trouble concentrating."

This time she flushed. "Would it be better if I didn't accompany you?"

Great. Now she was bringing up the fact that she noticed me noticing her. Her question implied that the reason I was having trouble concentrating was because of her.

"No no," I answered quickly. "It isn't you. All this life stuff… you know…"

She looked hurt. Idiotic moment number two.

I sighed as I pushed open the glass door to the history building and stepped outside into the cool air. I stopped and faced Xia after holding the door open for her. "Let me try again. I have a lot on my mind, and am finding myself distracted rather easily."

A tiny bit of excitement welled up in my stomach when the look in her eye told me she was expecting my eyes to drift away from hers when I said the word "distracted." The truth was that she *was* one of those distractions, and I would have wanted nothing more than to look over her body when I said that, but I controlled the impulse and held her gaze. I didn't want to make myself look any more stupid.

"But," I continued, "I would love someone to talk it over with. Care to join me for lunch?"

Bingo. Her resulting smile was radiant. Stupidity absolved. Normalcy restored.

"So what will we be having?"

We started walking again and I answered, "I make a killer grilled cheese."

The walk to the north campus housing wasn't far, and Xia and I contented ourselves with our own thoughts in silence while we walked. I knew it was probably strange of me not to think about the circumstances surrounding my life in those minutes, but it was a welcome break to forget about demons and magic for a while. I found myself thinking about what I imagined Xia thinking about.

We walked close to each other, which made me happy. Either she had forgiven me for my earlier indiscretions, or (the possibility I found much more likely) she was purposefully trying to understand how I felt about her. That, I deduced, would mean that she felt something for me.

But then I started to feel a little arrogant, imagining that I knew her thoughts and motivations. We had only known each other for a few days and it was very improbable that I knew her well enough to know anything about what she was thinking. Even still, the thought that she might be thinking about me as we walked together, bumping hands occasionally, perhaps purposefully, caused me to feel warmth and happiness that I had never experienced before. I was such a dork.

I found myself noticing all the other men on campus, noticing their eyes trail up and down her body as we walked, sizing *me* up afterwards. The warmth and the happiness mixed with the icy sting of overprotective jealousy. The odd emotional combination sat strangely comfortable with me.

When we got to the dorm building we opted to take the elevator to the third floor, where Nicholas, Quon, and I shared a room. Xia watched the numbers in the elevator climb with a seductive smirk on her face. I watched her.

Xia finally spoke as the elevator doors swung open, "You'd better watch the creepy stalker stare," she jested. "It scares some girls."

"Sorry," I said, done denying the fact that I was admiring her. "I didn't mean to creep you out."

Now Xia laughed, which wasn't exactly the reaction I had thought I would receive. "You had us throw a hammer at your head, but instead made it change directions mid-air, shatter a window, which you then put back together, and you think I'm creeped out that you find me attractive?"

Now I was laughing too. "I guess you have a point. I just didn't want you to think I'm the kind of guy that…"

"Stop," she cut me off. "All guys are 'that kind of guy' sometimes, and I'll let you in on a little bit of a secret: woman actually don't always mind… "

"…I know… sorry," I cut *her* off this time. I really didn't need a lecture into the psychology of how women view men. "And just for the record, you are very beautiful."

She took the compliment well, simply responding, "Thank you, I know. I dress this way for a reason… men are fun to tease."

She bit her lip playfully, more teasing, and went to open the door to my room, when I grabbed her hand. "Wait," I said, taking her hand gently off the knob.

I pointed to the red tack that had been pushed into the soft wood of the doorframe.

"College boy sign?" Xia chuckled. "I thought it was a sock on the doorknob."

"Socks are too obvious. Nicholas prefers a tack," was all I responded, because as if on cue, we heard a strong masculine grunt from beyond the door. "How about we hit up the cafeteria?"

When we got there, Xia ordered a vegetarian spinach

salad—light on the vinaigrette dressing. I couldn't help but notice how much attention she got from the guy behind the counter. He even had to remake her salad because, while being distracted by her cleavage, he accidentally used the real bacon bits instead of the imitation ones. My tuna sandwich was thrown together miserably… In fact, I was pretty sure I had ordered turkey.

"You know," Xia said after we had paid and filled our drink cups with the college's most recent concoction they had the nerve to call iced tea, "lunch in a college cafeteria is an experience not to be missed."

"Why's that?"

"It's like watching ravenous wolves," she chided.

"Is this some sort of commentary on people who eat meat?" I chuckled as we sat down.

Xia peeked at my tuna sandwich. "Not at all, actually. In fact, I wasn't even talking about the way people eat." She glanced back toward the counter, at the guy who was still staring at her. "So this nun…"

The change of subject was abrupt enough to catch me off guard. I flinched a little at being pulled back into the world of reality. Reality. Demons, death, and magic were reality. I didn't want to go back to that subject. I wanted to be a normal college guy having lunch with an abnormally beautiful college girl.

"How do they make imitation bacon bits anyway?" I asked, poking at one in her bowl. "I mean, they would have to use pig flavoring or something, right? Wouldn't that be even worse than the real thing? Killing a pig to make pig flavoring?"

She slapped my hand, knowing I was being playfully irreverent. "It's imitation smoke flavoring on crispy crumbs of red-dyed bread. When are you going to go see her?"

Ok. I would allow myself this conversation with her, not because I wanted to, but because talking about it seemed to excite her.

"This weekend, I think," I answered between bites of sandwich. "I really thought about doing it sooner, but I haven't been to work in long enough that my boss told me if I ever come back I'll have to work for minimum wage... so I think I'd better go back and try to smooth things over with him."

"Well you should show him the cuts on your chest and tell him you've been sick," Xia sympathized.

I laughed. "He's a pretty decent guy. I really don't think he'll give me much trouble. He didn't fire me now, did he?"

"What is it you do, exactly?"

I thought for a few seconds while trying to decide

267

how I could answer this and not sound like a total nerd, and without offending her. After swallowing the bite of sandwich I purposely took to buy me some time, I still had nothing. "I stock a local supermarket. And work with meat sometimes." Big whoop.

Xia didn't seem too disappointed. She was smart enough to understand that this was just a job to get me through college.

"And your boss owns the place?" she asked.

"Yeah. Owner and manager—and butcher," I grinned.

Xia's face twisted into an ill look. "If you EVER come home smelling like meat…" but she didn't finish her sentence.

She didn't need to. I smiled at the idea that she was thinking about being wherever I was when I came home. I got the feeling that it was now her turn to hastily stuff something into her mouth in order to keep quiet.

"I want to go with you," she blurted out awkwardly after clearing her throat with a gulp of iced tea. "To see the nun, I mean."

"Sister Mary Elizabeth," I corrected. "You probably wouldn't want to call her 'the nun' to her face. Really. She's a bit… opinionated. I don't even know that she'll be willing to talk to me."

"Well, Nicholas and I talked about it, and I think we both want to go. Strength in numbers, right? Not to mention the fact that you really can't just leave us at home wondering what is going on. You've involved us all now."

"What about Quon? And your schooling? How long are you in town anyway?"

Xia waved dismissively and her throat made a noise that matched her apathy. "Quon doesn't really seem to have an opinion about all this, but he's always been the least spiritual person in our family. Buddha himself could appear and he'd go take a nap. As for school? I took this semester off, and we have two months before the next one starts. I was thinking of maybe transferring—"

"Nicholas wanted to come?" I interrupted.

Before Xia had the chance to answer, an extremely bubbly blond dressed in a Santa hat knocked loudly on our table. I found the gesture not only odd, but unbelievably annoying.

"Hi guys," she started, without any observance for our former conversation. "I'm Brittany and I'm collecting donations for 'Change for Jesus.' Get it?" Her resulting chuckle was so condescending that I had to suppress my desire to punch her.

"Anyway, this year the Christian students have teamed up together to collect money to renovate an old church somewhere in the city. We've collected over three thousand dollars just on campus. Will you donate?"

I smiled. "The money is going to renovate a church? Not feed the hungry or clothe the poor?"

A look of complete seriousness fell over her face, "By helping Christians here you help Christians everywhere."

"We aren't interested," Xia glared sharply.

"But Thanksgiving is just a few days away," Brittany pointed to her Santa hat like she was making some sort of coherent statement, "now is the time for giving."

Her sugary-ness was too sweet to handle.

"We don't believe in Jesus. Xia's Wiccan, and I'm not religious," I said tersely.

Brittany's eyes grew big, but not in shock or surprise... I was pretty sure it was anger.

"But without Jesus you cannot be saved, for no man can enter the kingdom of God but by him. He performed many miracles, healing the sick and turning water into wine—"

"Here," I interrupted, reaching for my cup. "Will tea do?" I shook the cup three times, and peeled back the lid. Alcoholic dregs slid slowly back down the sides. "Now it's wine. See? Nothing special."

Brittany wasn't fazed. "It was always wine."

I reached for Xia's cup angrily. She graciously traded

me for the wine and snickered.

I repeated the trick, this time showing Brittany the tea first. When I showed her the transformed liquid, she glared at me with cougar-like intensity.

"You *dare* mock God?" she screamed loudly enough that half of the cafeteria stopped to stare, and the other half, wondering why the whole place just went silent, stared too.

"Yup," I replied, as matter-of-factly as I could. I wasn't upset or annoyed anymore. This was actually sort of fun.

Brittany took one step backward and pointed a finger at us. "He will judge you," she said, shaking uncontrollably. She glared at us a moment longer as if trying to leave us with a lasting impression of guilt before she then turned and stormed off.

"Too bad she didn't cry," Xia said, chuckling, once Brittany was out of earshot.

"If she would have, I might have felt bad. I don't mind religious people, it's the hypocrites I can't stand."

Xia took a sip of wine, her eyes deviously questioning.

"Brittany, for example," I continued, "really, *really*, enjoys her fornication."

Xia's brilliant smile flashed before her mouth burst

open into uncontrollable laughter. "How could you possibly know that?" she chided.

I grinned back. "The wind told me."

Xia hiccupped and then held up the glass of wine. "Just for future reference, I would have preferred a cabernet."

SIXTEEN

We talked long after our lunches were finished. I couldn't remember the last time I had so much fun. I couldn't help but laugh as the wine loosened Xia's tongue and her reservations began to crumble. She told me a rather elaborate story about her arrival to the US when she was two, which included details so minute and hilarious that I knew they had to be made up. For the past year and a half she had been living in Florida, going to a small private university, but had taken this last semester off to return to Japan to do some humanitarian work.

The walk back to the dormitory was brilliant. I don't know if it was the fact that she couldn't walk straight or if not walking straight was an excuse, but Xia pulled my arm over her shoulder and held on tightly to my waist the entire walk. The closeness was refreshing, even more refreshing than the scent of lilac shampoo that the wind picked up as it blew gently through Xia's hair. I think I was as intoxicated by her scent as she was from the twenty-four ounces or so of wine.

We entered the elevator in the lobby of a very quiet dorm building. After I pushed the button for the third floor and made some joke about us going to the penthouse, Xia shifted herself so that her arms were wrapped tightly around me and her head was resting on my chest.

"Hmmm," she sighed. "Let's take a nap."

I reeled over the suggestion and my hormones surged powerfully enough to make me dizzy, but real-life was quick to bring me down. "I have to go to work soon."

"Just for a few minutes," she cooed.

I hummed in agreement as the elevator doors slid open.

Cold air shot into the elevator as if someone had left a window open in the middle of an arctic winter. At first I thought the air conditioner must have been stuck at the lowest temperature setting, but once Xia moved away from me I felt how cold the air was—too cold to be coming from any air conditioner. My next exhale was visible.

I glanced down at Xia whose face was confused.

I took a step out of the elevator into a hallway that was lit only by a flickering florescent emergency light directly above my head. Xia carefully approached from behind. My immediate reflex was to keep her behind me by blocking her path with my left hand. The hallway had never had any windows, but usually, even without the lights, beams of light would mark the doorways that were the entrances to each room. I quickly doubted my own sense of time—but I quickly assured myself that it was still mid-day.

I listened intently but couldn't hear anything except a faint high-pitched ringing in my ears.

"Hello?" Xia yelled so loudly that it made me jump. My left hand instinctively went from her waist, where it was holding her behind me, to her mouth. I stole a look at her and shook my head in warning.

Something was definitely wrong. I hadn't noticed it sooner because I was so happy with Xia that I missed the gentle warnings that reverberated through the air. Now, I felt like I was standing in the middle of an earthquake; everything was buzzing frantically.

I took one step into the darkness. The carpet sloshed under the weight of my foot. Unthinking, I turned to examine the bottom of my shoe in the light. At first, I thought I had stepped in tar, the substance was so black in the dim light, but as a drop of liquid rolled off my shoe and onto the carpet below me, I saw a faint glimmer of rusty red.

Xia was no longer looking at me, but at the red stained carpet. Her face turned white before she sank to the floor.

Seeing her face caused panic to bubble up inside me and I found myself all-too-conscious of the fact that we were standing under the only working light in the hallway, our presence illuminated against the darkness. If something were in the hall it certainly would be aware of us.

I focused on the light above me, pulling the flickering light into my body and concentrating them in my hand. "Luthos," I yelled, and brilliant light flashed from my outstretched hand. The spell only lasted as long as a flash of lightning, but it was long enough to sear the image of the hallway onto my retinas.

The walls, the floors, and the ceiling were all smeared in sticky red. A body with indistinguishable features was lying in an unmoving heap at the end of the corridor. The trails of blood on the walls suggested it had been smeared, not splattered, and the carpets ran red so uniformly that I knew numerous bloody carcasses must have been drug off to some unknown location.

Xia must have seen the hallway too because she was now poised tensely against the wall, half hidden by the shadows. The muscles in her hand were so tight that it looked like she was reaching out with shaking claws instead of hands.

We couldn't stay here. I tapped the elevator button swiftly, but it didn't light up.

Xia's eyes pleaded with me. She was holding her breath as I tapped the button again and again. Nothing.

I muttered profanity under my breath.

I took Xia's outstretched hand and tried to pull her into me—my pathetic attempt at trying to make her feel safe. She didn't move.

Her lips slackened, and when I realized she was trying to say something, I moved closer. Her mascara was running in wet streaks down her cheeks. "Nicholas and Quon," her mouth moved.

Suddenly I was running, Xia in tow, directly into the darkness. The moment she said the names, a surge of adrenaline spurred my feet into action. The sticky carpet didn't help my feeling of being unable to get to them fast enough, every step was like getting stuck in a puddle of thick syrup.

I could see the shadowy outline of the wall that made out the end of the hall. Our room was the first door around the corner. I was in such a frantic state of mind that I only slightly noticed the air get colder as Xia and I leapt over a bloody body and burst through the unlocked door into the room.

My eyes had to adjust to the strange way the light came in through the blood-covered window. So much blood—the scene here was no different.

Xia gasped at the same time that I saw Nicholas—a red silhouette against an even redder backdrop.

Nicholas sat rigid on his bed, his knees pulled up to his chin, rocking slightly back and forth. I could see his dark eyes as they glowed red in the dim light, but they didn't look at us, only through us.

"Nicholas?" I asked softly, taking a cautious step forward. "Are you okay?"

His naked legs were covered in blood up to his knees, but it wasn't until I got closer that I noticed his heaving chest and twisted face were as well. At least he was breathing.

I ran toward the bed. "Are you hurt? Xia, get a blanket." I tried to pry his hands from around his legs so that I could lower them and find where the blood was coming from. When I touched him, he was colder than the air around us.

His face turned slowly toward me and his eyes finally fell on mine. His expression instantly softened, but only slightly. His body remained tense. With his muscles flexed,

I couldn't pry open his arms.

"I'm just glad you're alive," I said feeling relief. I stared directly at him, trying to use the strength in my eyes to get him to respond. "Who did this?"

Nicholas's face tensed again and his brow furrowed. His lips stretched into a straight line. I could see the strain in his neck muscles as he attempted to unclench his jaw.

"I did."

I wasn't sure I heard him correctly because the words came out with a gurgle of blood that spilled out of his mouth. He started to vomit uncontrollably. The tension in his body exploded and I took a few uncontrollable steps away from him.

Nicholas's eyes pleaded with me to understand as the force with which he was heaving threw him off the bed. He coughed up blood between gasps for air.

He was now on the floor on all fours, his chest and back rising with his raspy attempts to breathe. His entire body was smeared with blood.

"He's still here," he managed to choke out coherently, stronger than I would have expected, enough to make me flinch.

That was all he needed to say, and I understood. "None of this is *your* blood?"

Nicholas didn't look up at me, he was too busy

staring at the floor trying to decide if he was finished throwing up, but he shook his head.

"No. Not mine..." His stomach twisted again, and more blood lurched out of his mouth.

The whole scene was proving too much for Xia. I saw her collapse in my peripheral vision and her back rolled as she followed Nicholas's lead, spewing red liquid—not blood in her case—just wine.

"... need... get..." Nicholas mumbled as he rolled onto his back and painfully stretched his limbs.

I crossed the room and helped Xia to her feet, giving her a reassuring squeeze as I stared into her pale face. Her eyes were full of fear and questions, as I'm sure were mine, but there was a sense of profound control behind them, and I had no doubt I could count on her. I pulled a blanket from my bed and wrapped Nicholas's body. When I finally got him to his feet, I turned back to Xia.

"We should probably go somewhere warm and safe... public. Then we can sort out what happened."

She nodded her head once in acknowledgment and took one step toward me before I felt large, strong arms grab me from behind and pull me away from her.

I hit Nicholas's hard body at the same time he pressed his back onto the wall. I looked down to find his arms around my waist, the muscles tense like when we found him. I could feel fear ripple through his body.

"Nicholas!" I cried. "I can't breathe. Let me go."

But he didn't. Instead he just whispered in my ear, "He's coming, he's coming, he's coming."

My heart skipped a beat as everything went eerily silent. I thought I was screaming at Xia to get down, or hide, or who knows what, but any sound that came out of my mouth was instantly swallowed up by a more forceful presence—a silence that had a life of its own. I saw Xia dash toward us as the door burst open and all light was drawn from the room.

This demon, for I assumed it could be nothing else, had no human form. It was a void—a void that devoured all sound and light. Its presence filled the room so densely that it pushed out all the air. Nicholas was clenching his arms so tightly around me that pain was shooting through my hip and the lower half of my body was starting to tingle from lack of blood. Of course, he couldn't hear my petitions to release me.

And then there was a voice, soft like the wind, gentle like a breeze, "So it is true. Edmund lives."

The pressure in the room pulled back as the darkness receded. For a brief moment I thought someone must have come to help us because the red tinted light from the blood-streaked windows was slowly returning and I found myself able to swallow a deep breath of air. But I saw rather quickly that the darkness wasn't actually dissipating, just consolidating. Within seconds, every shadow around the room quivered with life.

Nicholas unexpectedly dropped me. Unfortunately my legs collapsed from underneath me as soon as they were asked to support my weight and I fell face first into a puddle of blood. Then they caught fire as my heart pumped life back into them.

"What do you want? Who are you?" I was finally able to ask.

"Blood," the shadows quivered as it responded. "I want the blood of all living creatures."

Nicholas was now inching toward the open door and Xia was curled in the fetal position in the center of the room. I couldn't see her face but I hoped she was okay.

"And your blood, Edmund," the creature continued, "your blood will fetch a great price. I will be rewarded handsomely."

"How do you know me?" I asked, trying to buy myself enough time to get us out of here safely.

"I know *of* you. The level walkers speak of you. Some have heard rumors but none have been able to enter this world as you have."

Now I was not only buying time, but intrigued. Still,

the answers to any questions I could ask were not worth the risk to the lives of my friends.

"Let me and my friends live and I will share my secret."

I assumed the sound the shadows made next was laughter, but it sounded more like a hiss.

"I will kill your friends and claim your soul along with all of its secrets."

I thought I had more time. I thought I would be able to do something to save Xia and Nicholas. I thought I could barter with the demon, but it moved too quickly. The quivering shadows around the room leaped forward, latching onto me. Their touch was so cold my skin burned. Their weight was so heavy, I felt myself collapse under the pressure—but something odd happened: when I collapsed, my body stayed standing, and then took a step toward Xia.

Now I knew what it was like to be possessed. My spirit crumbled under the crushing blow of the demon, and in doing so, I unwillingly relinquished control of my body to it. I could hear its thoughts in my head, screaming so loudly it drowned out my own.

"Such a glorious connection you have, Edmund. What a great, unused power. With my knowledge and your body, I will do amazing things."

... including killing my friends. The demon didn't

have to say that part. I knew all that it desired.

"Edmund?" Xia asked in fear as I came toward her.

I could feel the lust burning in my eyes, scared to realize that the lust for her body was partially my own, grateful that the lust for her blood was entirely the demon's. I knew she could see it as well.

"Edmund, no. What are you doing?" she took a fearful step back and I felt the demon relish in her discomfort.

No! I screamed, fighting for control. The demon was now in a body—my body. If someone could just cast an exorcism spell, the first spell I learned as a child in Orenda, all would be well. The demon laughed as I thought this, as I fought to get my own mouth to mutter the words.

I felt Nicholas grab me from behind in an attempt to stop me, but his arms were not strong like they had been a few minutes ago—his tense arms felt so fragile.

"I'll deal with you next, pet boy," I said, casting him aside easily.

I expected Xia to run, to cower, or to plead, but instead she stood and firmly planted her feet. "I'm sorry, Edmund," she whispered as I tried to fight my own hand from reaching out toward her.

"Hecate!" her voice boomed. "Hear your daughter. Deliver us from our enemy."

Her eyes softened as they met mine and the look in her eye told me this was going to hurt.

An ear-splitting howl sounded from behind me. The demon whirled, my body responding slower than it would have had I been in control. As I turned, I was bowled over by a large white dog.

I watched in horror as it ripped into my flesh, its pale blue eyes unblinking, never disconnecting from my own. I braced myself for pain but instead simply felt a slight slip, a crack in the shackles that the demon used to bind my body to his mind.

Shadows oozed out of my skin like liquid and started combining against the dog, but as they did I began to regain control over my own body.

"Xia!" I managed to cry out before being muzzled by the demon again, thrown back into my mental cage that I was fighting so frantically to escape. In my mind I saw two animals: the white dog on the outside clawing its way to the inside, and myself, clawing desperately at the cage in my mind, howling for escape.

Instead of running, Xia bolted to my side and grabbed my hand.

"If you can hear me Edmund, if you can fight for enough control, get us out of here! However you need to do it get us out of here!"

The dog continued to struggle against the shadows but was weakening. I could feel the effort of the demon's successful defense against Xia's beautifully conjured assault. All I could do was glance toward Nicholas, but it was enough for Xia to get the message. She called him over and gripped his hand in one of hers, while holding fast to mine with the other.

I hoped my miraculous escape from the demon in my small pickup truck would be enough experience to keep my friends from meeting an icy fate. Had they not been there when I inexplicably emerged in my dorm room I could have died, and I had no idea if someone would be there to save us all where my mind wanted to take us.

And then there was the issue of this mental block the demon was somehow able to cage me into. Would I be able to use his connection to me, and to the world he was from, while caged against my own body?

I hoped the demon was distracted enough. I could feel Xia's warm hand in my own, and with that thought turned my vision inward. I searched frantically for that silver strand of light that saved me, and almost killed me, the last time. When I found it, I tightened my hand and pulled Xia and Nicholas with me into the cold.

SEVENTEEN

The rolling hills where the wayward pines sheltered the damp earth that played host to hundreds of wild mushrooms were unmistakable, and the miles of sprawling sweet alfalfa fields were just a short journey to the west. When the wind blew just right, I could almost taste the morning dew.

"Where are we?" I heard Nicholas whisper to my right. He was standing, staring intently at me, his question more an accusation than a question.

"I'm not really sure. Somewhere between reality and a memory I think," I answered almost reverently, the last word punctuated with a quick inhale as the ring on my finger pulsed with icy frigidity.

"Come on," I didn't delay. "We need to get to the ruins about an hour north of here. They're this way."

"You've been here before?" Xia asked.

I felt sick. "Welcome to Orenda," I replied dryly. "Sort of. I think. At least my memory of it. I'm not really sure, actually. The fields are familiar, the mountains too, but at the same time everything is…" I had to wrestle for the right word, "…ghostlike."

I reached out to hit a tree branch as I walked to prove my point; it passed through my hand without moving.

"I'm pretty sure wherever we are just uses my memory as a representation. The last time I was here I spent three days trying to get back to my childhood home. I made it as far as the gates before the dogs…"

Xia wasn't about to let me get away with leaving my sentence unfinished, but instead of prodding me, she let her silence speak for her.

"… Let's just keep an eye out for the dogs," I finished, lightly touching the barely healed gashes on my chest.

"You didn't tell us any of this," Nicholas chided, stepping over a large rock in the path. I hadn't immediately noticed he was still naked, but that fact didn't seem to bother him much.

With nothing more than a thought and whisper, he was fully clothed again, but instead of a look of thanks or surprise, he simply stopped and glowered.

"Really? Stripes? Couldn't you have conjured up something Armani? Naked is better than Walmart stripes."

"Designer apparel wasn't my first concern. If this is all my imagination I'd rather you not run around it naked anymore."

My whole hand pulsed like I had plunged it into a bowl of ice water. Xia and Nicholas must have noticed me flinch.

"You'll start to feel cold soon," I explained, though I wasn't sure I was doing a good job of it. "The cold isn't so bad the first day here, but by the second you'll start to think you'll never feel warm again."

Nicholas continued to mutter under his breath about my choice of clothing for him while Xia's eyes exploded with understanding.

"You were here for three days last time. You thought you were actually at your childhood home, the place you remember but no one seems to know about, and you tried to get to the city?"

"Yes," I answered. "It took me a whole day to get to the town, but before I could get inside the gate the dogs attacked me. I spent a few hours trying to figure out how to get around them, but they just kept coming. Eventually the cold started to be too much, and I started looking for a way back to Earth."

"Back to *Earth?*" Xia practically exclaimed, slipping a little on the dirt path. She looked annoyed as she attempted to regain her balance. "We're not on Earth?"

I laughed, and wrapped my arm around her as a shiver exploded through her shoulders. "I don't know where we are. How else was I supposed to phrase it?"

"How did you find your way?" Nicholas asked.

I pointed upward, "The glow of silver."

When I had arrived to this ghostlike world the last time, I hadn't noticed that in addition to everything else that seemed wrong about this place, color was another one. It wasn't that things appeared in black or white, everything just looked at like an old faded photograph, followed by a layer of blue hue. The warping made the silver aura high above us almost fade out of existence, but it was visible against the raven black sky if you knew what you were looking for.

"It leads into the ancestral mountains," I said hoisting myself to a higher point on the trail and turning around to offer a hand to Xia and Nicholas. "There are some ruins and some caves that were sacred to the Orendan people. We can get back from there."

"Does the sun ever come up?" Nicholas grumbled. "I can barely see where I'm stepping."

"It is up," Xia said matter-of-factly.

"How did you know?" I was honestly surprised.

"Because this day just keeps getting better and better," she replied with a grin. "And I'd bet that when it sets, we won't be able to see anything."

I shot her a glance that confirmed her theory and heard her mutter under her breath.

"Why is it that the trees pass right through us, but we have to hike up the mountain?" Nicholas barked as he struggled up a steep incline.

"How am I supposed to know?"

"Well, it is *your* imagination. Can't you just make it flat?"

"It doesn't work like that."

"Why not?"

"How am I supposed to know?" I repeated, more firmly.

He huffed, but noticed my irritation so didn't say anything else.

We walked further along a path that twisted steeply along jagged rock. While the walk really wasn't that far, it didn't take long before my legs started to complain that they didn't particularly enjoy the constant straining they had to exert to keep up with the boulders, inclines, and loose gravel. It didn't help that I was pushing them faster than the last time I had been here; I didn't want to get caught on these trails again when the sun set because, even though it made the small silver strand that marked our path more visible, it made everything, including the obstacles, blend in among the black backdrop. Nicholas grunted on occasion but otherwise kept pace. I didn't doubt that his daily hours in the gym were of some benefit to him now, so his first couple of grunts really frayed my nerves, but what could I say to a big lug who probably had more muscle now than he neither needed, nor could haul around? Once I decided not to let him annoy me his huffs became background noise—a small signal to let me know he was still there a few steps behind us in the darkness.

And by us, I meant Xia and me. When she had slipped her hand into mine, I stiffened both in surprise and excitement. She was so quick and quiet I had hardly noticed her by my side. When I stole a glance at her, my surprise no doubt evident on my face, she gave a sly grin and a knowing, penetrating stare.

"My hand is cold," was all she had said, but when she looked away I saw a look in her eye that I cannot explain. Hope, perhaps. Maybe a little bit of fear. I had to contemplate how her look made me feel, but finally settled on a hope of my own—that her fear was fear of rejection… my rejection, not because of what she had seen or been through tonight, not because of what our future held, but because of the possibility that her future might not be intertwined with mine. And if that *was* her fear, I was happy. It was a fear we shared.

I realized it was presumptuous of me to read into a passing glance, especially while everything around us was fading to black and the night was casting shadows so that we were only able to see a few feet in front of us, but I know what I saw in Xia's eyes, and there was something unique about her, even here. It was almost as if the shadows dared not touch her face, and her eyes, though dark as cocoa, simply beamed.

I'm sure I've already discussed how beautiful Xia was, but I'm sure I'll do it again. Let's just say that even here, even after everything, I couldn't help but let my mind wander to scenarios that would be impolite to discuss in mixed company, and I felt major regret for the missed opportunity of that nap. Damned demons.

"Looks like we're getting close."

Nicholas's voice was jarring but composed—he was less tired than he wanted us to believe, his heavy steps and harsh breathing obviously dramatic flair, but he was right. The silver stream had grown wider and culminated in a ball of light between two cliffs that were so close together that you had to look hard to distinguish them or you would have thought the light was just a beam of moonlight rising above the horizon.

"That's it," I confirmed, turning to meet his eye, but as I did, I lost my footing and collapsed, hitting my shin on something hard, cold, and sharp.

I'm sure the sound that came out of my mouth as I reached for my leg sounded more like a hiss than the profane word I was thinking, but my mind immediately noticed that the blood dripping from the wound wasn't warm like it should have been. We had already been here long enough for our body temperatures to drop, which explained my dreamlike flow of thoughts. I still didn't curse my imaginings of Xia naked though…

But instead of logic telling me to get up and get to the caves quickly, another stream of thought occurred… one I had tried not to think about… another time when my blood felt this cold and had dripped, thick as syrup, to the ground. The most recent time I was here was when I had escaped the demon in my truck by somehow pushing my mind and body into this place, but there was another time when this place was real and alive and vibrant with color, when the dark sky didn't bring total darkness, when my friends and I frolicked under the moonlight and fell asleep amongst the pines… until the day I was murdered, and my blood ran as cold as the heart of the man who killed me.

As the blood from my leg struck the ground I could

almost hear the same pounding of the earth... my blood drops like a heavy stick striking a drum. I hadn't heard the earth speak like that to me in a long time... never in my current life. The sound was foreign and familiar to me at the same time, but the sense of the power in its whisper was intoxicating.

"Come on, Edmund. It doesn't look that bad. Can you walk?"

Xia's voice sounded as ridiculous as a soft bell trying to ring as loud as the drums in a symphony. Everything around me was alive and speaking. I could hear the trees in the valley miles away... they spoke of conquerors and slaves, of souls and demons, and of death.

The mountains shook with warnings and secrets. If they were a book, I could almost read what was printed, but the light was too dim and the text too small; all I understood were pieces.

The grassy meadows sang instead of spoke. Their voices were melodic and unified while everything together was carried on the wind.

And the wind was too overwhelming. I couldn't single one voice out or make sense of anything. I knew Xia and Nicholas were screaming at me. They obviously misunderstood the reason why I was grasping my ears, trying to drown out what was becoming white noise. It wasn't my ears that were hearing. I didn't know what it was, but Xia and Nicholas's frantic motions, red faces, and blasted screams only added to the ocean of noise that I didn't have the power to stop any more than I could stop the flow of the waves. Only one word kept being repeated, spoken—no cried—from the mountains, the meadows, the earth, the trees, and the rivers: Death. Death. Death.

And then I hear them... closer than I imagined... the cries of the dogs—the beasts that almost killed me the last time I was here. Their howling rang above all, and I knew, I just knew, that the noise created by the mountains, the meadows, the earth, the trees, and the rivers alerted them to our presence. They were coming for us. They, too, could hear.

My last thoughts were to focus on Xia, but she wasn't looking at me anymore. She was looking in the direction of the howl, her fear evident.

"Run!" I cried, hardly able to move. Somehow I would protect them as they raced for the caves that would bring them to safety. "Wait! You'll need the ring!" I couldn't say more, but I managed to tug it off and place it in Xia's hand... her almost frozen hand. I closed her fingers around the ring and turned down the path toward the sound of the dogs. I could hear the vibrations their huge paws made as they galloped towards us. I was unable to stand but I was able to crawl, and I would meet them with the power of the thumping earth if I had to. I felt Xia's hand on my shoulder, trying to pull me back, trying to make me go with them, but we didn't have time... the dogs would kill us all.

I made a choice. I knew the earth's drumming was a source of power, so I asked it to bring my friends to the caves... and to do it quickly.

The white noise turned to a rumble and I felt Xia's hand rip away from my shoulder. The earth would grant my request, not because I forced it to, but because it owed me, and it was almost like it was on my side, willing me to win.

But I could only ask for one favor. There was a balance that could not be broken that I understood with the beating of the drum in my head. So it was no surprise when I looked up to see a mouthful of fangs drooling over me. They came for me at the same time the rebound from my spell did, crushing me.

EIGHTEEN

Waking this time was an odd experience. I can't even say that I woke for certain, only that I became aware again. I was standing, wearing white, covered in blood, with a cleaver in my hand and half a slab of bright red meat lying in front of me.

The scene would curl the stomach of any normal person. To my right were sharp sticky knives and to my left was a large hook that looked like something out of a horror movie. Toward the edge of the table were perfectly cut and stacked steaks. I had even already wrapped and prepared a few T-bones and stamped them with a bright orange price sticker.

The whole scene was comforting to me. I was at work at the local grocery store. Cutting and restocking the meat was familiar.

When my boss walked into the fridge, he was cordial

and didn't seem too upset over the fact that I had not been at work lately. He didn't even look at me as he scraped the good scraps of meat onto a Styrofoam plate and labeled it 'stew.'

"I think that's enough, Edmund," he said. "I really appreciate you making it in today. Luckily it hasn't been too busy while you've been gone."

That was his non-confrontational way of reprimanding me, but even with the softness in tone, the words were meant to be sharp.

That was Henric's personality, though. He wasn't a domineering man, but that isn't to say that he was one you wanted to make angry. He was smarter than he let on. Even owning the supermarket was a tribute to his intellect. He bought it for less than half of what it was worth, partnering with a bank that he knew was in financial trouble… the bank just hadn't known it yet.

And he was smart enough to know that he could run the store without me, which made me all the more grateful for the job. Because of my school schedule, Henric often managed the market alone for days at a time, but he always welcomed me back whenever I could put in a few hours. I made up for my sporadic appearances by taking him out for drinks and telling him stories that I'm sure his rational mind thought were made up. Still, we had formed a strong bond and mutual understanding, though I dared not say we were friends. We were both too smart and got what we wanted, but we were different enough from each other to make our similarities entertaining.

There was also something secretive about Henric. I knew, for example, that Henric wasn't his real name. In fact, he wasn't even from Norway or wherever someone one might expect that sort of name to come from... he was from India. I knew nothing about his family, although I suspected he didn't have any... at least not in California, or the States, for all I knew.

"Are my friends still around?" I asked nonchalantly, trying to read a reaction.

Henric looked tired but his expression otherwise remained the same. "They're taking a nap in the back room I think. When you arrived they looked pretty haggard. I saw on the news there was some trouble over at the college. Nothing you were involved with I hope?"

His tone wasn't accusatory, just curious.

I could feel my mind start to race with the question. Henric asking meant it was a big deal. I should have felt anxious. Instead, I felt numb. I collected the knives and dropped them into a sink filled with hot soapy water.

"Nope. Xia and I were at lunch and hadn't been back all day, and I'm pretty sure Nicholas was hooking up with some guy in the steam room at the gym again." Honestly, I added the last part not only because it was true, but also because I always suspected that Henric might be gay. I tried to get him to react to such statements all the time but he never flinched. Just in case, I wanted to remind him that I had a gay best friend so that he would feel comfortable telling me more about his personal life if he *were* gay. There wasn't even a flicker in his eye or a slight pause in his smooth motion as he wiped down the cutting tables with disinfectant.

"I think the police wanted to talk to everyone who lived in the building," was Henric's only response.

"Well, then we should probably go talk to them." If I hadn't known better, I would have thought he was trying to get rid of us. I hung up my apron and washed my hands a final time before adding, "Do you need me to check inventory or stock the shelves?"

"Already did it yesterday. Maybe tomorrow?"

At least he wanted me back. "Okay."

"Oh, and Edmund? When you are gone for a few days, I tend to get a little worried. You've always done so well in the past, but at least try to call in every so often. Especially with all that has happened at the school recently, I wasn't sure where you were. I just want to know that you're okay."

301

He said it without any emotion, so matter-of-factly that I wasn't sure what to make of the statement but decided I was probably reading into everything too much.

"Sure. Hey, drinks Friday?"

"Of course. If you missed that, I'd have to file a missing person's report," he grinned.

I found Xia and Nicholas not sleeping, but looking rather bored, and perhaps a bit worried, in the break room. Xia was slouched over what looked like a terrible cup of coffee and Nicholas was sprawled across an old leather sofa Henric and I had rescued from the dumpster out back.

"Okay, how the *hell* did we get back here?" I asked with more force than I intended, my emotional numbness starting to wear off.

Xia and Nicholas's faces both widened into a shocked expression.

"Well at least you're talking again!" Nicholas exclaimed. "What was up with you?"

I had no idea what they were talking about but I wasn't about to let them answer my question with another question. "I'm glad you guys are okay. What happened?"

"It was pretty sweet," Xia answered, now animated. "I think you meant to send us to the cave... the portal back to our world?" she grasped at what exactly to call the cave in the side of the mountain that we'd been trying to reach. I couldn't think of a word or explanation that would help her. "Anyway, you ended up bringing the mountain to us!"

"Oops," I couldn't help but beam with pride.

"So we grabbed you and took you with us, but when we got back you were… different. You wouldn't acknowledge us, wouldn't answer our questions. All you kept saying was that you needed to get back to work."

Nicholas wasn't smiling, but his expression was soft. "You've spent the last six hours back there cutting up meat. Xia and I couldn't watch." He made a face and mimicked vomiting.

"Six hours?"

"Without saying a word," Xia whispered. "We were worried you were… broken or something."

"Asleep, more like it. At least that's what it felt like," I thought aloud.

"You were sleep butchering?" Nicholas laughed. "You've got some mad skills."

"Speaking of mad butchering skills," I interrupted, "why don't you tell us what happened back at the dorms?"

This was the kind of conversation that made Nicholas uncomfortable, but I figured if I sprang it on him he'd have less wiggle room. I was still surprised when he started talking without much protest.

"I figured you'd ask eventually, so I've been trying to piece it all together. Even now it all feels like a bad dream that has pieces missing. But I guess the past day or so has been like that for all of us."

I nodded almost involuntarily.

"Anyway, I went to the gym as usual, and there wasn't anything out of the ordinary. This guy kept smiling at me, working out next me, offering to spot," Nicholas grinned at the memory. "When he was standing over me at the bench, I could see up his gym shorts—"

"Do we really need those details?" I chuckled half-seriously.

"I do!" Xia bellowed, her eyes wild with lust.

Nicholas laughed and winked at her playfully, "Skank."

"Well, come on!" she chided, "We've been covered in blood, in Edmund's imagination—not a very sexy place, by the way—fought off shadow demons and half-werewolf-dog-things, it's about time we get to a little naked action."

We all laughed, and it felt good. I put an arm around Xia and gave her an affectionate squeeze.

"Well, it was nice. Really nice," Nicholas continued. "So I thought, why not see if he was interested in a bit of a more private show? He followed me to the steam room.

We fooled around for a bit before he asked if we could go somewhere…"

"And that's when Xia and I came home and saw the tack."

"Yeah, what is it with that anyway? I still would have preferred a sock on the doorknob. I thought college boys like gloating to all your buddies about getting laid."

Nicholas smirked, "A tack for tact."

"Well, the noises we heard weren't very tactful," Xia grinned lasciviously. "Was he any good?"

Nicholas's eyes glazed over momentarily while he thought about it. "A-maze-ing. His body was—"

"Again, details we don't care about," I interrupted. It wasn't so much that I was getting uncomfortable (in fact, watching Xia's reaction to the story was quite erotic). I just wanted to get to the important demon-possessed-me and made-me-kill-everyone stuff.

"I totally care about *all* these details," Xia spoke again, giving me a knowing look while her hand trailed slowly down her stomach. I couldn't help but swallow whatever it was I was going to say next.

Thankfully, Nicholas picked back up further down the story line, "Well, we were—" he looked at me uncomfortably.

"Having sex," I spoke for him.

305

"Yeah, and then he looked at me. His eyes looked weird. I thought at first that it was just the light from the window, but then it felt like something was stabbing into the back of my head. It hurt so bad that I lost consciousness. I don't remember much after that until a few minutes before you came in. It's all sort of disconnected."

"What do you remember?"

"It was like I was having a dream, and in the dream I was really hungry. Nothing I ate felt satisfying. There was this girl down the hall, and I've never felt that way about a girl before. She looked so amazing… but the lust I had for her wasn't sexual, it was… predatory."

Nicholas looked like he was going to be sick, like he hoped that he had said enough, but we waited and he eventually regained his composure.

"I think I ate her," he said, "and the jock down the hall, and the chess club president, and the head cheerleader… well… technically the cheerleader was being eaten by the jock down the hall first, you know? They were *together* together. Anyway, I *ate* ate them.

"And then I went back to the room, and people kept coming. I couldn't eat anymore because I was so full, but their blood was so warm."

"What did you do with the bodies?"

"I don't know," Nicholas was crying now. "I think he took them."

"Who?"

"The demon. I don't know his name. But the worst part was that he was looking for something. He wanted everyone dead so he could collect their souls. I remember him thinking that. It wasn't a hunger for flesh, blood, or murder that he had. It was a hunger for souls. He said with them he could do anything he wanted."

"And what did he want?" I asked cautiously.

Nicholas gave me a look of compassion and horror, one that communicated everything he needed to say even before he said it. "He kept repeating a name. Your name, Edmund."

NINETEEN

My eyes fluttered open just as Nicholas pulled a tight red polo over his broad shoulders. The orange light in the room looked florescent as it filtered through a high concentration of dust. Cheap motels always made me worry. I had to wiggle my nose a few times before I felt like I could breathe again after sleeping on a pillow I was sure played host to a New York-sized colony of dust mites. At least the sheets were crisp. I didn't dare move too much since Xia was comfortable in the nook at my bare shoulder. My arm tingled and felt a bit clammy, but I hadn't ever seen the rose color on Xia's cheeks that appeared only when she slept. Even in the orange light it was so beautiful a color that I dared not wake her for fear it would fade.

Nicholas had turned on the TV, but had it muted with captions. The news was currently scrolling text about twenty-nine students who had mysteriously gone missing from the dorms at UCSD. There was speculation that the disappearances were the result of some psych student's senior thesis, but it was hard to read the scrolling black-and-white text from the angle at which I was viewing the screen.

Xia stirred and pulled herself in even closer, her hand landing squarely on my groin. Nicholas stifled a chuckle as my eyes widened and I flushed.

He flashed me a toothy grin, taking a long moment to give me one of his "knowing" stare-downs. I smirked and stuck my tongue out, childish, but effective.

He winked at me and mimicked holding a phone to his ear while mouthing the word "mom" before he silently slipped out of the room into the bright morning.

I couldn't help but squirm as Xia's grip tightened. I looked down at her, expecting a sleep spasm to be to blame, but her clear cocoa eyes met mine directly.

I couldn't contain a smirk. "Good morning," I said.

"Seems to be for you," she glanced down at her hand.

I snorted. "Oh no, you're not pinning that on me. That was all you."

"Mmm hmm," she intoned with a sarcastic note. I couldn't help but notice she lingered a bit longer.

She stretched while I balled and released my fist to

get rid of the unpleasant feeling of the blood rushing back into my arm. She was right back against me after a few moments.

"These look like they are healing well." She lightly traced the lines of the wounds on my chest.

"Well, *that* feels a bit... tingly."

She withdrew her hand quickly, but I snatched it and used it to pull her on top of me. She half-shrieked and half-laughed, but didn't resist. The result was her straddling me, our faces so close together that I could feel her breath tickle my upper lip as she exhaled.

"Good morning," I repeated. It was stupid, but it was the only thing that came to mind, which now clearly focused only on how little clothing both of us were wearing and how full Xia's lips looked in the morning. Did they always look this way? Who knew? Who cared?

I caught a rather mischievous look in her eye just moments before she pressed her lips to mine. The look caused a thrill to ripple through my body, but the greater response was when I felt her melt into my embrace and give way to my lips.

There are many books written from the point of view of a woman during the fateful kiss between the romantic hero and his heroine. Pages have been written explaining the melding of souls, the buckling of knees, or the helpless sense of falling during a romantic embrace. Most of these descriptions make you assume the man is a fortress of stability and control, knowing exactly what effect he has on his heroine. Part of the romance and power of the scene is the heroine's perception of the manly, emotionless hero—but I'm here to tell you that as stanch and powerful as the hero may be, if he were anything like me, if his heroine meant half as much to him as he meant to her, he would also be weak in these moments, not powerless, and maybe his knees wouldn't falter, but he would give up every bit of power he had in his respective kingdom to make that connection last just one second longer.

Which is exactly why I felt nothing but extreme anger when Nicholas came back into the room and Xia pulled away.

"Oops, sorry! I can come back," he said.

I assume he was skulking back through the door, but my eyes were locked on Xia's as she responded, "It's okay, Nicholas. I was going to take a shower anyway."

When she disappeared into the bathroom, I found the closest thing and hurled it at Nicholas in fury. Unfortunately, it was only a pillow.

He cowered playfully and snickered, "I'm sorry, I'm sorry. That's why we have the red tack rule!"

"Where the *hell* am I supposed to get a red tack, you

little bastard?"

Nicholas bellowed with laughter and preemptively ducked. "I always carry one just in case. Why wouldn't you?"

I had thrown my last pillow and was half tempted to throw the phone. Instead, I catapulted myself back onto the mattress and joined him in laughter.

"It's not too late. She's just in there," Nicholas said, motioning toward the bathroom door. "Shower sex can be fun. I'm pretty sure you don't need an invitation."

"Call me an old romantic, but I think I'd prefer our first time to be in a sleazy hotel bed, not in a sleazy hotel bathroom."

Nicholas tugged at the wrapper to a protein bar he retrieved from his bag. "Suit yourself." He chewed for a minute before continuing, "Brunch with my mom is at eleven-thirty." His chewing slowed. He wasn't good at hiding the pensive look on his face. I wasn't going to like what he was about to say. "She wants you to come. She has some information about the college, and with the…" his words started to come with some difficulty, "… magic thing in common, she wants to talk."

He added a quick, "I don't know…anyway…" at the end with a dismissive tone.

I waited to answer until he looked at me. When he

did, I could see anticipation on his face, but it was also soft and hopeful like a puppy who knew he did something wrong but hoped you wouldn't notice.

I felt my nostrils flare and my eyelids tighten. I just nodded. "How much does she already know?"

I was sure Nicholas took another bite of his protein bar to avoid answering, so after a few moments I filled the awkward silence by asking the question again, this time more firmly.

"Everything I do."

I had to swallow to stop a profane word from escaping. "She knows about your possession?"

Nicholas nodded.

"Me?"

He nodded again.

"Orenda?"

He didn't nod, but he didn't need to anymore. His lack of denial was confirmation enough.

"I knew you were close, but I had no idea. You are hardly able to talk about this stuff with me."

"I never talked to her about it until I started talking with you. She's the only one who doesn't think all of this is entirely insane. I needed to talk to someone else I could trust."

He emphasized the word "else" so that I wouldn't

313

think he didn't trust me.

"You know I don't like this stuff. I don't want to know about it. I need to keep a good head on my shoulders too. Normally when you would go off on all of this, Quon and I would go out for a few drinks and make fun of you. We'd blow off some steam, remind ourselves that none of this exists. Now he isn't answering his phone, no one knows where he is. Xia doesn't seem concerned and he very well may be dead! He was always around to keep me grounded in *reality* and now he isn't. My mom has a way of making all of this seem less scary, so yes, I told her. She's here for all of us, and wants to be there for you. She's been living in this world for a long time so I want you to talk to her so she can put things into perspective for me."

Nicholas's rambling diatribe was so unlike him that all I could do was agree to meet his mother for brunch, not only because it was something I wanted to do (although I was feeling apprehensive and unprepared), but because I needed to keep him from having a breakdown.

"Okay," I spoke in a soothing tone. "I'll go."

***

I always considered Nicholas's reluctance to believe in magic odd, considering his mother was a practicing witch. I thought about the dichotomy this presented, but in my mind, being someone directly involved myself, I simply had to believe that either his mother wasn't very good at the craft or he was so deeply hurt by what happened to us in the orphanage that he blocked out not only those experiences, but any he had with his mother as well.

Still, thinking about how someone could believe completely opposite of what their life experiences had taught them gave me a headache. I often compared the thought process to any religion or faith, and saw the same dichotomy in the super zealous as they struggled with hypocrisy: sometimes in little things like how not to judge while being judgmental, and sometimes in larger things like how to continue an affair while preaching fidelity.

Obviously I had my own dichotomies to work out. I was literally two people. What greater dichotomy was there? Where did Edmund end and Alexander begin? Did Alexander even exist? Or was Edmund the imaginary figure? If I were to believe only what I was told was possible, then Edmund was nothing more than a dream and I was Alexander, with simply no memory of the first twelve years of my life.

But I knew differently and I had a select few experiences that confirmed my belief, not the least of which were my magical gifts. Comparing the importance of those few experiences with those in which Nicholas chose to place his faith helped me to understand him. The faith-building experiences that shaped my beliefs were founded in magic; his were founded anywhere else. I clung to my beliefs because of those experiences, and he did the same.

It became easier to see how Nicholas could dismiss the magic surrounding his life when we arrived at a small café for brunch and I saw his mother. Her skin was pale and smooth like porcelain, so untouched by the sun that it was almost translucent. The light in the room seemed to find the angles of her cheekbones in a way that made it look like she was glowing from the inside. Her deep burgundy lips were stunning, even from across the room of the little café we had entered. She looked up at us, her eyes smiling from beneath a large, floppy sunhat that seemed to fit the scene so perfectly I couldn't imagine her without it.

Quite honestly, she looked strikingly normal. Perhaps a bit more beautiful than average, but she certainly didn't look like a witch.

She stood when we entered, only to be dwarfed by her son as they embraced.

"Hi, Ma," Nicholas smiled as he engulfed her tiny

frame in his giant arms.

She chuckled joyfully and kissed his cheek, standing on the tips of her red stiletto shoes to reach him.

"Mom, this is Edmund and Xia," he continued by way of introduction. He then stepped aside as I came face-to-face with someone who struck me as remarkable. Perhaps what was most stunning were her piercing gray eyes, exactly the same shade as Nicholas's when he was a child, the color of rain clouds—not dark or threatening, but ones that accompany the smell of grass just before the fall of the first refreshing raindrops. I was immediately swept back in memory to the alfalfa fields in Orenda as the earthy smell flooded my nostrils.

"Call me Linda Rose, please. This is quite a pleasure." She stepped forward and embraced me without hesitation, deeply inhaling at the nape of my neck as she did. "I do so love the smell of rain, don't you?" she whispered into my ear.

"Aren't you a beauty? And so powerful!" Linda Rose chimed as she moved on to Xia. "Quite truly a warrior spirit. She's feisty, Edmund dear. You'll have quite a bit of fun with this one if you are up for the challenge."

Xia grinned at this, which caused me to melt, as usual.

"Well, let's take a seat, shall we?" It wasn't a question that expected an answer. "I ordered a pot of tea for the

317

table," she said while pouring herself a cup from a large metal pot, "but of course we can order coffee or whatever else you would like."

"I'm going to go get a sandwich. Edmund? Xia? Want me to order you anything?"

"Split a turkey bacon avocado?" I offered.

Xia flushed slightly green. "How about the vegetarian?"

"Still a bit queasy from the butcher?" Nicholas chuckled. "If it's any consolation, I've lost all taste for red meat."

Xia glared, her nose wrinkled in disgust. It was adorable.

"I'm afraid I've missed something," Linda Rose stated—or questioned—I wasn't sure which.

"It's too soon to make jokes," I chided Nicholas, "regarding recent events."

"Ah, I see," Linda Rose remarked quite seriously, although her lip turned upward slightly. It seemed Nicholas's twisted sense of humor was not lost on her. This small insight into her character settled my stomach some. "On that subject, I'll have you know the school called looking for Nicholas. I took the liberty of informing them that all three of you were staying with me, and that you were most distraught about not knowing when you would be allowed back into the dorms to collect your personal belongings. I told them you had come for Thanksgiving and had no knowledge of the events. They'll want to speak to all of you, of course, but I convinced them to hold off until after the break. You should stick to that story if you are questioned."

I was filled with gratitude.

"I'll have a vegetarian too, please, Nicholas," Linda Rose added, placing her napkin in her lap.

It was here, in this moment, when my stomach had just started to settle, that something quite subtle occurred, or at least it would have been subtle by anyone else's standards. Linda Rose picked up her spoon, shuffled a few spoonfuls of sugar into her tea and started to stir. While this event was not out of the ordinary or unexpected, what happened next was both.

Linda Rose lifted her hand from the spoon and simply hovered it over the cup while she turned to Xia and started asking something about her family. Unfortunately, I couldn't hear the question above the screaming.

The motion of the spoon was subtle, but it continued to stir, all the while screeching with a horrendous metallic moan. It was almost the same noise as the metal-on-metal sound you hear when your brake pads are getting too low, but the sound was amplified to a state that made my hair stand on end.

I looked around the café wildly. How could no one else hear the noise? Xia was chatting brightly with Linda Rose who smiled graciously before her mouth started forming words I couldn't hear. Nicholas was flirting with the barista, his back to us. All of the other patrons seemed unbothered.

"For the love of that poor spoon, stop!" I bellowed, slamming Linda Rose's hand down over the cup so hard that it tipped over and spilled the tea. It felt like time had stopped. The silence that now permeated the room was heavy. All eyes were trained on me. It became obvious I had yelled more loudly than I had thought.

Linda Rose maintained her composure, even with the spilled tea now running off the table onto her flowered sundress. She didn't look at me with any anger or malice, but instead with inquisition.

I became aware of my hand still clutched over hers and I released it awkwardly, offering no apology. "Couldn't you hear it screaming?" I asked in a whisper.

Only now did she move to clean up the tea. She started with a couple of napkins along the edge of the table, but a change in the air, and the feeling in the pit of my stomach, made it obvious that Linda Rose had no issue using magic to do everyday tasks. The tea fled from before her hand as she motioned it across the table, congregating into an easily seep-able puddle. Her power felt odd to me. It took me almost until she was finished adding a few more spoonfuls of sugar to the righted and refilled cup to find the right word for it: forceful. Her power required much more force than I would have expected from such a frail-looking woman. She was undoubtedly strong, her will obeyed as long as it remained unbroken, but she had to push hard to get magic to work for her. I wondered why she was so pushy. It seemed strange for what seemed like such a proper woman in every other aspect.

Linda Rose stirred her tea, by hand this time, until the café patrons returned to their normal conversations. Then she took a sip from her cup and asked me a very odd question.

"Edmund, do you think that spoon would have stirred for you, if you simply asked it to?"

The question was perplexing. "I couldn't know the answer for sure until I asked it to. I suppose now it would feel that it owes me a debt since I saved it from—" I didn't finish when I realized my thought was coming out as an accusation. Instead I said, "So I guess it probably would, as long as it wasn't too tired." I was trying to find a tactful way not to add *because you forced it to stir against its desires*, but since I doubted Linda Rose understood this, I hoped this point would be lost on her anyway. Surprisingly, it wasn't, as her next question hinted to understanding.

"Do things often obey you, simply because you ask?"

"I prefer to think we understand each other and have a relationship. If I respect something and it respects me, we can mutually benefit," I replied.

"Have you ever forced something to do something it didn't want to do?"

"I don't think I've ever had a reason to."

"And why not?"

I briefly scanned the room, stood up, and pulled a spoon off the table next to us. "Options," I responded, putting the spoon in her cup. It began stirring when I asked it to, just as I knew it would. "This one wanted to stir."

"How did you know this one, above all the others, wanted to stir?"

I hesitated. I had to think about this question. I had never really analyzed what it was that made my ability unique, what gave me the ability to communicate with the elements. Finally, when I could come up with nothing better, I responded, "Magic. I think that is what magic is… the feeling… the knowing… the understanding."

I wasn't sure if the answer satisfied her or not because Linda Rose fell into deep thought. Her eyes went vacant, but she rubbed her index finger and thumb together in small circles, a twitch I took as pensive. We sat in silence for a good while, Xia and I passing uncertain glances back and forth.

Linda Rose didn't break her concentrated look until Nicholas came back, placing a tray of sandwiches on the table. "I got his number, the coffee guy," he nudged me playfully. "What did I miss?"

I was just opening my mouth when Linda Rose answered, "Your friend here, Edmund, has a very ancient way of looking at magic—a way that is now only whispered about among very old and powerful practitioners of the craft. I've only heard rumors..." she left her sentence unfinished until I prodded.

"What rumors?"

"Well, witches, Edmund, like people, don't tend to be very observant of things like the feelings of a spoon. We believe very much in the elements, and in balance, but there aren't many of us who know exactly what that balance means or how to achieve it. We spend our entire lives trying to understand it. We often can only settle for balancing the things we do know, and hoping we do well enough with the rest."

"What's the best way to put it," Xia interrupted, hoping to clarify whatever it was Linda Rose was trying to convey. "We understand how elements work together and understand that there must be balance. We know how to use and summon them, but we don't really have the ability to *understand* them the way you do."

"Except for the Originals," Linda Rose added shortly, and the air went cold.

"The Originals?" I repeated.

"No one knows exactly how witchcraft came to be, Edmund. Some people think it started with a group of people who hoped to understand and worship nature. Bible believers would tell you Satan gave it to man. My coven believes it was taught by those to whom it just comes naturally, people we refer to as the Originals. If I were to ask you, Edmund, what the source of your abilities is, or who taught them to you, how would you answer?"

"It's simple understanding," I responded, because it was the only answer I could think to give that would be honest.

"And if you tried to teach me that understanding, would I be able to hear the spoons?"

"Probably not."

"And if you tried to teach me your abilities anyway?"

"Then you would end up in a café, forcing a spoon to stir, without the understanding necessary to know you should use the one from the table next to us instead," I answered, finally grasping where the conversation was going... where Linda Rose was gently guiding me.

"Not just understanding, Edmund, but ability. And the fact that you were born with that ability makes you an Original."

Linda Rose sat back, crossed her arms, and looked proud of herself.

"There are others?" I prodded.

"I would imagine there have been many. Adam would probably have been the first recorded. Moses, Noah, Jesus. I believe all miracles, all prophets, and all magic comes from the same source, the same understanding. It takes someone very special to master it and—as you said— *understand* it."

"It's not mastery," I felt defensive. "It's... purity."

"What do you mean?"

I had to seriously think before I spoke next, because I knew it would offend her, so I tried to make it sound like a compliment of sorts.

"You're very strong willed. It seems odd to me how forceful your will is. You're such a refined woman, but what I have seen of your practice so far is... I don't know how to put it non-offensively..."

"Say what you must," Linda Rose encouraged.

"Well, it's... rude. Harsh. I'd imagine you must

offend everything you use your magic on. The only reason you have any success is because your will is stronger than the will of… well… the spoon, for example."

"Witches take years to learn to master their will," she responded, but it wasn't defensive, it was explanatory.

"It feels wrong. It feels immoral. It feels like a form of slavery."

Linda Rose smiled and raised her eyebrows at me, a reaction I was not expecting.

"We could learn a lot from you, my dear boy. I would love to know if you could teach me some other way."

"You aren't from Orenda. I believe it is our people's ways you would have to learn."

"Ah yes. Orenda," Linda Rose's smile expanded into a knowing grin. "Actually, I do think I've been there. But you're right. I'm not *from* there."

She purposely paused here, lifting her teacup to her lips, building suspense for some revelation, or debating whether she was going to tell me where she was going with that at all. I could see that whatever she wanted to say was about to burst out—her eyes were bright and sparkling, her lips pressed together as she swallowed her tea, before her knowing grin returned.

"And you are from there?"

I was pretty sure I had already established that.

Linda Rose laughed at the quizzical look that must have been on my face.

"Oh, dear boy, must I really spell it out for you? I believe that I've been to the place you call Orenda. I believe it is the place we all go after we die, to wait our reincarnation. And if Orenda is my place to go to wait for reincarnation," her lips curled even further, "then this here, dear Edmund, is yours."

Something within me shifted with her words. For just a moment, perhaps, I lost control. Every single object, every element, every molecule spoke to me then, as if Linda Rose had cast a spell upon them all. In this small moment, my whole body convulsed with so much power that escaped from me in spite of me not wanting it to. Every single coffee cup exploded. The shrieks of the patrons couldn't drown out the voice in my head—the voice telling me that Linda Rose was telling the truth.

Then one voice, one object spoke louder than the others, it wasn't a person, but something that cried from Linda Rose's handbag. It spoke in a voice that was familiar to me.

"You have something for me," I said, refocused, my energy and abilities feeling sharp.

Linda Rose flashed her lovely smirk as she dabbed nonchalantly at the tea from her broken pot with a napkin that was already soaked through and not nearly big enough for the job. She did not look up. "I was told not to give it to you unless you asked," she said, reaching into her clutch and pulling out an object wrapped in a pressed handkerchief. She set it in front of me, careful to pick a spot that wasn't saturated with tea.

When I unfolded it, I felt my eyes widen. The look on my face must have been one of wonder or fear—because I was feeling both. There, now seemingly delicately placed in the center of a pure white kerchief, was an acorn.

"Where did you get this?" I asked with an undertone of anger that made me wished I had controlled the question better.

"Not where, but from whom." Linda Rose's tone was condescending... corrective. "A nice woman gave it to me in the Carlsbad Mountains. My coven was there last week. This woman spoke highly of you. I believe she was once a nun."

My vision blurred. Tears welled up in my eyes, threatening to spill over, but I didn't know why. I didn't feel sad or frustrated. I wasn't hurt. The amount of energy that suddenly entered the room was overwhelming. The frantic waitstaff was wiping down tables, the barista more interested in wiping down Nicholas. Xia and her collected energy still vibrated heavier than normal and Linda Rose seemed not only unbothered but prepared… she was using this energy. She wanted this.

"What was the nun's name? Mary Elizabeth?" I had planned on driving up to Los Angeles this weekend to see her as I had told Father Paul. So much had happened since I promised him I would go; that conversation seemed months ago, not just barely over a week.

"Chantale, I believe."

My eyes flashed with anger. I felt the emotion settle behind my pupils. It pushed out the tears that had been welling up there—making it hard for me to convey my anger with the appropriate stare. "Mary Chantale is dead."

"She said you'd say that. I'm afraid you're mistaken."

Anger mixed with relief and excitement. If Mary Chantale were alive, I had to find her. "Where?"

Linda Rose cocked an eyebrow. It was an odd expression and position for her to hold her face in; it made her porcelain appearance look asymmetrical and off-putting. "Ask the acorn. After all, if it can't tell you where it came from, then you're not the person she thought you were."

I didn't have a response. I didn't think I needed to say anything. I found myself standing, snatching the acorn, and turning to leave. Right before I headed for the door, my manners caught up with me. Luckily, this gave Xia and

Nicholas the hint that I was about to storm out, along with the time to quickly collect their belongings and follow me. "It was a pleasure to meet you," I said dryly before heading for the door.

TWENTY

It was going to be a busy day, and I couldn't sleep. The clock on the wall had an hour hand that seemed stuck at three a.m. for an eternity. My father's ring on my hand pulsed every time I was about to drift off to sleep, sending an icy spasm up my left arm, and the jolt would start my mind spinning and spinning. Orenda seemed close tonight—and I wondered if it had something to do with three a.m. also being the witching hour.

Xia was fast asleep, curled into my side. Her deep breathing reminded me of a cat's purr. If I had any doubt that the pulsing ring was bringing a true chill into the stale night air, it was confirmed by Xia's slight shiver every time it pulsed. First she would shiver, then she would pull herself in tighter to me. Whether or not this was an unconscious movement I didn't know, but either way I didn't mind.

At 3:26 I maneuvered a pillow into Xia's relaxed arms and slipped out of bed. I pulled on my jeans, keenly aware of the small lump the acorn made in my front pocket, and tied the laces tight on my favorite pair of red Converse shoes. I needed to go to Carlsbad to find where the acorn came from. I was certain I could find its parent tree among the mountain forest—although what else, if anything, I would find was entirely a mystery.

I needed to find Sister Chantale and Mary Elizabeth as well. I had held off long enough on seeing them. I hadn't purposely forgotten or pushed it off, but it did seem like every time I thought about going something catastrophic would happen—like Nicholas's possession or a trip between spaces to Orenda.

The ring pulsed again and my left arm responded with a wave of goose bumps.

I calculated my time. First the forest, which hopefully wouldn't take more than a few hours. Then, I would spend some time with Mary Elizabeth. I had her address somewhere. I patted down my pockets, already knowing I didn't have it on me. I would have to call Father Paul and get it from him on the way.

Finally, I had to have drinks with Henric. It was Friday and I had no doubt, with how little he had seen of me lately, that he would file that missing person's report if

I missed our routine trip to the bar. I'd get him drunk enough to ensure my job at the supermarket, then skip out back to Xia.

Xia. I caught myself looking at her the moment I thought her name even though I hadn't consciously moved my gaze toward her direction. The moonlight spilling through the window onto her soft skin made her face look paler than normal. Even in the moonlight her lips were fire red. The soft lines of her bare shoulders with the sheet draped across her breast surprised me because the softness seemed juxtaposed to her inner strength. My body ached to crawl back into bed with her, to press her smooth skin against mine, to part my lips with hers, and feel our inner fires ignite.

Instead, I pushed my keys into my pocket, ran my fingers through my hair, and silently left the room.

"Going somewhere?"

I was going to wake Nicholas up to tell him where I was going and when I would be back, but I didn't have to. His room was right next-door but he wasn't in it. Instead, he was leaning with one foot propped up against the building, inhaling deeply on a cigarette, his face half-shadowed by a baseball cap he was wearing to keep his unkempt hair from falling into his eyes.

I flinched at the unexpected sound of his voice,

dropping the hotel key. "Sheesh! What are you doing out here?"

"Couldn't sleep."

"Yeah, me either."

Nicholas motioned toward the inside of the room. "What about her? You wear her out?"

I couldn't help the slight curl of my lips. I was sure I was turning a lovely shade of red that would be obvious in the stark florescent lights that lit each of the hotel doorways. The light was harsh, too bright and clinical to my heavy eyes.

"Xia's sleeping fine."

"You going to Carlsbad?" Nicholas was good at deducing people's thoughts, but this in particular didn't strike me as odd. I didn't have any other place to go at the moment.

"Yeah."

Nicholas twisted his foot on the butt of the cigarette. I hated seeing him smoke. It meant his anxiety was high.

"Without us?"

"Yeah. I kinda need some time. I haven't really noticed the trees talking much lately, and if I'm going to find out where this acorn came from, I'm going to need some quiet, you know?" I wasn't lying.

Nicholas nodded. "You can't really focus with her

around?"

That wasn't a lie either, but was also a half-truth. "Not on what I need to focus on," I grinned.

"When will you be back?"

"I figure around dinner? We can maybe get together then and grab drinks with Henric after?"

"Nah, we already decided we aren't a fan of that guy," Nicholas grinned, pulling a pack of cigarettes out of the pocket of his basketball shorts. He slapped the pack a few times against his palm.

I waited until he had lit his next cigarette and expelled the first puff of smoke.

"Can I borrow your car?"

He smiled. "Sure. And don't worry about her. Xia and I can find some stuff to do today. I'll keep her entertained. You can report on what you find, if you don't think we'll be any help." Nicholas raised his eyebrow at me on that last part. "I'm sure we could all use a break from all of this *magic* shit for a while."

"Yeah, okay." I responded. "So," I motioned toward his room, "you alone in there?"

"Nope. Barista." This time it was his lip that curled, but he hid it by shoving the end of the cigarette back into his mouth and taking a slow drag.

"Well don't sleep in too long," I joked. "Xia wakes up

pretty early and I didn't leave a note."

"You should at least text her something in case I'm in the mood for a little morning exercise," Nicholas grinned, twisting his foot onto what I thought had been his second butt. Now that my eyes were adjusting to the outside light, I could tell it was more than his second—he had been at this for quite a while.

"Will do. Hey, take it easy on those."

Nicholas shrugged and looked down at all the cigarette butts that were littered around his feet.

"Hey, you be careful," he said, tossing the remainder of the pack into a nearby trash container.

"I'm tree hunting. What's the worst that could happen?"

"Well, if I recall correctly, didn't you catch on fire from that once?"

I grinned. "I'll be careful."

***

The drive to Carlsbad from San Diego is pleasant at three-something in the morning. The air is brisk and has a slight salty smell from the ocean, instead of the smell of exhaust that is so common on the California highways. My father's ring was pulsing so often that I had the passenger side window down and the heat on in the car to keep myself comfortable.

Eventually I found myself driving on some smaller, curving roads that inched toward a set of ridges to the east. Large trees became common along the countryside as a dense morning fog rolled across the mountains. I followed an unknown road for quite some distance until the fog became too thick and I was forced to pull over. Normally, this prospect would have been frightening—being alone very early in the morning with no other cars or people or signs of life, unable to drive and unable to see because of reduced visibility. But I knew something beyond *me* was happening. My father's ring was now sending constant streams of ice through my body and the acorn in my pocket hummed with life.

I pulled over and got out of the car, not surprised to find a hiking trail just inches from where I had parked.

I hiked until the first signs of the sun turned the pale white moonlight reflecting off the fog into a murky grey morning. It was actually easier to see in the moonlight because it didn't refract against the fog like the sunlight did—didn't hide the shadows of the trees that had been visible in the lesser light.

"Edmund," I heard a female whisper my name behind me in the fog, and the resulting chill my ring shot through me gave me more than goose bumps: it made the hair on the back of my neck stand on end like it does when I'm being watched.

I spun around and strained to see through the fog.

"Hello?" my voice creaked, barely above a whisper.

"Is it him?" another voice whispered, this time in front of me. I spun back forward in time to see a dark shadow flicker into oblivion... unless my eyes were just playing tricks on me.

I couldn't tell if the whispers were from real people or if they were carried on the fog like the tree's whispers were carried on the wind in Orenda, but I suspected no one out here would know who I was... unless Nicholas or Xia had come to look for me.

"Nicholas?" I asked, taking a step forward on the trail. I listened carefully for a response, for a rustle, for footfall on the path, but heard nothing. The world seemed almost too still, too quiet. So quiet in fact, that I could only hear my heartbeat in my ears when I tried to listen.

Then, as if by some change in the wind, the fog in front of me began to dissipate and a large, black figure started to materialize. At first, I thought that it was a person, but it soon became apparent that it was too large. Then, it sprouted giant arms... no... branches...

I strained to see the large tree, but while its silhouette was becoming clear, I couldn't make out details. Finally I could hear the slight rustle of its leaves carried on the soft breeze that had started to clear my path. I couldn't distinguish the individual leaves or see any color, but I could make out the shape of the tree and could tell that it was still a long way off—off the path, into the forest.

Something at the base of the tree caught my eye—movement. I couldn't tell if it was a trick of the fog or something really moving, but the base of the tree seemed to twist and turn, then rise up, then get smaller. I watched as a shadow stepped away from the trunk of the tree and divided into two.

They were people!

"Hello?" I called to them, my voice more confident this time.

There was no vocal answer but the two shadowy figures raised their hands and started waving at me.

My legs decided to start moving toward the tree when the acorn in my pocket began to hum again. It only took a few steps to realize that the tree was much further than I had originally thought, and was much larger.

Every step brought more of the tree into focus. Every step seemed to make it grow. With every step the acorn in my pocket buzzed with excitement and knowing. It knew something I didn't and it was excited to show me.

The two figures at the base of the tree danced. As I

339

got closer I started to make out human characteristics. One was much larger, the other more subdued. The one dancing was almost as excited as the acorn. Both shadows vibrated with the same intensity as the acorn in my pocket, or perhaps the vibration was actually coming from me. I couldn't tell.

Then, suddenly, one characteristic came into clarity that made me stop dead in my tracks. Amid the black-and-white world of fog and shadow, one color stood out as vividly as a color in a selective-color photograph; the larger figure had fiery red hair. I would know that shade anywhere.

"Ralph!" I burst out and started running.

It was like a nightmare and the best dream of my life at the same time. I could see them, Ralph and Hailey. They were unclear but they were there. I knew it.

The faster I ran, the further away they seemed to get. The tree, however, got closer, its giant black trunk obscuring my view of the dancing human shadows, one with red hair.

When I finally got to the oak tree, I could see that my two shadow friends were actually just smaller trees, one with fiery red leaves and the other with limber branches that swayed and danced even though the air felt still.

My heart fell and I couldn't help but feel

disappointment. I chided myself for missing my friends and for letting something so foolish get me excited. Yes, I longed for Hailey and Ralph both—but they were in another life. Now, I had friends here... Nicholas and Xia.

Still, the pep talk didn't fill the emptiness. It was more than just longing, or missing, or sadness, or loss. I felt out of place. I didn't belong.

My, my child. That is quite a burden you carry, the wind seemed to whisper.

And that feeling, that wonderful feeling of magic, filled my entire body. I knew that voice. I spun around to gaze at the oak tree.

"Mother Tree!" I gasped aloud, and this time, there was no holding back the tears. "But how?"

We trees remember, but you people forget. How is it that you remember?

I had no idea how to answer her riddle, but it didn't matter. I swung myself up into her branches and secured myself around her trunk in what must have resembled a hug. I wanted to be connected with her.

"Show me. Show me how you came to be here?"

And she did. I could feel what her life was like in Orenda, on the outskirts of the rolling alfalfa fields. I saw our previous encounter from beginning to end. I even felt the fire consume her.

The transformation from Orenda to this earth wasn't like I had expected, but then again, I didn't remember being born on earth myself, so I didn't really have any reason to have expectations. Mother Tree's birth here seemed quite ordinary, not fancy or transformative. In fact, it was almost as if her roots were so deep that when her life force encountered the flames of the fire, it retreated into the deepest parts of her roots, flipped inside out, then sprouted new life here.

And that life here simply made sense to her. There was no questioning within her about who she was or where she came from. Orenda wasn't her home; Earth wasn't her home. She just was.

That understanding made sense to her, but not to me. In that, we were different.

I wanted to be consumed by Mother Tree's understanding. I found myself wondering how many lifetimes she had seen—completely awestruck by the knowledge that a tree's lifetime could be hundreds upon hundreds of my years. Just the time she would have spent in Orenda alone would have been generations to any human, and the knowledge and memory that she carried with her from lifetime to lifetime must have been infinite.

Mother Tree responded with answers to my thoughts as quickly as I thought them. She could show me her life in

Orenda only because I had been there with her. If I could not remember that life, it would be against the laws of nature for her to show me more. I tried to prod at the memories prior to the lifetimes we shared, wondering why the laws were the way the laws were but found nothing but darkness, a barrier as thick and strong and dense as the heavy oak wood.

I opened my eyes to the sound of my name. At first, I wasn't sure if someone had actually spoken it or if Mother Tree was poking at some of my memories in a sort of playful retaliation because the voice was definitely from a memory.

"Edmund!" the voice sounded again, breathless with excitement and surprise.

I looked down into a pair of eyes sunk so far back into their sockets that at first glance I almost missed the kindness in them. The soft shape of the corners that once made them look like they were smiling had given way to gravity, and delicate wrinkles that were once easily covered with makeup were now canyons—canyons that looked like rivers of tears had worn through them.

But there was no mistaking the glimmer, the brightness, and the inner fire.

"Sister Chantale!" I exclaimed in complete shock.

"And Sister Elizabeth," a second, harsher voice

343

responded. I hadn't even noticed the other woman standing on the other side of the tree. Her voice was so jarring that I teetered on the branch I was balanced on.

I was down on the ground and in Sister Chantale's open arms before I even realized I was moving. She was no longer dressed in the nun habit but she still smelled of eucalyptus, just as she had when I was a child. My eyes stung with happiness.

"How? I mean... I saw you. I thought..." I couldn't bring myself to say that I thought she was dead.

"The Lord spared me that night, somehow," she responded. "All I remember is a sharp pain, then waking up in the hospital. They said I had a heart attack."

"That seems to be a common theme," I said, pulling away.

"What do you mean?" Sister Chantale responded, but before I had a chance to answer Sister Elizabeth was by my side.

"Got any hugs left for an old hag like me?" she grinned. I never remembered her being affectionate, but there was something familiar and warm when she hugged me and gave me a wet kiss on the cheek. She smelled like mothballs, a scent that I found to be extremely pungent, but also oddly calming. I caught myself wondering how it was that anyone even used mothballs anymore. Did clothes-eating moths still exist?

"I was actually on my way to see you. How...?" I began, but then decided I was asking the wrong question, "What are you doing here?"

It was Sister Chantale that answered. "Actually, we were looking for you."

"It was an odd coincidence, our running into Nicholas's mother," Sister Elizabeth explained. I realized about this time that I didn't even know their real names.

"Oh, don't bore him with the unnecessary details. Long story short, Elizabeth and I had faith that the acorn would find its way into your possession, and that it would lead you here."

"Elizabeth?" I gawked at Sister Elizabeth. "Your *real* name is Elizabeth?"

"It is now, my boy. Come, let's sit down. My hips are a bit sore from the hike. We've been coming up here for days hoping to find you. Took you long enough."

The fog hadn't yet yielded to the heat of the sun so the air felt murky and heavy. I couldn't tell if it was the fog playing with my vision, but when Elizabeth turned to walk into the fog, her eyes looked milky white, translucent and hauntingly dead. I shivered and reached for her hand, not in guidance or out of an emotional necessity, but because I had an overwhelming need to make sure it was still warm.

It was warm and clammy and the skin was loose around the bone as it gets with age, but I could still feel Elizabeth's heartbeat as it pushed blood through her fingers.

Elizabeth spun and looked at my hand in her own as if she expected someone else. The look in her eyes as she sized up the gesture was somewhere between surprise and sadness, but at least the color of her eyes looked normal now. She gave my hand a light squeeze of acknowledgment, then dropped it and turned back to the fog.

I glanced over at Sister Chantale, whose half-smile seemed forced. "So what is your name these days?" I asked lightheartedly.

The smile faded, which made the old wrinkled face appear ghost-like in the fog. All signs of life within her seemed carried in her lips. I hadn't noticed before how I only knew them to be upturned, which caused the wrinkles near the corner of her eyes to star outward. Without the smile, her face was less than expressionless.

"I actually took the name of my son, Simon. You must think that strange."

We had walked a few feet from the large oak tree to a place that had benches carved out of marble. As we sat down, I found myself cursing the fog—I would have loved to see where I was and what this place looked like in the light. Between the hiking trails, the large oak tree, and the benches, it must have been some sort of park, but everything was unfamiliar to me. Every few feet I may have been in a different world for all I knew. My entire point of view was lost. The shadow of the large oak tree had even given way to new fog wafting in from all around us. I could still see the shadow of the small tree with the orange leaves, though. I had to keep reminding myself that not only was there not a person standing over there, but that even if there was, it wouldn't have been Ralph.

Simon Chantale's hand on my knee brought me back to her comments.

"Actually, it answers a lot of questions for me. I went to see a priest at the school," I said.

"Father Paul. Yes, he called me," Elizabeth interrupted.

"Yes. He said that you were living with Simon. Obviously I knew Simon couldn't be…" I didn't finish the sentence again when Simon Chantale's face fell and her hand tightened on my knee.

"It made me curious," I settled, resting my hand on hers in a show of solidarity. "Then to find you, Sister Chantale… I'm sorry. Simon. I thought you were dead."

"In a lot of ways I am," the old woman responded

347

and her eyes seemed to glaze over like Elizabeth's had done.

I blinked and those eyes were looking directly at me, now shining, wet with tears.

"Now look at me," she chided herself, producing a handkerchief from her pocket and dabbing at her eyes.

I turned to Elizabeth who was watching Simon Chantale cry, judgmentally. She really was a bitch.

"Anyway," I interrupted Elizabeth's stare, purposely giving her a judging look of my own. She opened her mouth as if she were about to protest or make an excuse, but then closed it and waved her hand like she was waving her thought away.

I continued, "I wanted to come talk to you about the survivors from the orphanage."

"What survivors?" she asked, and the question almost seemed menacing, like a serial killer asking "what bodies?" It took me a minute to process that she didn't mean there were no survivors; she just didn't know that I was asking about all of them as a collective.

"All of them," I clarified, which seemed to satisfy her.

"Well, what would you like to know?"

"How many people survived," I started. "Their names and where they are, for example, would be helpful." I paused, and watched her reaction to the end of my question carefully. "How many have died of some sort of heart related issue?"

She didn't flinch. She knew.

I watched as her gaze drifted down to my father's ring. I felt it pulse, so icy on my finger that I flinched. Then her eyes snapped back up to mine—too quickly, like she hadn't actually wanted me to notice that she had noticed the ring.

"You still wear that?" she covered, her eyes a bit harder than they were when we had first started talking. Hard like the eyes I used to know when she was a nun. I could almost imagine her in her habit again, throwing chalk at my head.

"It's the only tie I have to my family."

"I see. Your family from another world," her condescending chuckle as she spoke the last word made a sour taste rise up from the pit of my stomach into my mouth. I inhaled and swallowed to get rid of it.

"Have you ever had the ring examined? Do you know what it's made of?" she continued.

"No." I had no idea where the line of questioning was supposed to be leading. I wanted to ask about the other children, about demons and heart attacks, about whether she had seen or had been in some sort of dark situation since the orphanage. Hell, I even wanted to save her life and warn her if something really was after the survivors.

"Pity. I was sure you were going to tell me it came from some ore found in the magical ancestral mountains of Orenda."

My ring pulsed and alarm bells went off in my head. I couldn't remember what parts of Orenda I had mentioned to Elizabeth, but I certainly didn't talk about the mountains. "You seem to know way more than you're letting on, *Sister*," I hissed the last word.

"Oh, come now," Simon Chantale was patting my hand lightly, sensing my anger bubbling. Somehow, the motion worked, and I inhaled and swallowed again although I couldn't seem to control my clenched jaw.

She continued, "We've been studying, Edmund. Ever since that day in the orphanage we've been looking for answers. We've been comparing notes and have learned quite a bit from the things you've said to us, especially in light of what we can remember and what we have in Father Michaels' journals. We've been searching for you for a long time, Edmund. We've been looking in the supernatural circles, the covens, the religious sects, everywhere we could think of to find answers."

"And what have you found?"

"You. Finally you."

"Well, I have to warn you," I stuttered, getting back

to the original point of our visit. "I think you're both in danger. If something is killing the survivors from the orphanage, you're both on a very short list."

"Actually," Elizabeth said, her voice back to being softer, her eyes back to a look of kindness, "we need to warn you. There are many people who have heard of you, Edmund. Many of them are Catholics who are highly interested in the orphanage. In those stories you're referred to mostly by your given name, Alexander. But oddly enough, there are also many witches who have heard your name and whose covens have been tasked to find you."

"Tasked by who?"

"Whom," Simon Chantale corrected, then blushed. "Sorry, sometimes the teacher in me gets out."

Elizabeth ignored her entirely. "Dark forces. Satanic influences. Covens are scared. Witches are dying."

"Linda Rose never said any of this," I said. I had a hard time believing covens of witches were searching for me or that witches were dying and Linda Rose didn't know about it.

Elizabeth did that hand motion again where she seemed to dismiss something. "No, no. We got to her and her coven first. We found them here, actually. That damned tree sure seems to mean something to a lot of people."

"We used the church records to find her before the other covens did," Simon Chantale clarified. "If they knew that she had any sort of connection with you, they would have already turned her against you or killed her in the process. Nicholas, too."

"So yes, people are dying. Heart attacks and all," Elizabeth's tone was devoid of emotion. She was delivering facts. "But no one is targeting survivors of the orphanage fiasco, they're targeting *you*."

"Who's targeting me?"

"Some covens are darker. Some witches are weaker. Some will believe anything that comes to them in spirit or as a spirit guide. The ones who don't know any better even allow themselves to be possessed for a modicum of power. Why do you think the church is so against witchcraft? It leads to gullibility."

"Funny," I allowed my thoughts to spill out of my head aloud, "a lot of people think the same thing about the Catholics."

Elizabeth's eyes narrowed, but her lips stayed silent. Then, she gave Simon Chantale a quick glance that conveyed something that had meaning to them.

"We need to leave. We've spent too much time with you already," Simon Chantale spoke gently.

"But, I have more questions."

"We've answered all that we can," she responded. "We needed to deliver our warning and we have done so."

"Well, can I see you again? I haven't even had a chance to tell you what you've meant to me, and what it means to me that you're alive."

"Come on, Chantale," Elizabeth chided, like a mother using a child's full name when they're in trouble.

"Good luck, dear boy," Simon Chantale whispered, kissing me on the cheek. Her lips were cold, unlike her hand, which now slipped off my knee as she stood.

"We'll see you soon," Elizabeth called, linking arms with Simon Chantale and walking off into the fog.

I was entirely shocked by their hasty departure. For a few minutes I sat on the marble bench as the thick fog swirled around me. Then, something odd hit me and I cried out into the fog, "Hey wait a minute! The trail is—" but there was no response. My voice reverberated as if the fog were an impenetrable wall. "—that way," I finished, although it was only loud enough for me to hear.

I had no idea where the two ex-nuns went, or where they were going, but wondered if there was another trail in the direction they headed, or if maybe they *had* gone the right way and I was just turned around. I decided I would try to find my way back to Mother Tree to get my bearings and thank her. I stood from the marble bench and took two steps before I tripped over something sticking up from the ground.

I caught myself as I tumbled, but my hands slipped over a smooth surface before finally grinding to a halt on the dirt and grass. My nose was inches from a slick granite slab that had a date carved into it.

It was a marker, too overgrown to be fully read. The date stamped in the stone was just nine years earlier, which made me wonder if I had stumbled onto the flagstone of the park marking the date it was completed, or some significant event that led to the park's dedication.

My shin ached from whatever it had contacted with, and I turned to find I had ripped my pants on a large rock, which, on closer inspection, had an oddly familiar shape. No, it wasn't a rock… it was a stone cross.

I was in a graveyard.

I sat, stunned from the fall but more bewildered, as a cold chill pulsed from my father's ring and shot straight up my spine. The fog was still swirling after my fall, and I could almost make out the name on the headstone I had tripped over.

The fog was thickening fast. I needed to get back down the mountain but my hunch, and my father's incredibly active and icy ring, pulled me toward the stone.

I got low to the ground where the fog was thinnest, my mind trying to make sense of what I was sure I couldn't be seeing. The stone read "Sister Mary Elizabeth, Taken home to God."

But there had to be plenty of Sister Mary Elizabeth's. This couldn't be the same Mary Elizabeth I was just talking to.

Just as I had that thought, a break between rolls of fog exposed a second stone. This one was undeniable. "Sister Mary Chantale. Now she sings with the angels."

TWENTY-ONE

The fog cleared as I came down off the mountain. I immediately got into Nicholas's car and sat stunned for a few moments listening to the sound of my heart pumping blood into my brain. My stomach felt tense, even though I left the contents of it somewhere back in the graveyard.

I couldn't decide what I had just seen. I'd encountered demons and shadows, all evil and destructive, but never a ghost—not like that. The nuns were warm. They smelled alive. They looked aged. Were they evil like the energumen of my childhood? Did Joshua send them? Did an angel? Did God?

I turned the key to the ignition and checked my phone, which I had stupidly left in the car. The battery gauge flashed red and the number on the clock surprised me. Eight p.m. I had been up on the mountain for over twelve hours.

I tried to organize my thoughts to account for the length of time. Maybe my conversation with Mother Tree had lasted longer than I had thought? Maybe somehow talking to the late Sister Mary Elizabeth and Sister Mary Chantale somehow sped up time? I didn't know and the cognitive dissonance was enough for me to consider on one final possibility: maybe I was going crazy.

I shoved that thought out of my head and settled on not knowing. My brain switched gears immediately as I scrolled through my text messages: five from Xia, three from Nicholas, and one from Henric.

Meet at the store for drinks?

I responded to that one first. *Running late. On my way. About an hour.*

I was halfway through Xia's second text message when the response came. *No problem. Working on a cow anyway. You can help me stock the meat first.*

Bastard was going to put me to work. I shifted into gear and pulled back onto the highway.

Xia's text messages got more frantic. They went from *I can't believe you are leaving me with Nicholas all day after the night we had. I told you I wanted to meet the nun*, to *If you seriously don't respond I'm going to call search and rescue.* I sent her a quick note to let her know I was okay and that I wouldn't stay long at the bar with Henric. I left out the ghosts for now. That wasn't exactly something I could figure out how to say over text message. I got halfway through writing "I love you" before I realized it, then paused while my head slowed, and at least one piece of my life became clear.

I was in love.

My finger hovered over the backspace key for a few moments before I finally decided to finish the sentence. Then it hovered over the send key for a few moments more, before I just closed the text window, leaving the message unsent. She deserved to hear it in person first anyway.

I took a deep breath as my foot pressed on the accelerator. I allowed the feeling of excitement to take the place of the knot in my stomach. I rested my head on the headrest and let all my busy, jumbled thoughts swirl around a single constant point: Xia.

I recalled the memory of her face, inches from mine in the moonlight; reminisced about the way her red lips explored my body; remembered what it was like to fold our bodies together. But my favorite memory was the way she looked at me that day in the cafeteria—the day I had turned the tea into wine. Then, I realized that she had been in love with me long before today. She was just waiting for me to realize it.

I picked my phone back up, and pressed send.

When I got to Henric's store, I had already decided I wasn't going to stay. I was going to tell Henric that we could have drinks another time. I wanted nothing more than to get home to Xia. A message or phone call wouldn't do. He would take that sort of thing personally. I would tell him in person and he would see the yearning in my eyes and the look on my face. I would use every ounce of persuasive magic I had in my eyes to get him to let me go to her... without firing me, of course.

It wasn't abnormal for Henric's car to be the only one parked behind the market. Usually, only he and I could stomach the walk through the back door. You had to pass through the butchery to get to the store from the back door and most employees preferred to park out in the front lot. I never really understood that, but I guess my experiences had given me a somewhat different view of death. The back door opened to a hallway that was lined with freezers, including one walk-in where we had full, bone-in animals. There was a small window through which you could see the carcasses hanging, but that wasn't the part the employees hated. The hallway then opened into a larger room that had an industrial sized meat grinder and a pulley system so the larger pieces of meat could be easily lifted into the grinder.

I had never noticed how eerie it appeared at night, the

large hooks casting menacing shadows from the nearby windows. When Xia, Nicholas, and I were here last, I hadn't remembered even coming through this room. On the far side of the wall was the meat trimming station room, where I had woken from my last trip from Orenda. The employee lounge separated the grinding room from the back of the store.

Light was spilling from a cracked doorway in the meat trimming room, and the whole place smelled of rust and blood. I checked the grinder, mostly out of habit. Meat had been ground there tonight—the grinder hadn't been cleaned, but the beef had already been taken and packaged. I picked up a paper wrapped package in each hand, heading toward the fridges.

"Don't bother with that now, I actually need your help in here," Henric's voice called from the trimming room. I shrugged and set the ground beef back onto the stack of neat rows.

"You couldn't have warned me that I would be working tonight? I wore my favorite pair of shoes," I joked, realizing my right pant leg was already ripped and somewhat bloody from my fall in the graveyard. I hoped I didn't already get blood on my shoes. I realized that Henric might also notice my ripped pants—my mind was already constructing a cover story.

"You know," I continued, "I was actually hoping I could take a rain check," I pulled the door open, prepared to give my best puppy-dog-sad-face look. Unfortunately, it was wasted.

The room was empty.

More than empty. The room was pristine. The metal cutting tables had been meticulously sanitized. The scent of bleach flooded my nostrils and nauseated me. The mental distractions I had been using washed away with the scent of the bleach, my mind thrown back into chaos. The pit in my stomach returned. Mixed with the smell of the cleaning agents, it caused my stomach to lurch.

I heaved, but swallowed it back and spun out of the room.

"Henric?"

He was there, right behind me, inches from my face. He shoved me against the wall, his body falling heavily into mine. I heard the sound of heavy chains. My mouth flooded with rusty liquid.

Henric's dark eyes were wild as I became aware of a sharp pain in my right shoulder. I tried to gasp but ended up splattering Henric's face with blood. My blood.

I looked down to see Henric's hands on one of the metallic hooks—a hook which he had just shoved under my shoulder, through my chest.

I felt a surge of adrenaline that tried, but failed, to cover the immense pain. My eyes started to darken and my knees gave way. I would have fallen except that my body registered somehow that if I fell I would catch my full weight on the hook—and I was already delirious from the fire that was shooting through my chest.

I tried to inhale but my breath made a gurgling noise and my mouth flooded with more rusty liquid. Henric started spinning—the whole room started spinning, and I fell forward into him.

"Hiya, Edmund. You've been one tough guy to find."

I didn't know if it was my delirium or if I was losing consciousness, but the voice wasn't Henric's.

"No, no. Don't pass out yet. We need to have a little chat."

He put his hand on the hook again and I felt it grow warm. My awareness returned as the pain lessened.

"That's better."

I was conscious enough to feel his hot breath in my face now, to feel the warm blood running down my hands. My brain was functioning enough to realize that my right lung must be punctured because every time I inhaled, blood bubbled upward into my mouth. I found that if I leaned toward the right and took shorter breaths it didn't feel like I was about to drown.

"Joshua," I choked out.

He put his hand on my forehead and tilted my head upward, pulling my eyes open to meet his in the process. They were a deep red, although I wasn't sure if they were really red, or if that was the only color my mind could see.

I started choking out the spell I had learned as a child, the spell to free someone from possession, but Joshua laughed.

"Stupid boy. I'm not one of *them*. That won't work on *me*."

My mind drifted to the time when I was a child, to my first death, the death that brought me to Earth. It didn't seem that long ago now. The memory was vivid, the red tint of the world as blood poured from a different wound was actually familiar. Was this my life, flashing before my eyes?

"That's it," Joshua said. "I need you to remember. How did you get here?"

But I couldn't remember. I didn't know. I was twelve before I remembered anything in the orphanage. The swirling blackness, the same blackness that accompanied words I knew but couldn't connect meaning to in the orphanage, returned now to eat away at my awareness. I knew I was in trouble when I started to find the dark oblivion comforting.

I heard the whirl of machinery coming to life and the hook tugged upward. Pain shot through my arm as the hook supported more of my weight. The pain brought me back to consciousness.

"Stay with me, boy. How did you remember who you were?"

My father's ring. Father Michaels had given it to me on the day of my communion.

The machine whirled again and my feet left the floor. They felt heavy and plump, like when the dentist numbs your face and you spend half an hour poking at it afraid he did something to make you fat.

"This ring?" Joshua questioned, sliding it from my finger. I felt it pulse cool one last time before the warmth of my own dripping blood replaced the sensation. My hands felt heavy now. I wasn't able to lift them.

"No," I choked out and my head rolled backward. "Mine..."

Joshua laughed, "Does this ring allow someone to enter into this level and not forget?"

His question was incoherent. His guess was as good as mine. All I cared about was that the ring was a gift from my father.

The rage returned. It bubbled to the surface like the blood bubbling from my mouth. It brought all of my feelings into clarity. For a few moments the world snapped back into place. I was higher now, a few feet off the ground. Joshua was taking off my clothes, but I didn't know why.

Then I noticed the link. He was probing my mind. He was reading my thoughts. My father's ring was now on his hand as he ripped off my shirt! The link between our minds worked both ways though, and as I questioned why he was taking off my clothes, I saw him glance toward the grinder.

I started kicking frantically, trying to free myself from the hook. The pain I felt as a result was dimmed by rage and terror. Joshua hit the button that lifted me higher into the air. I tried to cry out, but every time I did I was met with a mouthful of blood. I spit this mouthful in his direction.

The sound the grinder made when it started sent waves of electric fear through my body. But even through the roar of the machinery, I heard my cell phone buzz in the pocket of my pants that were lying in a heap beneath me.

Our minds connected; Joshua heard it, too. He glanced at me quickly, aware that the familiar sound of the phone had caused me to stop struggling. I knew I didn't want to endanger my friends so I had to keep my mind clear.

Joshua reached into my pocket and read the message.

I could see the words on the screen through his eyes. *I love you, too.*

Joshua smiled wickedly and started plotting the death of my friends.

"So you're loved, are you Edmund?" he spoke aloud, even though I could hear his thoughts. The sound of his voice and his thoughts created a delayed echo in my ears. "How will this poor girl feel when she learns that her great boy toy has abandoned her, just like you were abandoned by the last people you loved? "

Visions of my dead father, slouched over in his office chair, filled my mind. He didn't abandon me. He was murdered.

"Yes, that secret room in the parliament building. How do I get inside?"

Shit. I hadn't meant to give that up. I could feel Joshua probing for the entrance to the room, but I thought about the swirling blackness behind the word *scripture* in the orphanage instead.

"Stop fighting me, boy!" he screamed. Then his voice softened. "No matter. Think about the book. Your father's book. How do you read it?"

I found his question hilarious. He had had the book

for over twenty years now and still hadn't figured out how to read it?

Joshua lowered me toward the grinder. He knew I was mocking him. Unfortunately, I didn't know how to read the book; my father's letter had been cut short by his death—a death that Joshua had caused.

I would give him nothing else.

My feet caught fire as they hit the whirling blades—at least, that is about the only way I can describe it. The whole scene seemed to happen in slow motion, but while I could feel the pain and still see through my own eyes if I chose, I actually had the sensation that I was watching the entire last moments of my life from above, a bird's eye view of my death.

I continued to be worried for my friends, but I was no longer linked to Joshua's thoughts. Actually, I was no longer linked to any thoughts. All my worries, all my hatred, all my love, all my fear, were replaced by a blissful nothing—a clarity that came unexpectedly.

And then I was on the sidewalk in front of the store, watching Joshua in Henric's body placing packages of ground meat in the storefront window. Each paper-wrapped package had a daily special sticker price tag. I had to hand it to him—the window display had never looked more organized.

Above me was a silver river, much like the silver thread that wove through Orenda that I had followed twice to the mountains where I was able to jump between that world and this one. But above me now was not a silver thread—it was much larger, and I could feel it pulling at me with an attraction like a magnet, whether I wanted to follow it or not.

Xia and Nicholas were walking up the sidewalk. I tried to cry out to them, but they couldn't hear me.

"Don't go in there!" I yelled, but Joshua had already seen them coming up the sidewalk, and went out to meet them.

"Hi, Henric," Nicholas started.

"Stop, please! Run away."

"Have you seen Edmund?"

I noticed that as Joshua walked farther from me, the pull from the silver river got stronger. I knew it was the ring. The closer I stayed to it, the more control I could keep. The easier it was to stay in this world.

"Xia," I whispered near her ear. I could feel the warmth of her body. I was so close. How could she not feel me?

"No, he never showed up for drinks last night. I actually did file a missing persons report. I told him I would. If you haven't seen him, he must be in real trouble."

The look on Xia's face was filled with worry.

"Stop. I'm here."

She clung to her phone—I could see my last message to her on the screen.

My heart leaped…

She loved me.

…then fell.

I was dead.

"Well, if you hear anything, do you have my number?"

My connection to her had to be enough. She could see my aura before. She must be sensing something was wrong. She had to know.

"Go! Get away! Don't say anything else to him."

I moved closer to Joshua, hoping to read his expression, sense his thoughts. All I could feel was the damned ring he stole from me.

As if connected to it, I felt it pulse cold. Joshua's reaction was subtle—a slight tic in his eye—but Xia glanced down.

I couldn't believe how well she maintained her composure. If I didn't know any better I wouldn't have guessed she'd seen the ring. Her expression didn't change at all—but I knew she knew because instead of looking at her phone, at Nicholas, or at Henric, she looked past them and right at me.

She couldn't see me but she was trying. I smiled. I felt warmth, love, and sadness fill her body—but her expression didn't change.

"I'll call," Joshua responded coolly. "But tell him he's fired if he dares to show up again."

Xia turned and walked away. The farther she got, the more my heart broke. I longed to be near her, so I did what any man in love would do—I followed her.

Every step I took from Joshua and the ring was fraught with difficulty. The farther I got, the more the silver river pulled at my spirit. After a block it felt like I was fighting the current of a raging river. It didn't matter. I had to be with her. I had to find a way to get through. I had to stay. I had to ensure her safety, somehow.

It only took one step past an uncertain threshold, then I was pulled, willing or not, into the silver river. My vision burst into stunning white light as the current grabbed me. I watched Xia drift away as I was swept upward and the light in my eyes grew brighter. At the last moment, struggling to keep her in my sight, I thought maybe, just maybe, she turned around and looked at me as I was slipped into oblivion.

TWENTY-TWO

The silver river, it turned out, was literally a river. It alternated between a completely bright white and a totally annihilating darkness, creating a gentle rolling visual that was quite hypnotizing. I found myself standing on a bank, watching the silver liquid flow toward an unknown location. While I didn't know exactly where I was, there was something familiar about this place—something I once explained to Nicholas as the space between spaces. This was different, though; I wasn't just passing through or pushing an object into this space in order to then pull it out. The space was more defined now, like a tight container. I was stuck here.

The bank was on one of the corners of a supernatural river confluence. Two silver rivers flowed together here, but instead of merging into one stream, they simply crossed each other and continued flowing in their

371

respective directions. While the silver liquid resembled water, the way they crossed resembled an intersection of a road.

The two rivers bordered the corner I was standing on, and to my back was a steep cliff. There was a bit of room, so I wasn't in danger of falling. However, there was no real place for me to go.

I walked to the edge of the precipice after surveying my surroundings. I peered down into a red fiery glow that brought up memories of all those Catholic teachings about Hell and damnation. I wondered if I was doomed to wait here until I decided it was better to fling myself over the cliff and into the abyss... maybe this was the entrance to Hell and I was here because I'd had premarital sex or taken the Lord's name in vain one too many times.

Stuck as I was, I didn't feel any fear until I turned around and discovered an unexpected person. The figure stood silent and still, observing me. I hadn't noticed the figure because it resembled a shadow and was standing across one of the silver streams. The being wasn't much taller than I was, but now that I had noticed it, it took on a forceful and ominous presence that began to fill the space.

It walked, gliding across the silver stream. As it got closer and took shape, I couldn't believe my eyes—the stories and legends were true. I didn't know whether to be insanely terrified, or if I was supposed to feel no fear at all, or if I should laugh at the ridiculousness of it all.

The figure wore a cloak that resembled smoke. It was in a constant state of motion whether the figure was moving or not. The face was hooded so I couldn't make out any details, just a hollow blackness where the face should've been. Large black wings expanded as the creature flexed them commandingly, a feature that I did not recognize based on the usual archetypal depictions. The look was completed with a long, sharp-bladed scythe.

We stood staring at each other for a moment. I assessed my emotions, trying to put this effigial character into some sort of teaching or story that made sense. I certainly wasn't with God. I hoped I wasn't in Hell. I suppose I could have been in Purgatory or some sort of holding place, but where were my loved ones? All of the different belief systems I had been taught, and the single truth out of hundreds of religions was that there really was an Angel of Death who looked exactly like the sketches I used to see around Halloween.

"The Grim Reaper? Really?" I accidently said out loud with disbelief.

The dark figure took a step toward me.

The way he moved was majestic. The cloak surrounded him, moving effortlessly, as if it was thicker than air but not made of cloth.

I felt apprehension with each step of his approach, an escalating apprehension that raised the level of my fear. As he took a step forward I found myself stepping back until I was at the edge of the cliff. Still, the creature moved toward me. Was he there to make sure I went over into the fiery depths?

The dark mass moved fast, so fast that at the last moment, my foot slipped and I started to topple over the edge. I would have fallen, had I not been caught by the Reaper's long scythe.

He pulled me toward him, away from the ledge.

"Do you know who I am, mortal?" he spoke.

If I had blood, because at this point I didn't really know, it would have run chill. It didn't matter if I had a body or not, if I was in the flesh or out of the flesh—when this being spoke, my entire soul reacted with pins and needles racing up and down my arms. The majesty of that voice. The awe-inspiring sound. The familiarity…

"Dad?" I choked out, fighting for the word as it caught in my throat.

The Grim Reaper pulled me in closer. I was inches from the black void of his face before he lowered his hood.

Those were the eyes of my father.

My fear was instantly replaced with elation. I fell into him, embracing him. I never thought this would happen. My elation was unlike anything I had ever felt before. Finally, I had a piece of my family back, a piece I thought I had lost forever.

"Edmund!" he exclaimed. "Thank the Earth and the Heavens that it's finally you."

"Dad!" I returned the exclamation. "Wait. You're the Grim Reaper?"

I meant the question as a joke, the observation obvious. Instead, his face grew serious.

"We don't have much time. We have a lot to discuss. I need you to listen."

"Okay. But, you're *the* Grim Reaper. You look kind of ridiculous."

This time he smiled, but as he looked down at my hand, disappointment crossed his face. If there's one emotion a son doesn't want to see on his father's face when they are reunited after a long separation, it's disappointment.

"You don't have my ring."

"Joshua took it from me," I explained.

My father paused. "Hopefully it won't matter. The ring should find its way back. It belongs to you, not him."

"Actually, it belongs to you," I corrected, feeling

sentimental.

"No, my son, it doesn't. Listen, Edmund," my father laid the scythe at my feet before continuing. "The ring is the key to being able to cross physically into the earthly realm, a place we call 'the level of the body.' It's a level Joshua hasn't been able to find a way into yet."

"I don't understand. Joshua found a way in. He possessed Henric."

"Possessed in spirit, perhaps. Possession is a spiritual power—the power of the energumen. But to have all power over the level of the body, Joshua would have to go there physically."

He was talking too fast. I thought in death we had an eternity. Why was he talking so fast?

"Joshua is seeking power. He hopes to learn the magic of all the levels. He's already conquered the level of the spirit—the energumen. That is how he learned the power of possession."

"Yes, I know. He made a deal—"

"The energumen's knowledge in exchange for the spirits of men," my father interrupted. "Joshua was the Master Elder of the level of the spirit. Do you remember?"

"Orenda," I spoke, my teaching as a child striking a familiar chord. "You're the Master Elder of the level of the body?"

"I was, until Joshua killed me. Since that time I've been here, waiting for you."

"Wait, I don't understand."

"Instead of going to the level of the body like you did when you died, I was able to use my knowledge to come here. Every soul has a cycle. The human soul is born first on Earth. When they die, our family is responsible to help them cross safely to Orenda. Your mother—" his voice failed as his memories of her surfaced. "I'm sorry. I miss her."

"Me, too."

I watched him swallow his emotions, pushing them back down into the pit of his stomach. It was odd to watch someone else do something that I had always done. I didn't realize I'd *inherited* my ability to swallow my emotions with the identical physical gesture.

"She was amazing. I know you didn't know this, but her job was to help with the transition. She was so good at taking a person's beliefs and helping them to reconcile those beliefs with the reality of Orenda. She could convince anyone that they were exactly where they were supposed to be: heaven, Hades, Sheol, a waiting place to be reincarnated… your mother had explanations for them all. It was something in her eyes, I suppose. The way she would look at a person—she could convince them they were a giraffe."

I felt a strong connection to my mother as my father spoke. I learned more about her in that brief insight than I had ever known. Her life was always such a secret—just like my father's. Now I knew why, and the fact that we both had the ability to convince with our eyes was something we shared.

"The human cycle continues for as long as the soul had something to learn. Once in Orenda, the Council of Elders is responsible for a human's Planning, where the lessons of their next life are decided. Then the soul is sent back."

"Reincarnation?"

"Yes. Humans are supposed to live that existence, in a cycle of learning between Earth and Orenda. The mages, however, are not human. You, my son, are not human."

"Then what am I?"

"Your soul began in Orenda. We are not supposed to exist in the human cycle. We have our own cycle, but it was interrupted when Joshua traded the human souls to the energumen. There was a side effect. Murder was the dark magic Joshua used to gain control over the magic of the energumen, and with the first murder of a mage, our souls fell. When he killed us, he made it impossible for us to fulfill our birthrights. We can't complete our own cycles with the mess Joshua has made. The side effect of murder was that our souls were pushed into the human cycle."

"So other mages have been sent to Earth?"

"Yes."

"But won't they come back here when they die again? Can't you just take them back to Orenda?"

"There is a rule you must understand. Memory of a higher level of existence cannot be sustained when descending to a lower level. It's meant to be that way so that men don't remember their previous lives or the reality of Orenda. The soul imprints the experience but the body cannot remember. Now that Joshua has condemned our race to exist in the human cycle, none of them remember who they really are. That means that any mage who was killed will descend into the level of the body, and forget.

"Except you." My father beamed. "You were the first of our kind to experience the transition and remember everything."

"How?" I asked.

"It was my power that gave you that ability. Since I was the keeper of this crossroads, I knew how to cross between our world and theirs. I was gifted a ring by my father, who was gifted it by his. The ring has the power of our family, generations of our ancestors who learned to guide the spirits of the dead to Orenda by paying the price of this crossroads. Now, the ring allows the bearer to control this crossroads. Without it, there could be no Angel of Death.

"Look at this place. It is the crossroads between our world and theirs. Every crossroads has two Comings, and two Goings. Every crossroads is a sacred place, full of wonders… and dangers."

"Dangers?"

"You just came from the level of the body, one of the Comings of this crossroads. The other Coming belongs to the level of the spirit—the energumen's level. Since my death, I have been unable to help the spirits of men cross. Since my death the demons have claimed the spirits of the dead."

As he spoke, my father disrobed and held his cloak out to me.

"I died as you died. I was only able to hide here because of my intimate knowledge of this crossroads. It belongs to our family. But Joshua killed me with the fire he conjured. I have to complete my death. I have to transition to a lower level. I don't have the power to do the job our family was meant to do anymore. Until you can reclaim this crossroads, with all of the power of the Angel of Death, the energumen will continue to take the spirits of the men who die—and the mages too now that they have fallen into the human cycle. You, my son, must reclaim your rightful place. Since you died on earth, the energumen will come looking for your spirit. They are promised a spirit for every death. I have a plan to save you from them and complete my transition to a lower level. My death and transition will be our family's salvation—your salvation."

Realization dawned. My father was dead, but he hadn't yet been reborn. He had to go to a lower level like I did. The deal Joshua made with the energumen required the spirits of the dead, so they would come for a spirit. They would come for me.

My father had waited here for over twenty years. He waited for me to die in the level of the body, for me to come to this crossroads so that my sprit and my knowledge could return to Orenda. He intended on being taken by the energumen. He intended to take my place.

"The level of the spirit is below the level of the body?"

My father nodded.

"You're not going to the level of the body? You're going even lower? That means you'll forget."

A sad smile turned his lips as understanding filled my mind. The expression made him look old and tired. It must not have been easy for him to wait for me here all these years, knowing what would happen to him when I finally came. How many spirits of the men and women who died did he have to watch the energumen take—unable to save them?

"I will forget either way. You have something no one else has—not me, not Joshua. You have experienced and remembered death. You better understand it than anyone else—and with that understanding comes power. You have learned everything you need to learn to take my place as the Master Elder of the level of the body, the master of the death of the body."

My father placed the cloak in my hands. I shook my head. "I can't take it."

"You must. You must become the Reaper. You must stop Joshua and save the spirits of the dead. You must save me."

"How? How can I defeat him? How can I save you?"

"Joshua has no concept of the death you know intimately. He only inflicts it on others so that more spirits will die on Earth and then be taken by the energumen. He knows that death caused you to cross physically into that world, but he doesn't know how you remembered who you were. Even if he now knows the ring is the key, he is too afraid of death to find the door. That is his weakness, and your strength."

"If the energumen take you, you'll forget who you

are! How can I save you from that? How can I restore your memory?"

My father's composed demeanor broke. The look on his face said that this was a statement he already knew, but that was trying to bury. I felt his anticipation turn into fear.

He didn't answer my question. Instead his eyes brimmed with tears. "I'm sorry to place this responsibility on you. I wish I had the ability to go back to Orenda. I don't. I'm dead. There are no exceptions to death. I'm in the human cycle now. I must fall, as you fell."

"Why didn't you just keep the ring?" My question sounded accusatory. "Couldn't you have experienced death, kept your memory, and saved us?"

"Oh, Edmund. Then I would have lost *you*. If you forgot who you were, if the energumen took you, whom would I teach? Whom would I love? Who could claim their destiny as the Reaper? Children are meant to experience the loss of their parents. The love they have for their parents isn't the same as the love a parent has for their child. Parents are not supposed to lose their children. Had I lost you, I wouldn't have the strength to do what I'm now asking you to do. Besides, I'm old. My cycle was almost complete in Orenda. My time was coming, and my *son* is the only person entitled to inherit the responsibilities and privileges that come with being the Angel of Death. It had to be this way, or the Angel of Death would cease to be, and all human spirits would be lost forever."

"I understand," I said, hoping I wasn't lying.

"This was always your destiny, Edmund. You were always meant to take my place. My only regret is that I couldn't mentor you myself."

The look in his eye was somewhere between sadness and pride as I slipped on the smoky cloak.

"Raise the hood," he said, as a distant whine began echoing through the rocky cavern. "The scythe isn't meant to kill or strike down. It's to capture. To reap," my father explained, handing me the blade. "The energumen, while dark and fearsome, have a unique ability. You already know they can enter the land of the soul—our home. That is why we had to teach you the spell against them when you were young. But, as you now know, they are also the keepers of the secrets of the spirit. They command the power of possession, of being able to cross between the levels.

"The scythe is meant to capture them. When they come for me, you must catch one with the scythe. Then it will be under your control and will show you the way to Orenda. An energumen is the final price required to enter your home, Edmund."

The whine turned into a screech, like the sound I'd

heard bats make on the nature channel. It grew so loud that I had to fight the desire to cover my ears. In order to be heard, my father had to yell.

"If you miss your chance now, wait for another death. Another spirit will always come. You'll have infinite chances."

The sound of screeching took on life as it engulfed us. The air hummed and reverberated with it. The shadows on the rock walls and in the crevices came alive around us—shadow creatures with yellow eyes.

I watched my father's face. There were signs of fear but also of preparation. He had known this time would come. He had been waiting for it, preparing for it. He knew exactly how much time we would have together before the energumen would come for me, and I trusted that he prepared exactly what I needed to hear to fill my new responsibilities. He mouthed the words "I love you, son. I'm so proud of you," before the energumen took him over the cliff.

Shadows flew everywhere. The only source of light came from the blade of the scythe, which managed to find the light somehow. The creatures scattered away from the light, but I plunged the scythe into a group of them anyway, surprised when I caught one on my first swing. The blade hooked around the shadow creature and trapped him in a beam of light.

I felt a tug and then, with a blink, I was in the middle of an alfalfa field, lying on my back, my face tilted toward the sun and my hands and fingers weaving a comfortable pillow under my head. The bright sun was centered in the sky and was hot enough that I unbuttoned my shirt. I sat up and listened to the familiar sound of the wind as it spoke through the grass, trees, and fields.

Orenda wasn't colorless or cold like it was when I was just a visitor from another level. There was no silver light leading toward the mountains. My cloak and scythe weren't visible in the sunlight, but I could feel them as a part of me—as an extension of my hand, ready for use at a moment's notice.

It was an empowering feeling, finally knowing who I was. I felt the presence of responsibility mixed with possibility: possibility that I could be successful now that I understood the tools, possibility because I had hope, possibility because I was home.

I made my way to the city gates, which opened for me just like they used to when I was here as a child. The city was filled with men and women I now knew once lived and died on Earth. These were the people my father had saved at the crossroads. I wondered how many of them even remembered him. My wondering, however, was not left a question for long.

"It's been quite some time since we've had someone successfully cross over," one townswoman said to me.

"You must have been very righteous in life, with a world so wicked that most don't make it here. I'm very proud of you," another woman explained.

"Let me show you to where you will be staying for the next few days."

I was taken to a small residence, a house that wasn't far from where I had grown up. I wondered if Clayton still lived there.

"I have a million questions," I told the woman who was instructed to help me get settled.

"I know this might be overwhelming. Depending on your beliefs in life you may have some trouble adjusting or need someone to talk to. Don't worry, you can ask anything you want of your domestic, who will spend some extra time with you at the beginning to help you cope."

"My what?"

"Your domestic. All the people here have one. They're assigned to you to take care of you while you are here."

"I don't understand. They're like a servant?"

"Yes. One domestic is assigned to multiple families, of course. They will help you reconcile your beliefs now that you are here. I think you'll find that whatever your religion, Orenda will be much to your liking, if not exactly your idea of heaven."

The front door opened into a small living area. There was a staircase to an upstairs bedroom, but no kitchen. The beautiful backyard featured a gigantic pine tree that I could tell was missing the conversations it used to have with *my* people—the mages.

"Well, I'll leave you to get settled and instruct your domestic to come make introductions. Domestics have certain privileges here," this woman said with a bit of hesitation, "but don't be alarmed. They're perfectly safe."

Safe? I wasn't sure what to make of the last statement, but before I had the chance to ask, the woman was gone and I was alone.

Even though I was home—and I definitely was home—something felt out of place. I wasn't sure if it was because I had become accustomed to life in the level of the body, or if I longed for Orenda back in the day when my people filled this city. Maybe I was out of place with my new responsibilities and calling because, understand them as I might, I still had no idea how to fulfill them.

It was good to have an Orendan connection to the earth again, though. It wasn't that the connection was different, but I felt it stronger here both because it was familiar to me in this setting, and because I belonged here. It made me want to learn. I wanted to save the spirits of those crossing over. I wanted to defeat Joshua.

But where to start? Maybe that was why I felt out of place: I had no idea what to do next.

I found myself out in the garden, peering up into the large pine tree. I was about to close my eyes and start a conversation with it when I heard rustling sound behind me.

"Sir, I have been instructed to introduce myself. I am your domestic."

For a moment I thought the tree was going to speak to me; the wind changed but there was a strange emptiness in the tree, almost as if it had forgotten *how* to speak.

"Sir?" the voice came from behind me again. "Do you require anything?"

I touched the pine needles of the tree softly so that it knew I was there and respected it. I wanted it to know that I would listen if it desired to speak.

"No, I think I'm okay for now," I answered, turning toward the voice.

My heart skipped a beat. The woman standing in the doorway, calling herself my domestic, was my mother.

DEATH OF THE SPIRIT

CROSSING DEATH: BOOK TWO

COMING SOON

ABOUT THE AUTHOR

I've often been accused of having done more in my life than the average person my age but if I were completely honest, I'd have to tell you my secret: I'm really 392.

So after all this time, I'm a pretty crappy writer.

I have two books published and a bunch half written (when you have eternity, where's the reason to rush?). I've been favorably reviewed by horror greats like Nancy Kilpatrick, and my how-to-write-horror articles have been quoted in scholarly (aka community college freshmen's) papers.

I enjoy the occasional Bloody Mary, although a Bloody Kathy or Susan will suffice.

Mostly, I just try to keep a low profile so people don't figure out who I REALLY am.

Stalk Rick

Official Website: www.ricktheauthor.com
Facebook: www.facebook.com/rickchiantaretto
Goodreads: www.goodreads.com/ricktheauthor
Twitter: @RickTheAuthor

Also available by Rick Chiantaretto

Facade of Shadows
First Edition

Relaunch early 2014

See a mistake

As perfect as I want every book to be, something was missed. If you find an editing problem, please don't hesitate to email me at rick@rickchiantaretto.com with the mistake. I would love to reward you with some swag, free books, or maybe even eternal life (especially if your name is Mary. Did I mention how much I love a good Bloody Mary?).